ADVANCE PRAISE

Meta's experiences during a turbulent time in history stand as an example of exceptional bravery and courage. This is a story of a girl who, being half-German, had a different perspective on WWII. It details how the occupation affected her family, her community, her country, and her childhood. Her perseverance will encourage readers to find their own courage during difficult times, even if that means traveling across the globe to accomplish their dreams.

—**Tim Carver, Principal, Urbandale High School, Urbandale, IA**

A moving series of vignettes from the life of a girl living in the occupied Netherlands during World War II. Written in a candid fashion that is accessible and directly relatable for most people, it stands as a witness to both the solemnity, fear, and pain brought about by that terrible destruction of life and the beauty, joy, and fun that comes from time spent with family and friends. This book is ideal for homeschooling parents and teachers who are seeking for a way to communicate history with a grace and sensitivity that is largely absent from history books. It would also be of interest to people who are either interested in gaining a deeper understanding of their cultural heritage or would like to meaningfully experience the perspective of others.

—Francis Cooper, Community College Student, Des Moines, IA

A lovingly detailed memoir of a childhood that was ultimately wrecked by Hitler's invasion of the Netherlands. Meta's courage in the face of intense hardship is unforgettable.

—Gina Dalfonzo, Author of *Dorothy and Jack* and *One by One*, Editor, and Content Developer for *Plough Quarterly* and *The Great Courses*, Fairfax, VA

This book is such a personal narrative that people will find themselves sometimes hurting with Meta and other times laughing with her. Indeed, I often was laughing with tears in my eyes. Yes, Meta is plucky, but she also is willful AND she is treated unfairly. I was rooting for her all the time while at times thinking, "Oops, Meta, that is not quite what you should do!"

I have read many books about WWII, and I think that this book captures growing up—maturing—from 1935 through the war and after from a unique and appealing personal perspective that adds valuable insights for all of us. I heartily recommend it.

—Bruce Hann, Emeritus Professor of Creative Writing, Des Moines Area Community College, Ankeny, IA

It is impossible to read this compelling and captivating memoir without thinking of the current terror and brutality in Ukraine. Meta's story must be told and retold to ensure that it is not lost in time, not only as a reminder of the very dark and evil side of humanity, but of the buoyancy of the human spirit where light pierces darkness.

—Dr. Hemchand Gossai, Author of numerous books on the Jewish Bible, Holocaust expert, Professor of Liberal Arts, Northern Virginia Community College

Heartbreaking and yet filled with hope. Authors Caroline Crocker and Meta Evenbly share a story filled with recollections of a horrendous time in history. While reading, I was amazed and inspired by the courage and hope found. My tears led to smiles as I cheered for the family and their friends. This is an amazing book that reminded me to search for good even in the worst of times.

—Melissa Henderson, Author of inspirational children's books and magazine articles, Mount Pleasant, SC

This detailed and unflinching account of a child's life "under the jackboot" of Nazi oppression during WWII serves as a primary source in company with others such as those written by Anne Frank, Corrie Ten Boom, and Rutka Laskier. Extensive use of Dutch words, dialogue, and descriptions of home and family link contemporary readers with a time and place that might otherwise be inaccessible to many young people today.

—Amy Imbody, Founder and Director, Center for Redemptive Education, Ashland, VA

This moving and shocking memoir is an account of how Meta, the youngest daughter of a working-class Dutch postman and his German wife, experienced the Nazi occupation of the Netherlands. Its picture of the brutality of this occupation and the response of Dutch society is remarkable for its vividness, giving a clear picture of the evil of Nazism, something which is also recognized by Meta's mother's German relations immediately after the war. The memoir concludes with Meta's struggle to find a place for herself in the postwar world and her unsuccessful attempt to fulfill her dream of becoming a doctor. It is essential reading for all those interested in modern European history and the nature of German national socialism.

—Dr. Anthony Polonsky, Professor Emeritus of Holocaust Studies, Brandeis University; Chief Historian, Global Education Outreach Project, Museum of Polish Jews in Warsaw, Cambridge, MA

A delightful, fascinating book. From a historical viewpoint it draws the reader into the historical setting of World War II and provides valuable historical contextualization for the reader. For young people, hopefully it will spark curiosity to further research various aspects of life in the Netherlands during World War II. The Dutch words incorporated throughout the book make the reader feel as though he/she was there. The heroine is a spunky and bright light throughout the book. As a result of the compelling anecdotes from the story, I feel like I "know" Meta. But I'd like to know her better.

—Kristin Pushak, History teacher, Trinity Christian School, Fairfax, VA

Brave Face is about the worst and best of humanity: it is about fear, hunger, poverty, loss, heroism, sacrifice, and the delightful warmth of family life. Over time, and given the random confluence of luck and determination, one can survive and perhaps, with even more luck and determination, thrive. While academic texts certainly have their place, novels have the unique ability to draw a reader into the many human aspects of a story, even one as horrible and alien as the Holocaust. *Brave Face* brings the reader into a world that is still unimaginable to all but those few still alive who actually experienced World War II. It is recommended to any person who wants to understand how ordinary people can survive, and even thrive, after living through extraordinary times that reveal the worst and the best of humanity.

—Dr. John Schmitz, Author of *Enemies Among Us: The Relocation, Internment, and Repatriation of German, Italian and Japanese Americans during the Second World War* and Professor of History, Northern Virginia Community College

Set in the Netherlands' darkest days, this is a story of perseverance and a child's fearless attitude.

—Harm Timmerije, Administrator for the Facebook group My Dutch Heritage, Rotterdam, The Netherlands

Brave Face, a memoir cowritten by Caroline Crocker and her mother Meta Evenbly, is an eye-opening account from the perspective of Meta's childhood days in the Nazi-occupied Netherlands, as well as Germany. What makes this Holocaust memoir remarkable is that the reader sees through young Meta, a non-Jewish child, how the events of war, with its hatred and prejudices, impacts every single person, no matter one's faith, nationality, or age. A true treasure of history, both tragic and uplifting.

 —**Elaine Stock, author of the Resilient Women of WWII trilogy**

BRAVE FACE

THE INSPIRING WWII MEMOIR OF A
DUTCH/GERMAN CHILD

I. CAROLINE CROCKER

META A. EVENBLY

ISBN 9789493276673 (ebook)

ISBN 9789493276659 (paperback)

ISBN 9789493276666 (hardcover)

Publisher: Amsterdam Publishers, The Netherlands

info@amsterdampublishers.com

Brave Face is part of the series WW2 Historical Fiction

Cover image: Helitha Nilmalgoda

The stories in this book were inspired by real events in the life of Meta Bisschop Evenbly. The names used belong to actual people, most of whom are deceased. Every effort has been made to portray these people faithfully. The dialogue is a product of the authors' imaginations.

Illustrations are mostly from the author's family album, but also include some public domain photographs.

Book website: https://iammeta.org

First author blog: https://ramblingruminations.com

YouTube playlist: http://tiny.cc/jackboot

CONTENTS

READER INFORMATION

The events in this book took place in the Netherlands, so the book contains many Dutch words. They are defined the first time that they appear. If they are used again, we provided a glossary.

Please be aware that Meta's father is a man of strong opinions who uses equally strong language. After extensive conversations with those it may offend, we have decided to leave in some of his actual words for the sake of authenticity.

Several of Meta's friends, relatives and neighbors appear more than once. To help you keep track of them, we included an appendix.

"He will wipe every tear from their eyes, and death shall be no more, neither shall there be mourning, nor crying, nor pain anymore, for the former things have passed away." Rev. 21:4

FOREWORD

Although everyone is born, lives, dies, and is eventually forgotten, the world is impacted by their lives. Every new generation lives in its own time, under distinct circumstances, and in a different environment, but all arise from those who went before. Knowing the past therefore may increase our capacity to understand ourselves and our neighbors. It might even aid us in appreciating people from other cultures. And that can't help but have a positive impact on the world.

So, even though some of this story was painful to recall, I am sharing it with the hope that it will be helpful to the generations who come after me. For some people, it may help them to better empathize with those who suffer. For others, it may reassure them that they are not alone in their struggles. For all, I hope that it will solidify an intention to never let something like World War II happen again.

Writing this book was also beneficial to me personally. It helped me to more fully appreciate some of what made me who I am. Yes, I have two very full refrigerators—I have known starvation. Yes, I sometimes suspect people of cheating me—I have lived in the presence of members of the National Socialist Movement (NSBers). Yes, as a younger woman, I grieved over not having become a physician and indeed not even having a college degree. That's why I persisted in my studies and finally graduated at 59 years old. I've performed stretching exercises all my life—in case they might help me to literally rise above the results of childhood starvation and grow taller. My entire life has been affected by my struggle to overcome living under the "jackboots" of Nazi oppression, war, poverty, and discrimination.

Even though my family and I survived, and I was never in a concentration camp, the war changed me. It molded me. For good. For bad. It was part of what made me who I am. You see, I am Meta and always will be. My name is pronounced "May-tuh," which means, "pearl." Pearls look smooth, beautiful, and shiny, but like me, they grow as the result of difficulty. You would never know that in the middle of each pearl is a painful grain of sand or other irritant, but it's there. Just ask the oyster! Also like me, pearls not only have a brave face, but they're tough: they can be scratched, but not be crushed. I think my name is very appropriate. I am Meta, and I'm proud that I overcame my personal jackboots.

Meta A. Bisschop Evenbly

meta@iammeta.org

PREFACE

My mother, Meta, is a born storyteller. Throughout my childhood I heard many of the stories in this book. As I grew older, the thought that I should record them for future generations often entered my head, but it didn't stay there for long. That changed in 2017 when my beloved father passed away.

It was then too late to ask him about his childhood and the aunt, cousins, and friends who perished in Auschwitz. It was too late to probe into the details of the stories that he could not bring himself to relate until well after his hair had grown gray. World War II (WWII) veterans are now in their nineties; soon they will all be gone. Many of them never talked about their experiences with their children and grandchildren—they did not want to. But once again, in the United States, in Europe, and around the world, authoritarianism, nationalism, Holocaust denial, antisemitism, and many other kinds of discrimination have taken root and are spreading. Everyone must hear what those who experienced WWII have to say.

I began this book by writing those stories that I could remember. Meta read the resulting document, filled in some details, corrected others, and gave me more stories. Next, I researched the historical context and checked that the incidents were in the right order (Meta adjusted the manuscript wherever I went wrong). During the process,

Meta remembered and shared more about her childhood, and I added those stories, too. This cyclical and close collaboration continued for over two years. Eventually, *Brave Face* was complete. Looking back, I can honestly say that it was a privilege, a pleasure, and an unforgettable experience to co-author this book with Meta. I am proud to be her daughter.

Brave Face is more than a collaborative memoir. Because of its unique perspective and subject matter, it also speaks loudly to several contemporary issues. As I write this preface, Russia is bombing Ukraine and bringing devastation to the lives of countless innocents, be they Ukrainian or Russian. Like Meta, if they survive, many will spend years, if not their entire lives, trying to overcome the damage inflicted upon them by the leadership and actions of a nationalistic megalomaniac. As the true story of a child who grew up in the Netherlands during WWII, which was orchestrated by another megalomaniac, this book is our contribution to a vital conversation.

Most WWII books either highlight the Jewish experience or focus on military aspects of the war. In either case, they rightfully point out the extreme inhumanity of the Holocaust and, peripherally, the senselessness of claiming the superiority of one people group over another. *Brave Face* approaches these same themes from a different perspective. Meta was a working-class child whose life was upended by forces beyond her ability to understand. She was traumatized by the horror of what was happening around her; thought deeply about the guilt expressed by her German relatives; and grieved over the loss of Jewish neighbors and classmates. She had intimate knowledge of the fact that bigotry and extreme nationalism led to the inhumanity that is embodied in fascism.

Unfortunately, the end of the war did not eradicate all of the attitudes that led to it. The Nazis had been defeated, but seeds of their despicable bigotry lingered. Those whom Meta considered friends ostracized her fiancé because, with his half-Jewish mother, he wasn't a Roman Catholic. A teacher's prejudice against anyone who could speak German spread to her students so that none of them would engage with Meta. Eventually, their actions forced Meta to leave the selective high school which could have provided her with the education she needed to become a physician. Sadly, the fundamental attitudes that lead to fascism are not unique to any one country. My work on *Brave Face* has given me much food for thought.

Today, many heated political discussions feature immigration and refugee issues. Meta's mother, Augustine, grew up as part of a very large Polish family that immigrated to Germany before Augustine was born. Augustine immigrated to the Netherlands from Germany when she was only 17 years old. After Meta married, she immigrated to Canada. My family moved to the USA when I was a child. As an adult, I immigrated to England, eventually married a British man, and my children were born there. We then moved to the US and adopted an immigrant from Bulgaria. It seems that immigration is a family tradition.

Immigration issues are also important in *Brave Face*. There is no doubt that having a German mother was more beneficial than detrimental during the war: Augustine could sometimes deflect the attention of the occupying soldiers away from Meta's father and his activities. After the war, however, being an immigrant from Germany had its challenges. Dutch people were understandably angry with Germany, and this anger sometimes manifested as unfair prejudice against anyone with a German connection. Of course, many in their small community knew and loved Augustine, but not everyone.

In *Brave Face*, Meta encountered many people who struggled because they were immigrants. In the Catholic high school, bullies beat up her very timid sister simply because her mother was a German immigrant. Right across the street from her home in Scheveningen, Meta witnessed neighborhood children disrespecting a refugee from Romania because he had an accent. Even her good friend Jan had to be careful not to be too friendly with Meta, simply because his family were from Indonesia.

These days we hear much about the need for equity: for women, for those under a burden of poverty, for people of color, for those with different sexual orientations. This is not a new problem. As an observant youngster, Meta was cognizant of the inequity of the treatment she received simply because she was both female and poor. At a very tender age Meta wailed out that she wanted to be a boy, but that was only the beginning of the struggle. Throughout her young life, when Meta excelled at sports and enjoyed adventures, she was told to "act like a lady." There's no doubt that she has thoroughly enjoyed her roles as wife, mother, grandmother, and great grandmother, but being expected to fit into a gender stereotype has always been a trial to her.

Inequity due to poverty also had an impact on Meta. Although her father worked long hours for the post office, hand-me-down clothes, holey shoes, and once-a-week meat were the peacetime norm. When teenage Meta and her sister got jobs, they were expected to give what was earned to the family, and they did. Augustine taught her children both extreme frugality and how to make the best of what they had. Nevertheless, her children suffered. In the way of young children, Meta was particularly offended because she was never given chocolate during catechism class. Poor children were only considered worthy of hard candies.

While the poverty that Meta's family experienced before and after the war wasn't life-threatening, the psychological trauma of always being considered less than others was significant. It meant that Meta took the declaration that their part of the country would not be liberated until much later, because they were not of strategic importance, as a personal slight that still hurts today. On the bright side, even though childhood poverty left her with a permanent fear of not having enough money to sustain life, she has lots of chocolate in her pantry. And her great grandchildren know it.

According to the Children's Defense Fund, almost 11 million children in the USA go to bed hungry. And we are isolated from the effects of the wars we fight. Because food and medicine are two of the first commodities to become scarce during war, and her family did not have relatives in the country, it was worse for Meta. Ration cards are worthless when the stores are empty. In *Brave Face,* the absence of food, the lengths the family went to in order to get it during the Hunger Winter, and the resultant lingering weakness and disease, are described in vivid detail. Hearing Meta talk about the devastation of extreme hunger and even near-death reminded me of the plight of those today who, through war, politics, or famine, have little or no access to food, medicine, heat, and clean water.

Even as her life story points a gentle finger at many human rights issues, I believe that, through this book, Meta will inspire others with the hard-won lessons she passed down to me. Never feel sorry for yourself and never give up. Remember that appearances matter. Enjoy what you can, when you can, and with whom you can. With the help of others, sheer determination, and a bit of luck, perhaps you too will not only overcome your personal "jackboots," but also be able to assist others in overcoming theirs.

I. Caroline Evenbly Crocker, PhD

caroline@iammeta.org

Beelden uit mijn kinderjaren
Uit mijn jeugd zo vrij en blij
Trekken somtijds kalm en rustig
Aan mijn peinzend hoofd voorbij

Ik denk nog dikwijls aan die dagen
Vol geluk en stille vreê
Hoe verheugd ik steeds ontwaakte
In ons hutje bij de zee
Hoe verheugd ik steeds ontwaakte
In ons hutje, ons hutje bij de zee

Visions from my childhood years
From my youth, so free and happy,
Sometimes file, quiet and peaceful
Through my pensive mind

I often think about those days
Full of happiness and peace
How joyfully I awoke
In our little cabin by the sea
How joyfully I awoke
In our little cabin by the sea

1

THE VIEW FROM THE WINDOW

I shivered; my forehead pressed to the front window of our row house over the butcher's shop on the Weimerstraat in Den Haag. A single leaf floated through the misty morning air. Just around the corner, patrolling the Franklinstraat, two German soldiers with rifles slung over their shoulders paced the red-bricked street up and down, up and down. No other people were within view.

"*Mamma, kom snel* [Mamma, come quickly]," I called. "*Wat is er buiten aan de hand* [What's going on outside]?"

Mamma sat motionless with unfocused eyes and tightly folded hands.

"Get away from that window, Meta!" my father barked from across the room.

I took a quick step back.

My mother rose from her chair and pulled me away from the window. She picked me up, straining me tightly to her chest.

Then no one spoke.

I tried to peek outside over Mamma's shoulder, but the net curtains obscured my view.

My father went to the window, watched for a few minutes, turned and silently beckoned Mamma, who deposited me into her chair and joined him.

After giving me a warning frown, my teenaged sister Corrie went to stand next to Mamma.

There they stood, all peering through the tiny crack between the net curtains, being very careful to remain concealed. I noticed they were no longer watching me.

Quickly, I took my chance, moving towards the side of the window. My other sister Sieglinde followed, whispering, "Meta, we're not allowed. We're too young!"

I ignored her. Pushing the heavy top curtain aside, I slipped behind it and looked out.

Sieglinde took her usual place behind me, holding onto my dress and timidly peeking over my shoulder.

The Nazi soldiers continued their marching; their shiny black jackboots snapped an ominous rhythm audible through the drafty window. As the mantel clock chimed 12, the hair on the back of my neck stood on end.

Just then, I spotted a man coming down the Franklinstraat towards our street, pedaling his wooden-wheeled bicycle so furiously that his legs were a blur. Where could he be going all alone and in such a hurry?

Momentarily distracted by my racing thoughts, the ear-piercing report of machine gun fire made me jump. Sieglinde gasped. The man fell to the ground; his bicycle slid away from under him. He lay flat on his back in the middle of an ever-growing circle of blood. My stomach clenched and cold sweat broke out on my forehead.

"Swine!" Pappa hissed through his teeth.

Mamma murmured, "They were waiting for him," as she twisted her apron between her fingers.

I turned back to the window, my eyes drawn as if by magnets, and my breaths almost deafening in the silence.

The soldiers slowly backed away while watching the man cautiously.

"*Lafaards* [cowards]! Afraid of a dead man!" my father spat with his fists so tightly clenched that his knuckles were white.

One of the soldiers pointed his machine gun from a distance and emptied it into the man's chest. After waiting for quite some time, both soldiers approached and turned the dead body over with their feet. The second soldier, his jackboots now covered in blood, fired his entire magazine of bullets into the man's back.

The soldiers backed away and waited again, all the while scrutinizing their handiwork. I wondered why. Were they genuinely expecting there to be any life left?

After what seemed like an eternity, they once again approached the mangled corpse. Each soldier grasped one of the man's feet, and they dragged him over the street and up onto the sidewalk, leaving a trail of blood in his wake. His arms flopped over his head, and his face bounced on the pavement as they went. The soldiers slung the body into the ice cream parlor on the corner as if he were no more than a piece of trash. They picked up his broken bicycle and threw it onto the sidewalk. There it remained, a forlorn testament to that day's activities.

I let out a whimper. Sieglinde clutched my hand and trembled while silent tears made rivers down her cheeks.

Mamma came over, knelt in front of us, and gently wiped our wet cheeks. Picking me up and, holding my sister's hand, she took us back to her chair, well away from the offending window. I sat myself on my mother's cozy lap while Sieglinde perched on the arm of the chair. Mamma silently enclosed us with her shaking arms. Corrie stood with her head pillowed on Pappa's shoulder, trying valiantly—but unsuccessfully—to gulp back her sobs. There were no words of comfort; there could be none.

I witnessed my first murder at just six years old. Now, 80 years later, the memory still makes me cry. World War II changed my life.

2

HOW IT ALL BEGAN

Pappa often told me I was born with my eyes and my mouth wide open. This is how he said it happened.

In January of 1935, Mamma divulged a secret to seven-year-old Corrie and two-year-old Sieglinde. "You girls are going to get a new sister or brother today. When the doctor arrives, I want you to sit quietly in the kitchen with Pappa."

The doctor arrived at lunchtime, and Pappa showed him to the living room of our upper-floor row house in the Zutphensestraat. It was the only heated room in the house. My mother, by now moaning and even crying out in pain, lay on the divan.

After spending a long day in the kitchen while Pappa was pacing the floor, Corrie wringing her hands, and Sieglinde sucking on her finger, ear-piercing wailing alerted everyone: the newest member of the family had been born.

The doctor popped his head into the kitchen. "Meneer Bisschop, congratulations. You have a daughter. Come and meet her!"

My father didn't have to be asked twice. Despite his short stature, he took long strides to reach my mother's side, his wavy chestnut hair bouncing with each step. Corrie followed, peering around the corner into the living room. Pappa kissed his wife's forehead and whispered,

"Well done, Guusje!" He rubbed her limp hand gently. "How are you doing? Are you okay now?"

Mamma inhaled deeply before forcing a smile. "I'm still alive. I suppose that's all anyone could ask. Meet *unser kleiner Spatz* ['our little sparrow' in German]. Now we have drei Grazien ['three Graces' in German]."

Pappa tenderly stroked his wife's cheek before turning his attention to me. In the manner of all babies, I was frantically searching for food while lying in my mamma's arms. Pappa lifted me up, kissed my forehead, inhaled my newborn fragrance, and passed me back to Mamma. "I think she's hungry, but Corrie and Sieglinde want to meet her. Are you ready for them?"

Mamma closed her eyes and nodded feebly.

Pappa burst into the kitchen with a giant smile on his face and stars in his blue eyes. He bent down and enveloped my sisters in an exuberant hug. Sieglinde pulled on his shirt. "Baby?"

Pappa nodded his head and chuckled. "*Ja*, you have a sister, and she has a good set of lungs. Come meet her."

Corrie and Sieglinde tiptoed in, clutching Pappa's hands.

Mamma, with her mahogany hair forming a wavy fan around her pale face, lay on the divan while holding a tiny blanket-wrapped bundle.

"Why is she so red and wrinkled?" Corrie worried.

Pappa laughed. "She'll look better soon."

Cautiously, Sieglinde drew near and gazed in astonishment at her new sister as I wailed out my dissatisfaction with life. Sieglinde's eyes filled, and she stepped back. "Baby no like me."

Pappa pushed Siegie forward again. "She just doesn't know you yet. There's no reason to cry. Try holding her hand."

My sister took her chubby, slightly wet, first finger out of her mouth and placed it into the palm of one of my furiously waving hands. Her mouth formed an "O" as my tiny digits curled around her finger. Wonder of wonders, I stopped crying. While my enraptured sister continued loaning me her finger, Pappa lifted me from Mamma's arms and carefully lowered me into my crib. Sieglinde smiled as I held her finger tightly, my eyelids drooped, and I peacefully fell asleep on my seagrass stuffed mattress.

"Mamma," she lisped. "Baby my friend."

~

"Dickie, come!" I called, dropping to my bottom on the front step and patting the place next to me. Mamma had given me permission to play outside, provided I stay where she could see me on the narrow sidewalk directly in front of our house. Dickie, with his brown eyes and dark hair, lived a few doors down. He toddled over and plonked himself on the curb, making his rosy cheeks vibrate. We held hands with our chubby tights-covered legs sticking straight out in front of us.

As our neighbors strolled by, they smiled indulgently, some even giving us a wink. I sat up straighter, reveling in the attention. A gray-haired lady on her way back from the corner bakery paused to chat. "What are your names, *Kindertjes* [Children]?" she enquired, leaning on her cane.

Dickie hid his face in my shoulder and didn't say a word. Despite only being two years old, I raised my pointed chin, looked her in the eye and announced, "I Meta."

The woman burst into good-natured cackles and agreed. "So you are. I think very much so as well!" She bent down, shook the hand I proffered, wished both of us a good day and proceeded on down the street.

I nudged Dickie and issued a command. "We sing!" In our baby voices, we piped out, "*De motten die motten kapot* [The moths they have to die]" over and over again, giggling as we warbled the silly play on words. I'd seen my father chuckle as he boomed the song out while inspecting his woolen clothes for moth holes, so knew for sure that the song was absolutely hilarious.

I puffed out my chest and sang louder, especially as I noticed several neighbors peering out of their windows. Being sure that they really liked our singing, I elbowed Dickie to belt the song out with me. Soon both of us were shout-singing, "*DE MOTTEN DIE MOTTEN KAPOT!*"

Eventually, Mamma called down from the window, "That's quite enough. I'm getting a headache. Why don't you play ball?"

~

The sun blazed overhead in a virtually cloudless blue sky. When Mamma suggested we all go on a picnic instead of to church, nobody dissented.

My statuesque mother was already dressed in her pretty, woolen Sunday dress while Pappa wore his gray suit with a white shirt and blue tie.

"My drei Grazien, put on your clean dresses," Mamma instructed, her gentle blue eyes twinkling. "We want to look our best for our outing."

I watched as Corrie adorned her own hair with a fancy new ribbon, and my mother brushed Sieglinde's ringlets until they shone like gold. My sisters looked so pretty; I felt so plain. Finally, clasping my squirming body between her knees, Mamma combed my straight caramel-colored hair and tied it with a new red ribbon. My favorite color!

Pappa gave me an indulgent smile as I twirled in delight. Winking, he tugged my hair. "I hope it isn't windy outside because, with such a huge, wide bow on your head, and as small as you are, you might fly away."

I visualized the strong sea wind, a virtually constant feature of the coastal area where we lived in Scheveningen, lifting me off my feet. Floating along through the air was an exciting prospect, but... "Could that happen, Pappa?"

Pappa chuckled and didn't answer. I frowned, pulled the collar of my dress up to my mouth, and chewed on it. At three years old, this was a real concern.

Mamma picked up the picnic basket with the bread, cheese and apples and issued marching orders as we proceeded down the stairs. "Spilletje (my nickname), stop chewing your clothes. Corrie, make sure the door is locked once we're out. Cor, hold on to Meta *alsjeblieft* [please]—you know how she is. Sieglinde, hold Meta's other hand."

Good, for now I was in no imminent danger. My father would hold me down. Being safe in the midst of my family, I soon forgot my fears and began to skip down the road.

Crossing the street where we lived, we started along the Zwarte Pad, which leads through the sand dunes directly to the beach.

"Hey Meta and Siegie, did you guys know the sand dunes protect Holland from flooding?" Corrie had her big sister voice on.

"*Ja*, everybody knows that!" Siegie responded. "I even know that a lot of our very flat country is below it."

I ignored them, focusing instead on the stubby tree just ahead. It was slanted, forced to grow that way by the wind. But could it be climbed? I pulled free to run over and try.

"Spilletje, come back here. Stay on the path."

So, we all walked between the sandy hills, the smell of the sea mixing with that of Pappa's cigarette, the fragrant wild flowers, and acrid odor of the hot sun beating on the Zwarte Pad. Once Pappa had chosen a picnic spot he deemed ideal, one sheltered from the sea wind, Mamma spread out the woolen blanket.

The adults and Corrie sat enjoying the peace of the day while Sieglinde and I built a sandcastle and decorated it with rocks and flowers.

"There, it's done." Sieglinde stood back to admire our work.

I danced with delight as I stuck a final flower in the top.

"Meta, be careful! You'll knock it over."

Now my legs were itching to embark on the next activity. "Mamma, Pappa, may I go and pick blackberries? Some of them look ripe."

Pappa shaded his eyes with his hand as he responded, "Yes, just make sure that wherever you go you can still see us. Then you'll know that we can see you. Sieglinde, go with her."

My sister and I raced towards the nearest blackberry bushes and picked and picked. We stuffed our mouths full, and purple juice ran down our chins onto our clothes. Our fingers were purple, too.

"Oh look, more over there!" I ran to the next bunch of bushes, ready to continue gathering the fragrant fruit.

"Meta, this is far enough. I can't see Pappa. You know what he said. That means he can't see us, either."

I shrugged. "I hear him whistling. So, it'll be okay."

"They didn't say to stay where we can hear them! We have to be able to see them. I don't want you to get in trouble again," Sieglinde whined.

I'd already moved on to the next set of bushes. Sieglinde followed, her mouth turned down at the corners.

Just then Pappa stopped whistling. I looked around fearfully, immediately putting my collar in my mouth, turning it purple, too.

"Um Siegie? Do you know where Mamma and Pappa are?"

"I told you so..." Sieglinde began, putting her hands on her hips.

Tears welled up in my sky-blue eyes.

"Ukkies [little ones], come and have some lunch!" Mamma's trill was a welcome sound.

Sieglinde took my hand, we sprinted in the direction of her voice, and both of us plopped down onto the picnic blanket. We choked down the freshly baked bread and Edam cheese, because wasting food was never an option with parents who had frequently experienced hunger as children.

It had now been several weeks since our picnic and high time I checked on our sandcastle.

"Mamma, *alsjeblieft*, may I go play in the dunes?"

Mamma didn't answer. She was busy tidying up after breakfast, singing a German folk song while she worked.

"Please, Mamma? I really want to. I'm big now. See?" I stretched to be as tall as I could. "And I'll be good. I promise." I tugged on my mother's skirt to make sure I had her full attention.

Crouching down, Mamma held my chin and looked into my eyes. "You really want to, don't you? And you are getting pretty old..." She hesitated before giving a decisive nod. "Oh, all right—I think you're

9

big enough." She pinched my cheek. "Only if Sieglinde goes with you."

I scampered to give my sister the wonderful news. Sieglinde and I grabbed our coats, said goodbye to Mamma, who told us to be back by lunchtime, and we left for the dunes—all by ourselves. Up until we reached the Zwarte Pad, every time we looked over our shoulders, we saw Mamma watching us from the front window.

The pale sun was still low in the grayish sky and the cold wind bitter. I shivered since we'd been in far too much of a hurry to do up our coats.

"Meta, slow down." Sieglinde stopped walking to button our outer garments, adjust our hats so they covered our ears and tuck our scarves more closely around our necks.

I danced from foot to foot. "Siegie, hurry! I want to watch the fishing boats go out to sea."

"It's much too late for that. They anchor in the harbor before light to bring their fish to the market."

Thunderclouds gathered on my face, and Sieglinde hurriedly continued, "Maybe we can see the *nettenboetsters* [women mending fishing nets]. You'll love seeing them work in their Scheveningen costumes."

Easily distracted, I shouted, "That'd be great. Oh, listen! I hear them singing!"

Sieglinde followed as I scrambled to the summit of the nearest dune.

There they were, perched on top of fishing nets piled high on their horse-drawn carriages. I watched closely as the women unloaded the nets, then plonked myself down to better observe them, my legs straight out in front of me.

"Meta, we can't stay here. It's rude to stare at people like that!"

"They don't care. Probably can't even see us." I lay down on my stomach with my chin propped in my hands.

After noticing that the *nettenboetsters* didn't appear to mind curious children watching them, Sieglinde, sighing, sat beside me.

The women first heaved the huge wet fishing nets over the fence and several bushes. Chattering and singing as they worked, they carefully checked them and mended all the holes where the fabric was torn.

Siegie whispered, "They have to be careful to get all the holes because herring are so slender."

"Yuck!" I'd recently tried salted herring, which my parents told me was a Dutch delicacy.

I watched carefully, desperately wishing I could assist them, but not daring to ask. I knew they'd say what everyone always did: "You're too small." When my curiosity had been thoroughly satisfied, I suggested that we now go to the beach.

"*Nee*, Meta! We can't do that. Mamma didn't give permission!" Sieglinde jumped to her feet, curls bouncing as she shook her head.

"Just for a short time—she won't know. We'll be back in time for lunch," I wheedled. The adventure was irresistible.

Sieglinde put her hands on her hips and once more opened her mouth. Noticing that she wasn't convinced, I alternately stamped both my feet, emphasizing each word: "I want to go!"

Sieglinde shrugged and sighed. "Oh, all right, just for a short while."

Running down the long, shallow, concrete stairway, we caught sight of the yellow-sand beach, which stretched for many kilometers. Apart from the ever-present seagulls, the only life we saw was a man with a wooden handcart, looking for valuables washed ashore after shipwrecks. I wondered what he would do with the things he picked up.

The tide was out, and the wet sand full of tiny, fragile, blue, white, pink, and brown seashells. I scurried around, busily collecting those that begged me to take them home.

Showing the contents of my skirt to my sister, I said, "Look, Sieglinde, maybe I can decorate the table with these!"

"What? Use your head! If you show Mamma the shells, she'll know we were on the beach. No wonder you're always getting in trouble. Think before you act! I don't want Pappa to spank you again." Mamma rarely hit us, but Pappa was a very different story.

She had a point. I deposited the shells into my coat pocket and determined to store them in my own special treasure box under my bed.

The day quickly grew warmer as the sun climbed higher in the sky and the morning mist dissipated. Hastily removing my hat, scarf, shoes, and socks, but not my coat (it wasn't that warm), I waded into the frigid water.

Sieglinde shook her finger as she hurled warnings at me. "Meta, that's a bad idea. Watch out! Don't go too far. Pappa said we should never go deeper than our knees. And that's when he's with us!"

"Yeah, yeah, yeah. I know. I know. The undercurrent... Bla-di-bla bla bla."

Now, Sieglinde was right, and I definitely had no desire to drown. Neither of us could swim—the sea was too wild and cold for Pappa to be able to teach his small girls. So, I was extra cautious and satisfied myself with only immersing my feet. The water curled around my bright-red toes, and my feet sunk lower and lower as the sand washed away from under them. The cold water made my bones ache.

After a very short time, I nonchalantly strolled back to where Sieglinde was sitting and situated myself next to her. We lay back in the soft sand, listened to the rhythm of the waves, smelled the salt in the air and watched the fluffy clouds go by. The sunshine warmed our faces so that we grew sleepy and eventually had a little snooze.

The sun was high by the time Sieglinde woke up and stretched luxuriously. Already awake, I was lying still while watching her out of the corner of my eye. Sieglinde sat up abruptly.

"Meta, you should have woken me. I can hear your tummy rumbling. Get up!" My sister shook my shoulder. "Hurry! It's late. Mamma will be angry with us!"

I rolled over to examine a few more shells. "I'm hurrying." I yawned before slowly brushing the sand off my feet, pulling on my socks and shoes, and picking up my hat and scarf.

"Come on, Slow Poke! We're going to have to run."

I got up quickly. "Oh no! What if she says we missed lunch? We'll have to eat our lunch for dinner! I'm starving!"

With Sieglinde dragging me by the hand, we sped back home.

3

FAMILY LIFE

Soon we were in front of the row of houses which ended with our small home on the Leeuwardensestraat. Red-tile-roofed houses made of red brick walls with green-painted doors lined the street on our side and beige brick walls with brown doors the other. There were no front yards at all, although some houses had a small window box for flowers.

Therefore, I assumed the whole world was constructed of gray cement tiles, like the sidewalks, and red bricks, like the streets. The dirt in the parks and gardens would have been brought in specially to grow plants. Now I stopped to think.

"Siegie, where did they find all the dirt to put in parks and flower boxes?"

She frowned. Although I had a surprisingly large vocabulary for such a young child, my pronunciation left much to be desired. "I don't understand. What do you mean?"

After sighing deeply, I explained my hypothesis to Sieglinde.

"Oh Meta, you're so silly! The world is made of dirt and water. Under the streets and sidewalks, there's dirt."

"No, under ours there's sand. I saw it."

Sieglinde rolled her eyes, reached through the brass mail slot in our front door, pulled on the rope right behind it. Without her even touching the doorknob, the door swung open. "Under the sand there's dirt."

"No, there's water."

Now I began to worry about everything being built on the sea. Grabbing the corner of my collar, I had a quick chew as we stepped through the door into a small hallway and started up the steep stairway. Mamma's bicycle with its two extra seats for children hung on the wall, and I gave the front wheel a spin. Pappa was at work delivering mail, so the space for his black bicycle was vacant.

Sien den Dulk and her family lived in the ground floor home below us. They had a separate entrance two doors down from ours, but their living room was next to our stairs. I was strictly forbidden to tap the walls on my way up, but did it anyway, grinning when I heard our long-suffering neighbor's wrathful shout. "Stop that, Meta!"

"Mamma, we're home!" I called out as I reached the top of the stairs and turned right into the hall. Removing my coat, I peeked in the door on my left to see if Mamma was in the kitchen. Yes! I flung myself into her waiting arms while Sieglinde quietly hung up her coat and put away her other outer garments. Mine were dropped onto a kitchen chair. Mamma scooped them up and put them in their proper places with a little shake of her head. I couldn't reach the coat hook anyway.

"Where have you been? You were supposed to have been home for lunch. It's two o'clock now. I was beginning to get worried!" Mamma put her hands on her hips.

Thankfully, the doorbell rang before I was forced to answer.

"It's a bit early for Agnes. I wonder who it could be," Mamma murmured. As she headed to the living room window, Mamma paused, turned and pointed at us. "You two, go into the kitchen and eat your bread. I saved lunch for you."

Sieglinde and I exchanged a look. Phew! We were allowed to eat.

My mother peered out of the window and threw up her hands. "Oh, it's Tante Agnes at the door! And it looks like she brought your dresses. I wonder why she's here so early."

Mamma quickly removed her apron and hung it on a hook on the back of the kitchen door. Then she hurried to the top of the entry staircase and pulled one end of the rope that had been threaded from the front doorknob, up the railing, all the way to the top of the stairway. When Mamma pulled on the top end of the rope, the door opened like magic.

"Come in, Agnes," Mamma called down the stairs. My mother's Titian-haired sister put her umbrella in the brass stand and lumbered up the stairs, bringing the carrier bag of dresses with her. She and Mamma had an arrangement: my mother would purchase enough fabric to make clothing both for her own small ones and for Agnes's daughter, Albertine. Agnes would sew the dresses or skirts, retain one as payment for her labor, and give the others to us. Because we only got a new dress twice a year, I danced with excitement to see my new dress while Sieglinde stood quietly watching, her finger in her mouth.

"Let me take your coat," Mamma said as she gave her sister three kisses. "I'll put the kettle on. We'll have a nice piece of cake. You can take a cake home for your family, as well. I baked two!" She turned to us. "Girls, go eat your lunches. I won't remind you again."

Mamma put her sister's hat and gloves on the top shelf of coat rack, which was high on the wall at the top of the stairs. She hung her coat on the sixth hook, which was reserved for guests. My aunt peered into the little oval mirror in the center of the coat rack while smoothing her windblown hair.

"Mamma, look, white stuff on her sleeve!"

Mamma frowned and shook her head slightly.

I snapped my mouth closed.

The bottom halves of the stairway, hall and kitchen walls were painted with high-gloss leaded paint so they could be washed. Necessitated by the rainy climate, the top halves of those walls were not painted, but whitewashed with a chalky powder that absorbed the moisture.

As the portly Tante Agnes squeezed past the bicycle on the wall, her right sleeve had brushed up against the whitewash. Mamma matter-of-factly grabbed a brush and cleaned the sleeve. Agnes never even noticed, being busy exclaiming over Sieglinde's ringlets.

The whitewashed walls had another important use, at least at our house. My father had a special place under the thin, colorful rug behind the coat rack that protected the hung coats from the whitewash, where he scraped the wall with a knife and then ate the powder that flaked off into his hand to cure his heartburn. It worked pretty well.

"Agnes, come into the kitchen and keep me company while I make the tea and set out the cake," Mamma invited.

"Gusti, did you hear the latest from Germany?" Agnes looked uncharacteristically solemn. (Mamma's name was Auguste, but she was called Gusti by her German relatives, Guusje by her husband, and Guusta by her Dutch friends.)

Mamma didn't notice. "Come, sit. Siegie and Meta, you too."

Agnes entered our brightly decorated kitchen, and Mamma quickly moved a stray scrubbing brush to its proper place under the sink behind the green-checkered curtain that hid cleaning products, two large enamel pots, and a pail for storing root vegetables and potatoes.

Agnes made herself comfortable on one of the wooden chairs placed at the far end of the table while Sieglinde and I shared the other chair.

"Um, Gusti..." Tante Agnes's voice trailed off.

I could see that Mamma was still too busy bustling around to listen.

My aunt sighed.

Nibbling on my bread and cheese, my eyes wandered until they came to rest on the slightly patched pans on the shelf over my head. I smiled, remembering that, only last week, Mamma took a pan outside after hearing the repair man's special cry as he walked down the street. Sieglinde and I watched as he measured the hole in the pan and took out two appropriately sized patches, each constructed of two metal discs with white asbestos fabric sandwiched between them. He placed a patch on either side of the hole, screwed the patches together, and the pan was almost as good as new.

While my aunt updated my mother on Albertine's latest accomplishments, Mamma put her apron on. She took out the tins with the poppy seed cakes that she'd baked yesterday and wrapped one cake in brown paper. She sliced two big, one medium, and two smaller pieces from the other and put them onto a plate on the tray. I'd just finished my lunch, but my mouth was watering, and I did a little dance of delight. We were going to have tea and cake with the grown-ups!

"Come Agnes, let's go and sit comfortably."

I skipped ahead of everyone. The gas burners were all that warmed the kitchen and, when Mamma turned the burner off after the water boiled, it quickly grew chilly. I had goosebumps.

Crossing the hall, on their left, the ladies passed the tiny WC, where the toilet with its huge tank of water suspended overhead and our birthday calendar could be found. That way, we could see whose birthday was coming up while we were otherwise engaged.

Mamma carefully carried the tray of tea and cake into the warm living room, where her artistic flair was once again in evidence. The predominantly red wallpaper coordinated with the Axminster rug covering the linoleum floor. The theme was continued in the bright red, floor-length velvet curtains hanging next to the windows overlooking the street. The room was crowded with furniture, but *gezellig* [cozy and comfortable].

Mamma put the tray down on the dining table. "Thank you, Corrie, this is beautiful," she said, noticing how Corrie had set it with a white cloth, fancy tea cups with saucers, delicate cake plates, and tiny forks, all taken from the tea cabinet.

"Come my drei Grazien, sit down. Have a nice cup of tea with your aunt and me," Mamma invited, with a sweep of her hand.

Sieglinde and I immediately took our seats and began speaking German carefully with proper diction as we imagined ladies would, crooking our little fingers while we daintily sipped milky tea and nibbled our cake. Unfortunately, this did not mean I was unaware of my mother and aunt's conversation, which was also entirely conducted in their mother tongue, German.

"Oh my, Gusti, I believe Corrie has grown even in the week since I saw her last. She's such a beautiful young lady—so elegant."

"Yes, Cor and I are very proud of her. Why, you should see the work she brings home from school! She's obviously very intelligent."

I quickly lost interest, as I'd been hearing the same all my life. I muttered under my breath, "The prettiest, the cleverest, the tallest, the best. Bla-di-bla bla bla." Fortunately, Mamma didn't hear me.

Sieglinde stifled a giggle. Corrie delicately wiped her lips, squinted her eyes at me, and sweetly asked to be excused from the table. As I watched her, she put her hands behind her back and sauntered over to survey the ornaments displayed in the rounded, etched, glass-fronted cabinets which formed the top part of our large oak buffet.

Then, catching sight of her own reflection in the oval mirror inset, she adjusted her hair, pinched her cheeks and pursed her lips. I giggled, and Corrie stopped immediately, whirling to look at me with daggers in her eyes before huffily clearing the cake plates from the table.

In my opinion, however, the best thing about the buffet and matching tea cabinet was the teardrop-shaped brass handles which were fastened into the wood at the top and sported a small ball at the bottom. They looked just like breasts with noticeable nipples at the bottom. I'd never seen my parents unclothed, but I knew what breasts looked like—just like those handles.

Tante Agnes leaned forward. "Gusti, I need to talk with you about something else..."

"You two can go play." Mamma excused Sieglinde and me from the table. My sister immediately headed for one of the easy chairs flanking the smoking table, a beautiful little oak table with an etched brass top. The large amber-colored, glass ashtray that graced the middle was solely for Pappa's use. As was usual for her, Siegie curled up by the window and read a book.

Seeing that my playmate was otherwise occupied, I rifled through the games, books, atlases, and crafting materials kept in the cupboard with the gas meter, wrinkling my nose at the smell of gas. I briefly considered counting the coins Pappa put there so Mamma could pay for that week's gas, but she was looking at me.

Shrugging, I hefted down an atlas and carried it to the warmest place in the room, one of the cozy chairs placed next to the *kachel* [coal-burning stove]. Gazing at its glowing mica windows, I imagined traveling to a place where the sun shone as hot as the *kachel*—maybe Kenya or Egypt.

Meanwhile, Mamma and Tante Agnes continued their interminable conversation.

"I just got a letter from Paula. She says the family is well, but since Hitler took over control of the German military, the country is in chaos. People are being fired from the government for all kinds of reasons, but especially for not subscribing to the Nazi nonsense."

"Cor has been talking about this. He's worried the Führer won't stop with just annexing Austria. But I'm more concerned that those back home won't keep their mouths shut—and be punished!"

I promptly closed my mouth. I knew all about punishment since Pappa believed that sparing the rod would definitely spoil the child. For the rest, while at my tender age I knew Pappa hated a man called Hitler who lived in Germany, the continuation of this conversation lost my interest.

Sieglinde and I went into the tiny room off of the living room which did double duty as a playroom and a sickroom to play together while listening for the sound of my aunt's bag being opened. We lined our blocks up on the narrow divan, which was decorated with a blanket with a brightly colored Japanese design.

Just then, we heard the women get up. I raced out of the room. Yes! Tante Agnes was picking up her bag from the hallway and carrying it to the dining table. We three girls drew near. I held my breath. Tante Agnes reached in, winked at me, and pulled out the first dress—mine. It was beautiful: soft yellow cotton with a white collar and matching cuffs.

Sieglinde's dress was identical to mine and Corrie's was light purple, the colors of Spring. Each of us thanked our aunt, and then, after pressing the cake into her hands, Mamma went down the stairs with her sister, stood on the front step, and waved until she was out of sight.

Pappa came home a few minutes later, put his bicycle on the wall, hung up his cape in the hall, and messed up my hair.

"Pappa!" I giggled.

"What?"

"Oh good, Cor, you're home." Mamma gave him a quick kiss. "Agnes came over with news from Germany—it's not good."

"Why doesn't that surprise me? I'll just get changed, and we can talk while I start on the vegetables."

Pappa came down a few minutes later and took his usual place at the kitchen table, peeling potatoes with a cigarette in his mouth and his head slightly bent.

"Pappa," I said, leaning on his chair. "The smoke is making ringlets around your ear."

"That way it doesn't go into my eyes." Pappa smiled before blowing a perfect smoke ring. "Now, let your mother and I catch up while we make dinner."

"What are we having?"

"Potato pancakes."

"Siegie," I yelled, running into the living room. "It's potato pancakes!" On weekdays, we usually had boiled or fried potatoes, a cooked vegetable such as Belgian endive, gravy for flavor and a salad. But it seemed that today we were celebrating our new dresses.

"Meta, out! You know it's dangerous in here with all the hot water."

It was Monday. Laundry day, when some of the laundry was pre-soaked to loosen the dirt and very soiled items were boiled in big pots on top of the stove. Although Corrie was allowed in the kitchen, Sieglinde and I were relegated to the living room.

On Tuesday, by the time we came down, the kitchen smelled wonderfully clean. Pappa, whose shift work enabled him to do much of the housework, had already poured the bleach in which the white linens had been soaking into the kitchen sink, filled the bucket with fresh water, and rinsed the linens. While we ate breakfast, he heated up two pots of soapy water, putting the white laundry into one and the colored into the other. Mamma swished the laundry around using a long wooden stick, lifted each article of clothing out with the same stick, and passed it to Pappa. Standing by the sink while whistling a happy tune, Pappa rubbed the laundry up and down on a ribbed laundry board to clean the dirtiest spots. Mamma's hands grew red and chapped, and her hair curled in wet tendrils around her face.

"Mamma, may I help *alsjeblieft?*" Playing with all that water looked like fun.

"*Ja* Mamma, *alstublieft!*" Siegie joined in. (In Dutch, parents and people older than yourself are generally addressed formally. God, however, is addressed in the familiar. My parents gave us a choice as to what form we would use for them. I chose familiar and Sieglinde chose formal.)

"*Nee*, laundry is grown-up work, but look here. You can have this bowl with some soap, and you and Siegie can wash your dolls' sheets, provided you stay by the table where it's safe."

We set to work scrubbing the handkerchiefs, slopping water on the floor until our teeth began to chatter. The balcony door was open to let the steam escape, even though it was bitterly cold and rainy outside. We decided to finish our game by wringing out our laundry and letting it dry by the *kachel*.

After Pappa had wrung out the laundry until it was virtually dry already, Mamma folded it. The next day she hung it on lines strung across the balcony. All too soon we heard a protest from below. "Woman, can't you double your sheets?"

"Of course not. Then they wouldn't dry before it rains. I'll get them in as soon as I can, Sientje. *Rustig aan* [Be patient]." Mamma gave me a wink.

Only a few hours later while we were eating lunch, Mevrouw den Dulk again called for Mamma. "Your sheets are dry. Get them in now, or they'll be dirty again. I'm going to beat my rugs."

Mamma bustled to take her sheets in, speaking loudly as she did so. "That ridiculous woman needs to learn some patience."

I was proud that, despite our relative poverty, our clothes were always clean and ironed. Our family put a high priority on keeping up appearances, if you like, putting on a brave face.

Every Friday, we cleaned the house. "Siegie, come carry this bucket of water downstairs. Spilletje, there's one for you, too. Come back for the soap. You both can wash in front of the house."

Sieglinde and I walked down our staircase with pails of water, sloshing them onto the stoop and making a mess with the soap. The water ran down onto the sidewalk. We went up for more water, rinsed the front stoop, and we were done. The stoop sparkled, but of course we were filthy and wet. So was the stairway.

Sieglinde and I ran upstairs to get dry and then went down to hang around the kitchen. We were ready for the best part of Friday to begin. Mamma was doing the weekly baking. I inhaled deeply—how wonderful the house smelled, both clean and fragrant with baking! "Mamma, can we lick the bowl? We need to check if the cake will be *lekker* [good-tasting]."

Mamma smiled gently. After making sure the spoon had a generous amount of mixture on it, she gave Sieglinde the bowl and me the wooden spoon.

"Well, how is it? Good enough?"

"Mmm, I think I need to check it again."

Mamma gave me a gentle swat. "Out! I need to make dinner. Maybe you can taste a little for dessert."

Saturday was the day for our weekly bath. "Wake up, Sleepyheads! Come down for breakfast." The big metal tub was already on the kitchen floor, and Pappa was busy filling it with water heated in the two large pots. When we were done eating our porridge, Pappa, Sieglinde and I left the kitchen.

Corrie, being the eldest, had her bath first. After the water was changed, Sieglinde and I got into the tub together. Mamma shampooed our hair, wiped our faces, and helped us wash our bodies, using a special facecloth that she could slip over her hand. She then rubbed us dry with a thin towel before handing us our freshly washed clothing.

We girls sat by the *kachel* to dry our hair while we watched Pappa polishing and buffing the copper and brass. By the time he finished the doorknobs, stair rods, mailbox, doorbell, and umbrella stand, my hair was dry. I followed him into the kitchen for the last chore of the week: preparing all the meals that we would eat on Sunday when no work was allowed.

"Guusje, I heard some bad news about Germany today at work."

"Oh, not again!"

"*Ja,* England, Italy and France have given in to *die schoft* [the bastard], Hitler. He's been allowed to annex Sudetenland. I have a bad feeling about where this is leading."

"Hmm, I'll write to Paula tonight and see if she knows anything more. Living in Germany, she should. Now, it's time to eat. No more of this talk."

I felt the hair stand up on the back of my neck. Although our weekly routine gave me a pleasantly secure feeling, even at my young age, I knew something bad was approaching.

After a dinner of pancakes, Mamma dampened my hair and rolled it up in strips of cotton to dry overnight.

"Mamma, it hurts to sleep with these in my hair."

"If you want to be pretty, you need to suffer pain."

Sunday was supposed to be a complete day of rest for us and our neighbors, except the Jews, who rested on Saturdays. In the morning, each member of the family took turns washing in the kitchen sink. I sat on the counter and put my feet in the sink to get them clean.

While Mamma removed the strips from our hair, Corrie folded the table rug, put on the white tablecloth and set the table. I looked in the mirror. Yes, my hair was curly, and I knew I looked pretty for now. If it rained, all my suffering would have been for nothing. Unlike Corrie with her waves and Sieglinde with her ringlets, I wasn't naturally beautiful.

After breakfast together in our snug living room, we walked the short distance to Onze Lieve Vrouw van Lourdes, a Roman Catholic church on Harstenhoek Plein. I prayed frequently, but didn't know much about Christianity, and the very long Latin Mass didn't enlighten me at all. My family paid a penny per person to sit on the back pew. We couldn't afford the 25 cents each for the front pews.

"Meta, sit quietly. Stop fiddling!" Corrie put a restraining hand on my leg. "Learn some patience and act like a lady!"

I sat thinking about all I saw. Why did I have to be pretty, if we had to sit at the back where nobody could see us—and I couldn't see what was happening up front? Just as I turned to ask Corrie, the service ended. Finally.

After a special lunch that included both meat and dessert, we always spent Sunday afternoon partaking in a quiet activity. Since it was summer, and the weather was cooperative, we went to the beach armed with a large bottle of sparkling lemonade purchased at the corner grocery store on the corner. I was glad it wasn't raining since virtually all the shops were closed, and then everyone stayed at home, as well. When that happened, Sunday was anything but the highlight of the week; it was miserable! But there was one Sunday that I never forgot.

4

THE YOUNGEST DAUGHTER

Today we were going to visit Pappa's sister Tante Mientje and her family.

We'd barely set off when I began complaining, "Mamma, I'm tired. Lift me up, please. Can we take a streetcar?" I held my arms up.

"You're okay for now, Spilletje. We just started." Mamma was normally a soft-touch, but the journey was far too lengthy to manage while carrying a child.

I knew that no means no, so I skipped along the sidewalk, enjoying that it was made of black diamond-shaped stones that looked just like Wybertjes (a kind of black licorice).

"Oh Sieglinde, look at that!" I stopped abruptly in front of an advertising column featuring Camel cigarettes, the kind Pappa always smoked unless he was rolling his own.

Sieglinde read: "More doctors smoke Camels than any other kind of cigarette."

I giggled at the thought of a physician smoking a camel and mimicked what that might look like.

Siegie rolled her eyes. "They don't mean that! They're saying that Camel cigarettes are healthy!"

"Hmm, healthy. I wonder if you could eat them? Ha, ha, eating a cigarette!"

Hand-in-hand Sieglinde and I ran around and around the advertising pillar, laughing and singing, "Healthy, healthy, healthy."

Corrie shook her head.

Pappa glanced over his shoulder. "Girls, keep up. Walk in front of us. Chin up. Tummy in. Shoulders back."

As we came to the Scheveningse *bosjes* [woods], I cast my eyes from side-to-side while I marched hand-in-hand with my sister, enjoying the pretty red and white mushrooms and the shapes of the tree trunks.

I soon forgot the requisite posture, pointing into the trees. "Sieglinde, I saw a fairy. She was eating those white berries—the ones that pop when we step on them." I made a popping sound to illustrate. "I heard it."

"There's no such thing as fairies, is there?" Sieglinde's eyes grew big, and her finger found its way into her mouth.

"*Ja*, of course there are. Gnomes are real, too. What do you think made that hole in the tree over there?"

Time passed quickly as I spun tales about the gnomes and fairies who come out at night, dance in the moonlight, and have feasts of berries and honey.

All too soon, we emerged from the woods. Sieglinde and I held our noses as we passed the pissoir and crossed the road that led to the Peace Palace. From then on, for the rest of our journey, we walked beside canals.

Now it was my turn to be frightened, and I slipped my hand into Mamma's. On a previous walk, my father told me that, when the canals were dredged, they often found the bodies of missing people. I imagined the slime-covered corpses being loaded onto flat boats and shivered as we passed by the dark green water, making sure to walk as far away from the banks as possible, all while chewing on my collar.

Finally, we arrived at my aunt's home on the 's-Gravenzandelaan in Den Haag. Two of my cousins, Ciska and Willie, joyfully greeted us as they threw open their door.

My dark-haired cousin Joop swung me up into his arms, and I wound my arms around his neck to better give him an enthusiastic smacking kiss on the cheek. Joop laughed and carried me over to the portrait of my deceased grandmother, Helena ten Bosch. It was our little tradition.

"Who's that?" he asked me.

"It's Oma, and she looks like me and Ciska! Her daughter was called Helena, just like her, but she died of the 'flu. Her children live in an orphanage, and last week they came to visit us. They're called Ciska and Henkie—hey, just like your Ciska!"

Joop tickled my side. "*Ja*, I know them. They're my cousins, too, and they come here often. And you're right—we recycle names in this family. Your father was named after his grandmother and grandfather, and you were named after your pappa's second name!"

"I am Meta Antonia Bisschop! Did you know my whole family has the same last name as me?" I pointed to another picture. "Show me that one! It's my favorite."

"What, this one? Well, Opa [grandfather] made this picture of a sailboat. It's made entirely of postage stamps."

I gazed at all the postage stamps, which came from all over the world, trying to memorize the picture. "One day, I'm going everywhere those stamps came from. Maybe even in a sailboat!"

"It's time for the special treat!" Tante Mientje announced. "Sit down, everyone."

My older cousins played musical instruments, and they'd prepared a concert for us. Joop put me down, drew up a chair and sat. I immediately plonked myself down onto his lap. At 14 years old, he was definitely my hero.

Afterwards, the adults retired to the lounge to have some tea, listen to opera and chat. Overhearing them discussing the German composers, I assumed that the people they were talking about were probably my uncles. "Corrie, have you ever met any of those uncles?"

"Silly! Not every German is our uncle. Why don't you go play blocks with the other little girls, Meta?"

After watching them while I chewed my collar, I decided to join the small boys in setting up a train set that meandered through the hallway and even into the kitchen. Much more interesting.

Then it began to rain. That wasn't unexpected, but, if it continued, would mean an unpleasant walk back. Next it began to pour. The rain became so loud that it was hard to hear anything else, and everyone grew silent.

Attracted by the booming thunder, my cousins and I pressed our noses to the window and watched the lightning as it lit the now-darkened sky. A particularly loud crash caused me to flee and bury my head in Mamma's lap.

"Come away! Stand here, far from the windows," my father ordered.

Suddenly, there was a deafening crash just above our heads. I peeked up from my mother's lap and saw something like a glowing ball fall through the second floor onto the first-floor landing. There was now a hole in the ceiling.

Everyone hurried to look where the strange object went, me clutching Mamma's hand. I wrinkled my nose at the smell of the scorched path the ball-like thing left behind as it rolled through the hall and bounced down the entry stairs. We peered down and there, in the entry hall, was a black, tennis ball-sized metallic sphere which was glowing red in spots. Fortunately, because the floor was made of stone, there was no danger of fire. Still, no one touched it until much later.

Once the storm stopped, my family and I donned our coats and set off for home. The journey seemed even longer on the way back. "Mamma, pick me up!" I begged, shuffling along with drooping shoulders. Mamma hoisted me up and carried me on her hip for a block or two. Then she passed me over to Pappa, who lifted me over his head so I could perch on his shoulders. By then, I really was exhausted. I pillowed my head on his and closed my eyes. It was late when we arrived at home—way past bedtime.

Sieglinde and I changed into our nightgowns, which had been pre-warmed on top of the *kachel* while we were still in the living room. We kissed our parents good night and started up the narrow, steep stairway leading to our bedroom in the attic. The light was broken, the stairs dark, and my heart beating fast.

"Bang! Bang!"

"What was that?" Screaming, we darted up the stairs in terror.

Then we heard our parents and Corrie snickering, and we knew.

They'd banged on the living room wall next to the stairs, just to scare us. The big people thought that it was funny to alarm us, but we ukkies did not agree.

~

The watery sun was peeping through our window.

"Girls, wake up!"

Shivering, we pulled on our winter dresses and our one pair of shoes before sitting and sliding down the stairs to splash water on our faces and brush our teeth at the kitchen sink. At least that water was warm. The room was toasty, too, because before he left for work, Pappa lit all four burners on the stove.

"*Goedemorgen*, Mamma," Sieglinde and I chorused together. I took a deep breath of the scent of Pappa that lingered in the kitchen: sandalwood shaving cream and cigarette smoke. Wonderful! That smell and Mamma's tight embrace made me feel cozy all over.

Corrie came down a few minutes later and mumbled, "*Morgen*" to everyone present. The tea kettle began its merry tune, and my mouth watered, thinking about the hot, sweet tea that was being prepared. Since it was a weekday, Mamma had set the breakfast table in the kitchen.

Today we were having milk bread. I grinned and silently pointed at the "MB" that was written on the bottom of the loaf before pointing to myself and nodding. I'd just learned my letters, so I was pretending that "MB" stood for "Meta Bisschop."

Corrie was quick to put me in my place. "Just because it says 'MB,' it doesn't mean they're your initials, Meta. 'MB' stands for *melk brood!*"

Mamma wasn't looking, so I stuck my tongue out at her.

"Mamma..." Corrie began.

Mamma interrupted. "Less talking. More eating." She liked to listen to the marches playing on the radio and have her breakfast in peace.

After crossing my eyes at my big sister, I looked at the two *boterhammen* [slices of bread] Mamma put on my plate. One had cheese on it and the other had *muisjes*. This word literally means mice, but is actually chocolate or flavored sugar in the shape of rice.

I picked my knife up with my right hand and my fork with my left, carefully cut a piece off of my bread with chocolate, and politely put the tasty morsel in my mouth with my fork as we'd been taught.

Sieglinde nudged me. I turned to her indignantly, and she pointed at my mouth. I had a bit of a cold and apparently was chewing with my mouth open. I quickly closed it. My parents insisted that we behave like proper ladies and always set a good example; excellent table manners were a mark of true class. Fortunately, neither Mamma nor Corrie noticed my misdemeanor.

After breakfast, Sieglinde and I raced up the stairs to collect our dolls, the doll baby carriage and the crib, which were kept in the closet in our bedroom.

Sieglinde's doll was named Rietje, and mine was Grietje. I detested that name because in my mind "Rietje" denoted someone from the upper-classes, but "Grietje" was used by the working class. My parents taught us that behavior, not poverty, determined one's station in life, but I knew that names matter, too.

After all, my mother always spoke *Hochdeutsch* [high German] and insisted we always spoke proper Dutch. Mamma only used the Scheveningen dialect when feuding with the neighbors; Sieglinde and I used it when play-acting—we were good at it, too!

About the name of my doll, I was the youngest member of the family, so had no choice. I climbed onto the dining table and sat cross-legged with my nose buried in the fresh flowers while fuming about my position in life: the youngest, the smallest, the least heard, the one with straight hair. At least, I thought, Grietje's face was prettier than Rietje's. She was probably cleverer, too!

"Spilletje, what're you doing?" Mamma smiled fondly.

I didn't answer. She never seemed to mind me enjoying whichever seasonal decoration was there, and I knew she couldn't read my mind.

"Meta, remember we were going to play with our dolls?" Sieglinde whined.

I clambered down from the table, and Mamma moved the vase of flowers and covered the dining table with a huge cloth that reached to the floor.

Siegie and I crawled into our "house" under the table.

"Okay, Meta, I'm Grietje's aunt, and you can be Rietje's aunt," instructed Sieglinde.

"Again? How about we also pretend I'm the big sister this time?"

"That'd be silly. I'm older."

My shoulders slumped, but I knew she was right.

"Meta, Rietje is sick! Please come to the doctor with me." Sieglinde was using her special "aunt" voice.

"Okay, can I put Grietje in with Rietje in her baby carriage? It's too cold to carry my baby in my arms. Let's stop by the shops on our way home. We need potatoes."

After wrapping our dolls in scraps of an old blanket, we put them in the baby carriage, grabbed our pretend shopping bags, crawled out from under the table, and walked to the "doctor's office" by the window.

Just then Mamma called out, "I'm going to the Stevinstraat to pick up flour and sugar. Corrie is in charge, so do what she tells you. Be good."

I heard Corrie groan, "Just what I wanted to do on my day off school!"

Nonetheless, after Mamma adjusted her hat, she put on her long black coat and left.

I waited quietly until I heard the door click closed behind Mamma. "Hey Siegie, are you hungry? Let's buy *spekulaasjes* [spice cookies]. One for you, one for me, and a half for each of our babies."

Corrie heard. "Meta, it isn't time for a cup of tea, and Mamma didn't say you could have a snack. Wait until she gets home."

I stuck my tongue out at Corrie, took Sieglinde's hand, made my way to the kitchen, and firmly closed the door.

Corrie jumped up and slamming the kitchen door open, stood with her hands on her hips. "You have to do what I say. Mamma said so."

Ah, but Mamma wasn't there. What might happen if I disobeyed my big sister? Would having a *spekulaasje* be worth it? Totally! I made

31

a move towards the cookie box. What could Corrie do? Would she do anything? I wondered.

Oh yes, she did do something. Corrie grabbed me with her right hand and Sieglinde with her left. She dragged us to the divan and growled, "Sit!"

As soon as Corrie loosened her grip on me, I got up. For good measure, I blew a raspberry at her.

Sieglinde muttered under her breath, "Meta, don't. I don't want you to get in trouble."

Corrie reacted immediately, grabbing me by the hair. Just in case, she took a handful of Sieglinde's hair as well, forced me to sit down again, and sat between us.

I howled and bawled. Sieglinde cried and moaned. It was all to no avail.

"Scream all you want. You're staying right here!" Corrie's face was the color of a beetroot.

Corrie, Sieglinde and I remained in position until Mamma came home.

"What is going on here? Let go of their hair, Corrie!"

"Mamma, Meta was being an absolute monster. She..."

"I don't need to hear. I know." Mamma turned to me. "Meta, when I'm out you have to do what Corrie says. She's in charge. And if I ever again hear you don't, I'll tell your father."

I quickly put my hands over my bottom. "Yes, Mamma."

Mamma turned to put away the groceries, and I took the opportunity to cross my eyes at my big sister.

"Mamma..."

"Enough, Corrie. I'm sure they'll be good in the future."

Corrie would have to babysit again. Poor me. Poor Sieglinde. Poor Corrie!

Of course, Corrie did love us, and I admired my biggest sister, but I was also envious of her. I so much wished I were as special and beautiful and clever and tall and privileged as Corrie. I watched and listened to Corrie very carefully, imitating the postures she adopted and the sounds that she made when she was singing in her beautiful voice, but I was still short and found it impossible to carry a tune. I sounded just like a croaking frog!

And oh, how I wanted to be dressed in her beautiful clothes! After Aunt Agnes sewed or Mamma knit something, Corrie always got it first. Then the clothes were passed down to Sieglinde, who was a little plump. By the time a dress or sweater or sometimes even shoes came to me, they were faded, stretched-out and threadbare.

One day, my dream nearly came true. Mamma had just finished ironing the clean laundry and there on the top was a dress that I'd always admired when Corrie wore it. I stretched out my hand and stroked the silky, shiny, brown and gold fabric. Of course, it would be passed to Sieglinde, but I just needed to touch it first.

Mamma watched me for a minute, smiled and handed me the dress. "Spilletje, this is yours. It's much too small on Corrie, so I took it in for you."

"What? What about Sieglinde?" Could I be hearing things?

"*Nee,* it won't fit her properly. Corrie told me how you've always loved this dress, so it's yours. Try it on."

I quickly slipped into the gorgeous dress and pirouetted to show Mamma how the skirt flared. Admittedly, it was still a little on the large side, but I just tightened the belt.

"You look lovely, Meta." Mamma touched my cheek tenderly.

"I'm going to show my friends!"

Holding up the skirt of my new dress so I wouldn't trip, I tore down the stairs to share my joy with my friends Beppie and Alie van Kruijsen.

I rang the doorbell at Leeuwardensestraat 17 while shouting their names. As I heard Alie and Beppie running down their hallway, I quickly smoothed my skirt for maximum effect. But when they opened the door, their dog Fifi squeezed past their legs and immediately began to snarl at me. A skinny white dog with black patches, Fifi was notorious in the neighborhood, having bitten several people. My heart leapt into my throat, and I quickly turned to flee. The monster dog from Hell was faster.

Fifi sank her teeth into my thigh and, as I tried to shake her off, my wonderful dress tore. Once Beppie and Alie managed to disconnect their dog from me, I limped down the street with my head hanging, opened my front door, went in, gingerly lowered myself onto the stairs and wailed out my heartbreak.

5

THE INSIGNIFICANT ONE

Mamma heard my cries and rushed down the stairs to ascertain what had happened. Noticing the blood smears on my skirt, she was very worried that I'd been bitten badly. But my tears were for the dress.

Once my eyes were dry, I tried to cheer myself up. I pulled out one of the bricks in the road. "Sieglinde, look here. Let's play marbles and see if we can get them into this hole."

"*Nee,* yesterday Beppie, Alie and I set up a hopscotch game. I want to play that. Fifi is inside now."

We went a few houses down where they'd drawn chalk squares on the street. Soon a whole group of children joined in our game. Because only bicycles, horses, carts and wagons used the streets, we were entirely safe—apart from the horse poop, of course.

I derived much pleasure from the carts promenading down the street every weekday, each operator shouting out his own particular cry or working his own noisemaker. The milkman, baker and greengrocer came by in the mornings and the people collecting trash, like rags, vegetable trimmings and metal, in the afternoons.

The housewares and drugstore wagon which rattled by every Friday afternoon was one of my favorites. "The household wagon is outside. I can hear it. *Alsjeblieft* Mamma, may I have some money to buy *drop* [licorice]?" I danced from foot to foot.

Mamma dug in the bottom of her purse for some change. "*Ja*, I think a cent would be more than enough. Be sure to share what you buy with your sisters."

I took the money and shouted, "*Dank je wel* [thank you], Mamma!" over my shoulder as I flew down the stairs. Seven pieces of double-salt *drop*—my favorite—seemed good. I straightaway popped a piece in my mouth, leaving two pieces for each of us. I stuffed those in my pocket so my hands were free for what always came next.

While pretending to be involved in a game of marbles, I waited for the merchant to close his wagon. Done. At my signal, my friends and I made our move. We climbed up to, and stood on, the running board, anchoring ourselves by holding on to the horizontal ladder on the outside of the wagon's back doors.

Sieglinde stayed on the sidewalk with her finger in her mouth, fearfully watching the row of stowaway children. I grinned at her and waved as the wagon began to move onward. I knew that from his vantage point the scowling vendor couldn't see us, but when he took out the long horse whip and aimed it backwards over the wagon, I realized he was on to our game. Everyone who was hitching a ride hurriedly jumped off and ran.

"Quick, come away, Meta," Sieglinde panted as she tried to pull me along faster. "Mamma warned you before. That man is mean and wants to hit you all with his horse whip; you could've been hurt!"

"Wait, stop! There's something I need to do." I paused to stick out my tongue right before the wagon disappeared around the corner.

Just then, Corrie came outside. "Meta, stop it! I saw you on that wagon. What were you thinking of? You're acting like a boy again!"

"So?" I shrugged. "Why shouldn't I?" But deep inside I worried. Maybe there'd been a mistake, and I should've been a boy. I certainly didn't feel comfortable in my rather diminutive body. With my love of running, jumping, playing ball and especially risky adventures, I'd overheard neighbors saying I was a tomboy. I wasn't really sure what that meant, only that once again I wasn't good enough.

"Meta, come! The library wagon is here!"

Sieglinde and I ran downstairs and stood with baited breath by the side of the road until the driver pulled on the horse's reins, and it creaked to a stop. Climbing up to enter, we breathed in the slightly musty smell and gazed at the brightly colored books covering every wall of the wagon. In a matter of minutes, Sieglinde staggered up to the librarian, arms laden with books.

I borrowed just one—a travel book with photographs of exotic locations. "This will be perfect for tomorrow," I told Sieglinde.

As we were on our way home with our books, the street organ came. Hearing the tinkling, crashing, repetitious music, we stood entranced, watching the animated figures dance. The organ grinder walked from house to house with his tin cup asking for money, but he only got a copper from Mamma if Pappa wasn't looking.

I was curled up in a cozy chair and visiting amazing places in my mind's eye when a cart unsurpassed by any other trundled down our street. The clanging of the bell as the white-coated vendor hit it again and again with a small hammer made my mouth water. I knew that a wheeled icebox containing ice cream was attached to the front of his bicycle.

"Mamma, Pappa, he's here!" My sisters and I scampered to the window and gazed longingly. We didn't dare ask, knowing that money was tight.

Pappa smiled. "Corrie, go and buy ice cream for dessert: three double thick and two singles."

All the ice creams were vanilla encased in a layer of chocolate. The difference was that the double thick ice cream was twice as big as the single, which came on a stick. You can guess who got one of the small ice creams for dessert.

"*Dank je wel*, Pappa," I said with slightly rounded shoulders. When he wasn't looking, I crossed my eyes at Siegie. I knew we could've eaten a big one, but we were small and never got the chance to try.

∽

The drizzle hadn't let up all day, which made it seem even more frigid than it was. Because it was Fall, the sun had set early. My lips curled up at the corners. Twilight was my favorite time of day, and it was my favorite day of the week, Saturday. Mamma turned on the little table lamps, which gave off a soft, gentle light.

Our whole family sat by the stove and paid rapt attention to the radio play, the children enjoying a cup of weak tea, and Mamma and Pappa a glass of red wine. Then in our clean shiny house, with the smell of baking still in the air, we had our very special evening meal of rice with cinnamon and brown sugar. After dinner, Pappa sat back, crossed his legs and smoked a cigarette while he read *De Leugenaar* (the newspaper, which Pappa had renamed The Liar) and we girls played board games.

"Oh no," Pappa groaned.

"What is it, Cor?"

"Hitler is at it again. He deported thousands more Polish Jews."

"Those poor people. My sister wrote that most of the people he expelled last time weren't allowed to cross the border into Poland. Where will these new ones go?"

"*Vuile rot Mof* [dirty rotten German]!" Pappa spat.

Mamma sighed. "Oh Cor, I do wish you wouldn't use that word about Germans. But I do wonder where Hitler's hatred will end. Jews. Czechs. My family came to Germany from Poland. Will they be under threat next?"

Pappa shook his head as he stood to take Mamma into his arms. "I think they'll be okay, because they're not in one of his target groups. If they keep their heads down." He shrugged. "But who knows?"

The following day our half-cousins Ciska and Henkie came to visit. We were playing quietly when Mamma called us.

"Dinner's ready. Come sit down at the table."

I stood and admired the dining table, which sported a clean, ironed, white tablecloth, with cloth napkins folded and neatly placed beside the fork.

"Sit down, Spilletje."

I obeyed, and my parents began bringing out our weekly feast in steaming pots and pans containing potatoes, vegetables, and meat. All were placed on cloth trivets on the table. Meat, usually beef hash, a pork chop or a small ball of fried hamburger, was a Sunday treat and my mouth watered in anticipation.

Mamma portioned out the food, we said the 'Our Father' while holding hands, we all told each other, "*Eet smakelijk* [Enjoy your meal]" and we began. We started with bone broth soup. Then I dug into my favorite, the meat, while Siegie saved her favorite for last. Children were not allowed to speak during meals so while the adults conversed, we ate silently making sure not to smack our lips, crunch our food or, horror-of-horrors, burp. Any infraction earned a very stern look from Pappa. Or worse.

Finally, Mamma pushed back her chair, rose from the table and disappeared into the kitchen. I sat on the edge of my seat waiting. She returned carrying a bowl filled to the top with a brown and white confection.

"Chocolate pudding with whipped cream. My favorite!" I shouted, hoping that having said this my mother might at least give me the same size portion as everyone else.

I paid close attention to her actions, but Mamma spooned out five large portions of dessert and two small ones. This is becoming altogether too much, I thought. Ciska and Henkie aren't that much older than me and I know I can eat more—I'll have to take matters into my own hands! Decision made; I nodded my head.

Waiting until neither parent was looking, I leaned over and spat on one of the larger portions. I figured that, when Mamma gave that bowl to my sister or a half-cousin, they would just pass it over to me. They didn't.

"Hey, Meta just spat in that dessert!" Henkie and Corrie shouted almost simultaneously, pointing at my work.

Mamma froze and then slowly turned to look at me. I felt my color rise, but tried to look innocent. Would she let me have the relevant bowl? After all, nobody else would want it, and she never wasted food. No. Saying nothing, Mamma grabbed that beautiful dessert and threw it away.

"Meta," Pappa said sternly, adding insult to injury, "apologize for spitting in the dessert."

"Sorry," I muttered. That's what I said. What I thought was

different. You can tell me what to do, and you can tell me what to say. But you can't tell me what to think. And I think this is unfair. I crossed my arms over my chest.

My mother added a bit from each remaining large dessert to one of the small ones and gave everyone, except me, a bowl.

I sat with steam coming out of my ears while acting like I didn't care that the rest was enjoying their chocolate pudding and whipped cream. It's not fair, just like the ice cream. Corrie doesn't need more sweets than me. She even has more toys! Nothing is fair. I hate being small, I thought to myself. I knew that any verbalized protests would not be tolerated.

As I watched everyone scrape the last of their dessert out of their dishes, it became absolutely impossible to hold my thoughts captive inside my head. When I grow up, I will never ever take the smallest dessert. In fact, I'll always take the biggest. Always. I lifted my chin, decisively.

Corrie snorted.

I slithered down in my seat so I could reach and kicked her under the table.

"Ouch!" Tears sprung into Corrie's eyes.

"Meta," Pappa ordered, "go to your room."

I stomped towards the stairs, muttering under my breath.

"Don't make me come up after you. You won't like it!"

Waking up a few days after this incident, I knew it was going to be a dreadful day. My nose was running, my head hurt, I was coughing, and I felt so, so cold, even in my cozy bed. "Mamma," I croaked miserably, hoping she was near enough to hear me.

Sieglinde lifted herself onto one elbow and peered blearily at me. "What's wrong, Meta?"

"I'm siiiick!"

Sieglinde immediately leapt out of bed and rushed downstairs to tell Mamma. Almost instantaneously, I heard familiar footsteps mounting the steep stairs to our room. I soon felt her cool hand against my cheek. Why did she feel so cold? Had she been hanging out the laundry? I tried to remember what day it was.

"*Ach, kindje toch* [Oh, child]," Mamma whispered. "Open your eyes, Spilletje. I'm going to wrap you in a blanket, and Pappa will carry you down. Then he will go and ask the doctor to come."

I'd always dreamt of having the privilege of lying on the divan in the tiny room, but this was anything but fun. Shivering until my teeth chattered, I curled up to try and get warm, but Mamma said I was too hot already. She and Pappa washed my face, neck, and arms down with what felt like icy water. As they worked, I heard them muttering about getting my fever down while my sisters whispered in the living room. Then I began to cough.

Mamma helped me sit up and issued instructions over her shoulder. "Cor, the cough syrup is on the shelf in the kitchen. Could you bring it and a spoon *alsjeblieft*?"

Usually, I would love this because the cough medicine wasn't really medicine, but liquid licorice in sugar syrup. It tasted delicious, and to tell the truth I sometimes used to sneak some when I wasn't even sick. So did Pappa! But now I turned away from the spoonful of delicious syrup, too miserable to eat or drink anything.

The doorbell rang, and Corrie invited Dr. Mees, our family doctor, to come in. After checking my ears and finding them clear, he just scratched his head and said that my parents should keep my fever down and let him know if I got worse. I lay there for three days and nights with Mamma and Pappa taking turns sponging me down and stroking my head, never leaving me alone even for a minute.

Feverishly, I called out for my sister. "Sieglinde, Sieglinde, come!"

She peeked around the door, but wasn't allowed to come in, because nobody knew what I had.

"I'm worried. Her fever is less, but she's still so sick. Should we call the doctor again?"

Pappa's brow furrowed. "She's not getting worse. That's a good sign, isn't it?"

On the fourth day, my parents finally knew what was wrong with me and that there was little a doctor could do. My face was covered in

41

red spots. By the end of the day, the spots had spread over my entire body, and my fever spiked: I had the measles.

Corrie was taking a turn sitting with me when Mamma showed Mevrouw den Dulk, who'd heard I was sick, in, whispering, "She may still be sleeping."

Our neighbor approached my sickbed cautiously, peering at me to ascertain if I indeed had the measles. "Ja, she looks just like my children did when they had them."

I woke up and began to scratch. The rash itched so badly!

"Don't scratch," Mevrouw den Dulk said. Then she proceeded to dig a chocolate bar and a roll of *zuurtjes* [boiled candy] out of her purse. "I'm so sorry you're sick. Would you like to choose one of these to help you feel better?"

Well, I was never too sick for candy. And I love, love, loved chocolate. But Corrie intervened. "Meta, choose the *zuurtjes*. They'll feel good on your throat."

Reluctantly, I chose the *zuurtjes,* and my sisters were happy to help me eat them. I did regret missing out on the chocolate, but I was the youngest...

My parents were in the living room huddled around the radio, Mamma pale with her lips pinched tightly together and Pappa's face resembling a thundercloud. The announcer was talking about Kristallnacht.

When the radio program was over, Pappa and Mamma started discussing, their voices tight with passion. I wanted to know what was going on, so crept under the dining table to watch and listen. Mamma had tears on her cheeks, and Pappa was hugging her, even as he continued to mutter under his breath. Sieglinde joined me; we looked at each other, mystified.

Corrie, who'd been reading in the tiny room, came into the living room and noticed what was happening. "Pappa? Mamma? What's going on? What are you talking about?"

Pappa exhaled noisily. "You might as well know. You soon will, anyway. Remember last summer when we were in Germany, and your mother's relatives were talking about all the difficulties they were experiencing?"

"Umm, I remember that they were worried Adolf Hitler was going to start another war." Corrie's face lost its color and she gasped. "He didn't, did he? Start another war?"

Pappa shook his head. "*Nee*, not yet. But *die schoft* is blaming all of Germany's problems on the Jewish people: losing the Great War, their loss of face and their economic struggles. He's even been suggesting the Jews want to control the world. And the problem is, because he keeps saying it over and over again, people are beginning to believe him. Fools!" Pappa hit his forehead with his hand before his voice tailed off. "And now this…"

"What was the radio saying? What happened?" Corrie's voice rose as she wrung her hands.

Even though my sister was now 11 years old, Mamma sat down and pulled her onto her lap as she explained, "Last night the Nazis organized an attack on Jews in Germany, Austria and Sudetenland. Shops, homes, synagogues—all were destroyed—even civilians joined in. Afterwards, there was broken glass everywhere—that's why they are calling it Kristallnacht."

Pappa's lips were white. "The announcer also said that Jewish men were taken from their families. Presumably, they were put in the concentration camps that your mother's relatives told us about. It's immoral!"

Corrie pushed Mamma's arms away and stood up, now trembling like a leaf. "So, will there be war? But in Germany. Not here, right?"

Mamma took a deep breath. "We can only hope not." She again took Corrie's hands.

Pappa's fist hit the table, and I jumped. He began pacing the room with his hands clutched behind his back. "Who do they think they are? That they can just destroy other people and their property? And what are the idiotic German people thinking, going along with *die vuile schoft* and his nonsense?"

While my parents and Corrie had been speaking, I'd begun to emerge from my hiding place under the table, wanting to hear every word, but now I shrank back and put my collar in my mouth. Pappa's anger always frightened me. With my arms around my knees, I chewed furiously and made sure to keep my eyes lowered.

Mamma protested, "Cor, Cor, calm down. Not all Germans are bad. Many disagree with what Hitler is doing. My family certainly doesn't like him and his policies. You've heard my brothers talk."

"Yeah, but their fool friends bought into Hitler's garbage," Pappa sneered.

"Well, what do you want me to do about it? Go drown myself?" Mamma's chest was heaving. She jumped up and made her way to the door, pulling her handkerchief from her apron pocket and dabbing her eyes.

Pappa's breathing slowed down, and he stopped pacing. "Stop! Oh, don't cry. *Alsjeblieft!* I'm sorry. Guusje, you're living proof that some Germans are good—a few anyway. You're the best woman in the whole wide world."

My father again took my mother into his arms as he grumbled, "I don't trust Hitler. That ridiculous man said that he wanted more room for the 'true Germans' to live. I'm so worried that Austria and Sudetenland won't be enough to satisfy him."

Mamma sighed and put her head on Pappa's shoulder. "Cor, I hope you're wrong."

The argument was over, but the sick feeling in the pit of my stomach had only just begun.

6

WHAT HAPPENED IN GERMANY

"Guusje, are you sure about going to Germany again this summer? Relationships are already tense, and I wouldn't be surprised if someone would declare war before we get home. I'm sure Hitler's only just begun." Pappa's forehead was creased.

Mamma put her hands on her hips. "Cor, we just have to go. If there's going to be war, I want to see my brothers and sisters now. They may not be alive afterwards!" She folded her hands as if praying. "It's only one day away."

"But Guusje, what about the *kindertjes*? Think..."

Tears sprung to Mamma's eyes, and she interrupted Pappa. "I have thought! Wilhelm specially asked us to come and stay with him. And I said yes. We can't let him down after I already agreed. *Alsjeblieft*, Cor!"

Pappa inhaled deeply and shook his head. "All right then, Guusje. Have it your way. Let's just hope the *idioot* is satisfied and will leave our little country alone."

So it was that our family traveled on a train to Bottrop, a small mining town, to stay with Onkel Wilhelm Weidemann and his wife, Liesbeth. They lived in an enormous two-story home with a one-room grocery store that was just across the street from the home where my mother grew up. Onkel was much older than Mamma;

their two sons, Emil and Bruno, were already grown-up and lived in a different city.

During the days while our parents chatted with relatives and our outgoing uncle worked, we girls wandered around his store, gazing at the huge bins and tubs filled with various foodstuffs.

"Ah, here comes Frau Weisz. I wonder if her poor son is feeling better. He was so sick with scarlet fever—we thought that he might even die!" Onkel Wilhelm mused as he arranged the window display. Walking as if she were in a great hurry, Frau Weisz smoothed her long, gray skirt and adjusted the blue kerchief on her head before opening the door, causing a clear bell to sound.

"*Heil Hitler!*"

My eyes widened at this strange greeting. How would my uncle respond?

Onkel smiled warmly. "*Guten Tag,* Frau Weisz. How's your son? Liesbeth and I have been thinking about him."

"Thank you, Herr Weidemann. He's much better. Soon, he'll be running around with his friends."

"I'm so glad to hear it. When he's well, be sure to send him in for a little bag of candy—free!"

"Why, thank you. You're very kind. I will!"

Frau Weisz approached the counter and Ilse, the sales girl, came forward. "*Guten Tag,* Frau Weisz. How may I help you?"

"*Guten Tag,* Ilse. So, the little Dutch girls are here again, Herr Weidemann. I guess your sister is visiting." Frau Weisz gave us a kind smile. "A kilogram of flour and a half kilo of sugar please."

Ilse weighed the sugar in a pointed paper bag, closed it and placed it upside down on the counter. I watched closely to see if the bag would empty. It didn't—no sugar fell out at all. Ilse weighed the flour in a regular bag and folded the top over before handing it over to her customer.

"Will there be anything else, Frau Weisz?"

"Hmm, yes. I think I'd like a *Holzhandgriffzuckerlutschbonbon* [wooden-handled sugar sucking candy] for my son. It'll help his throat feel better."

Ilse put the lollipop into a little brown bag and handed it to Frau

Weisz as well. Frau Weisz paid, stuffed everything into her cloth shopping bag, wished us all a good day and off she went—in a hurry, of course.

The candy in my uncle's store was displayed on the countertop in large glass jars. I again wished that I were taller; I couldn't reach high enough to help myself, even on my tippy toes. Not that this would have been allowed.

A wooden barrel filled with lemonade powder stood just in front of the counter. That was more accessible. I checked whether the coast was clear. It was. Onkel Wilhelm had disappeared into the shop's backroom to get a refill for the sugar barrel. Ilse was cleaning the windows and distracted by some children playing in the street. Corrie was sitting outside on the curb with her chin in her hands.

Time to make my move. I stretched as high as I could go and reached inside the barrel. Yup, I was tall enough for this—I was touching the powder! I quickly withdrew my hand, licked my finger, stood on my toes, and again stretched to reach inside the barrel. I dipped my wet finger into the white lemonade powder. It turned yellow! Sucking the powder that stuck to my finger off, I closed my eyes blissfully.

Sieglinde had been looking around at the other side of the shop, so I sidled over. "Siegie, come here!" I whispered in Dutch. "Try this!"

She followed me to the lemonade barrel, and I showed her what to do.

"I don't think we're allowed. We might get caught!" Sieglinde whispered.

I looked around. "No one's looking." I stuck my finger in again and sucked it. "Mmm, *lekker!*" I rolled my eyes to demonstrate my ecstasy.

Taking a cautious peek over her shoulder and confirming that indeed no one was looking at us, Sieglinde also stuck her finger in her mouth, put her wet finger into the powder and sucked it off. Just then, Ilse turned around, so we nonchalantly wandered away.

When Ilse finished for the day, and Onkel was once again in the back room, we showed Corrie what we'd been doing. To our utter astonishment, our big sister joined in. We all had several licks before

Onkel Wilhelm came back to close the shop. Quickly putting our yellow-stained hands behind our backs, we smiled innocently.

~

Strolling around the town with Mamma, Corrie said, "Mamma, I think that Onkel Wilhelm must be very wealthy. He has his grocery store in Bottrop, but Tante Liesbeth said they also have one in Recklinghausen. Two stores, and his house is absolutely huge!"

"Yes, he's doing very well for himself. He made quite a bit as a naturopathic doctor, but then bought a store. Eventually, he purchased another which your cousin Emil runs. With him and Ilse doing most of the work, Onkel Wilhelm still has some spare time, which admittedly he sometimes spends indulging himself." Mamma tweaked my cheek.

I grinned remembering how, the previous evening at dinner, the family had made fun of my handsome uncle for bathing his feet in 4711 Eau de Cologne. The beautiful, lemony smell followed him wherever he went. Privately I thought Pappa smelled better, even if Onkel was rich.

Besides stores, Onkel Wilhelm also owned a horse, which he kept in his paddock and rode every morning after breakfast. Only two days after the lemonade tasting, my uncle asked me to come outside with him immediately after I finished eating. I hung back a little and exchanged a fearful glance with Sieglinde. Had he found out about the lemonade? Or was he angry that I'd rudely spat out the bitter homemade beer Tante Liesbeth had again given me for breakfast?

Mamma stood up from the table, took me by the hand, and we followed Onkel Wilhelm to the field behind the store. There we waited for a while, watching the quietly grazing horse, who totally ignored us.

Onkel Wilhelm went on to the barn while whistling a happy tune. I grew increasingly worried. What was he doing? He'd been gone for a long time. Was he looking for a big stick to beat me? I sidled closer to Mamma.

When my uncle returned with a saddle in his hands that he then put on the horse, I breathed a sigh of relief. Holding onto Onkel Wilhelm's trousers, I drew closer and closer to the enormous brown horse, until I was almost directly underneath her.

"Oh Mamma, look how tall she is. Her legs look like trees! And what a big, fat tummy!" I giggled as I reached up to touch it.

Mamma quickly pulled me away. "Don't stand underneath, Spilletje. That isn't safe. She could kick you."

Onkel swung himself onto the horse, and I stepped further back, expecting him to ride away. He didn't. Before I grew conscious of what was happening, Mamma hoisted me up and placed me directly in front of my uncle.

I clutched her in terror. What was she thinking? This animal was enormous!

"It's alright. You're safe," Mamma said, peeling my fingers, one at a time, off her shirt. I quickly grabbed my uncle's pant legs, gripping them so tightly that my knuckles turned white.

Then that huge beast began to move. I couldn't say anything, because there was no spit in my mouth, and closed my eyes tightly. Onkel and I went on what I guessed was his usual morning ride through the fields. Eventually, I relaxed a little and opened one eye.

Finally, it was over, and we returned to where Mamma was waiting near to the paddock. Onkel passed me down, and I clung to my mother.

"It went well, Gusti. I think Meta enjoyed the ride. I certainly did." Onkel's face was glowing, but he obviously hadn't been able to see my face.

Once we were alone, I told Mamma what I really thought. "I never want to go riding again. I was so scared of the horse. She was so, so, so high up!" I stood on my toes with my arms over my head to show her what I meant.

Stroking my hair, Mamma responded, "Schatje [Sweetheart], Onkel Wilhelm loves you so much. You remind him of his little daughter—the one who died of the measles when she was only three. Let him take you riding. I wouldn't let you go if it wasn't safe."

But I was not Onkel Wilhelm's daughter. I am Meta. I was happy to have been chosen and it was fun to be up so high, but... I didn't say anything but, with my eyes narrowed and my lips pressed together, I silently vowed that I would never ride that animal again. Never, ever.

~

The following morning, before my uncle finished his breakfast, I made my move. I put Grietje under my arm, left the house, and walked and walked. At four years old, I didn't know where I was going, but I knew I was not going towards that paddock. I was running away.

It became very hot as the sun rose, so I headed for the nearby woods, where I vaguely remembered that the family often had picnics. Ending up on a hill, called the Donnersberg by local people, I lay down in the soft, green grass, listened to the buzz of insects all around me, and fell asleep. I heard the story of what happened next many times throughout my childhood.

My uncle, finding me missing when he was ready to go riding, grew worried. He asked my mother where I was.

"I don't know. I thought she was with you. I haven't seen her in quite a while, not since breakfast. Corrie, have you seen Meta?"

Corrie shook her head and asked Sieglinde. "Do you know where Meta is?"

She didn't.

The grown-ups began searching. They investigated all of my favorite places, under my bed, in the store and in the barn. I was nowhere to be found.

"Corrie, where could she be? Will we ever find her? What if she's hurt?" Sieglinde's lips trembled.

"Don't worry. The grown-ups haven't stopped looking for her. I'm sure they'll find the little scamp." Corrie took Sieglinde's hand. "Come with me; we'll look in the barn again."

Pappa went door-to-door, asking the neighbors if they'd seen me or if I was there. Morning turned into afternoon, and the search became more desperate.

Recalling my favorite places, Mamma had an idea. "Wilhelm, let's have a look at the Donnersberg."

"It's too far away. She could never have gone there. How would she know the way?"

"Please!" Mamma clasped her hands under her chin. "We've sought her everywhere else."

The two adults hunted through the grasses of the Donnersberg until they heard someone crying. They followed the sound, and there I was. I'd woken up, was hungry, but didn't know how to get back.

Wordlessly, I held my arms up, and Mamma scooped me up. I was safe, if a little sunburnt. It was 4 pm.

"Cor, we found her," Mamma sobbed while running towards my father, who'd returned to the house. Pappa held us both tightly. He declared, "She'll never have to go on that horse again." Music to my ears.

Hearing a raised voice, curiosity propelled me to wander sleepily into my aunt and uncle's dining room. The noise was coming from the radio; it was Adolf Hitler with his mesmerizing voice, whipping up support for das Reich and proclaiming how he would save the chosen people, the Aryans. He was calling for all young people to join the Hitler Youth. As he joked around, I could hear a crowd cheering in the background.

The adults in the room sat immobile and in cold silence. Pappa's lips were white, and his fists clenched.

I startled as Onkel Wilhelm stood up so suddenly that he knocked his chair over and viciously swiped the radio off. "*Scheiße*! [sh*t] "How can anyone believe this baloney? That Germans are the top of the evolutionary tree? As a scientifically trained person, I can tell them that the idea is ludicrous! That *Arschloch* [a**hole] will bring even more trouble down on the heads of Germans with his nationalistic nonsense." His normally attractive face was bright red and his eyes bulging.

Tante Liesbeth motioned with her long, thin hands and whispered, "Keep your voice down, Wil. The neighbors may be listening."

Onkel's eyes grew wide as he scanned the windows. He'd been shouting.

My aunt reached across the table to my mother and whispered, "Gusti, if there's war, the young men in our family will have no choice but join the army—even though we don't believe in the cause. You understand that, right? We don't agree, but we may end up fighting against you!" Her eyes grew wild at the thought.

Mamma didn't answer, but the tears rolled down her cheeks as she pulled her hand away. I slid over to put my hand into hers. Sieglinde stood nearby with her finger in her mouth while Corrie twisted her handkerchief into knots.

Wilhelm spoke in a barely audible voice. "You have to understand, Gusti. We know what happens to people who speak up or protest. Emil and Bruno will be forced to choose between killing or being killed. It's so hopeless." He leaned forward on the table and put his head in his hands.

I was as fluent in German as in Dutch, but I still wondered what he could mean. Why would my cousins have to kill people? Who would make them do such a thing and how?

"The problem is many people believe what Hitler is saying. My friend Johanna told me that the schools restrict who and what can be taught. Innocent children are brainwashed to follow the 'Great Leader,' as if he were a god while their parents do nothing." Liesbeth shook her head. "Not that we're doing much," she murmured under her breath with a shrug.

Wilhelm's brow furrowed. "Several men in Bottrop have fallen for his promises. Bruno told us that some of his friends joined up, and now they're officers in the German army. They strut around like ridiculous peacocks." He paused and lowered his voice still further. "It's essential that we're very careful about what's said in this house. You never know who's listening."

Mamma had been translating into Pappa's ear, but now he motioned the conversation to a close. "Well, let's wait and see. We've talked enough."

A few days later, the German government issued a directive ordering all foreigners to leave the country immediately. Theoretically, Mamma and her children could remain, but Pappa definitely had to go home. For our family, separation was not an option nor would my father let his family stay in "enemy" territory.

We prepared to leave, quickly packing our suitcases and gathering food sufficient for the journey. Mamma tearfully hugged and kissed our German relatives. Hurrying from Bottrop to the railway station in Oberhausen, we planned on catching a train to Den Haag.

No trains were available. As train after train, all filled with soldiers, left for Poland, my parents and we three girls waited on the platform at the station for a day, a night, and another day.

We were anything but comfortable as we first sat, then slept, on the hard, wooden benches, with our heads pillowed on our parents' laps. Pappa and Mamma didn't sleep, but whispered in worried voices.

On the morning of the second day, I opened my eyes to again see shiny black boots marching past me, *click, clack, click, clack*. The train station was still packed with neatly dressed soldiers wearing gray-green dress uniforms, each with a rifle slung over his shoulder. The soldiers were singing, always singing.

"The *idioten*," Pappa whispered under his breath. "Singing, they are going to their graves."

Sieglinde and I watched the men with round eyes and butterflies in our tummies. One of the tall, blond soldiers narrowed his ice-blue eyes as he surveyed our bedraggled family. He pressed his razor-thin lips together and his nostrils flared in disgust before he turned to bark another order at his marching companions.

The jackboot drum beat combined eerily with the singing to make me shiver.

Mamma busily arranged and rearranged her hat and scarf and our clothing, her face as white as chalk. Pappa's shoulders were rounded as he chain-smoked while pacing the platform. Corrie sat with her arms wrapped around Sieglinde and me. "*Rustig aan*, stop squirming. We don't want to upset Mamma even more."

53

"But Corrie, *der Stiefel* ['the Boot' in German] keeps glaring at me," I whispered under my breath.

Corrie glanced up briefly to see where my eyes were fastened. "Don't be silly, Meta. Why would a soldier look at a little girl like you?" But I could see her hands trembling, and I knew. Some people hate without reason, and they might hate me, too.

And still, there were no empty trains. Mamma offered us some bread and cheese. The rocks in my stomach stopped me from eating even a bite.

Finally... there was a train going to the Netherlands, and it had some room for passengers.

"Quick. Get in!" Pappa pushed us through the crowd, extending his arms on either side of his little flock, and we practically fell in just before the doors were closed. The train was so crowded that Pappa and us girls had to stand all the way back to Den Haag.

"Cor," Mamma beckoned him to bend over as she whispered, "I'm worried the *kinderen* might be interrogated when we arrive. Remember how careful we needed to be during the last war?"

"They're sensible girls. Teach them what they need to know, and they'll do it." Pappa pushed us towards our mother.

Whispering under her breath, Mamma taught us to say: "*Ich weiß es nicht,*" ['I don't know' in German] and "*Ik weet het niet,*" [the same in Dutch]. She rehearsed us again and again. That was to be the answer to all questions that we may be asked.

On September 1, 1939, the day that we arrived home, Hitler's armies invaded Poland. Two days later, England and France declared war on Germany.

7

THE LAST SINTERKLAAS

Sieglinde and I stood around Mamma's knee as she once again described the events to come. "Any day now, Sinterklaas and his helpers will arrive from Spain. He comes on a steam ship, but no one ever knows when he'll land or in which city."

"Mamma, will he come this year? Will he remember? Will he come to our house?" I was dancing from foot to foot as the questions fell from my lips.

Mamma smiled mysteriously. "Oh hush, Meta! Of course, he'll come to our house. Well, I expect that he will, anyway. He does every year, doesn't he?"

When Pappa got home, he relayed exciting news. "He landed! Sinterklaas. The ship came into Rotterdam harbor this year. He, all his helpers, and *Schimmel* [his white dappled horse] are now in Holland."

It was raining outside, but Sieglinde and I noticed that, right after breakfast, Mamma was preparing to go shopping. Corrie was at school.

"Mamma, can we come? Can we come?"

"All right. Put on your coats, Ukkies. It's cold out there."

As Mamma strolled down the Stevinstraat with her hand over her ear to keep out the cold wind, Sieglinde and I skipped ahead, holding hands, our eyes round with wonder. The shop windows were filled with chocolate initials and sugar candy shaped like animals. Mamma caught up with us when we stopped to gaze appreciatively.

"Which color would you like to try?"

I swallowed as I silently feasted my eyes. Sieglinde pointed to a yellow horse.

"No Siegie, I want pink! Pink is the best-tasting."

Mamma smiled and bought each of us our own sugar animal. Sieglinde nibbled hers while I wolfed mine down.

Mamma also purchased a chocolate *borstplaat* [candy similar to fudge] heart because, she explained, that was Pappa's favorite. We stood nearby and inhaled lungfuls of the scrumptiously scented air.

Next, we visited the bakery. "Look Mamma! 'M' for Meta. They're all mine!" I was pointing at a *banketletter* [puff pastry filled with almond paste] in the shape of an 'M' in the window.

"Ouch, Meta. Be careful! You jumped on my foot!"

Mamma laughed. "Spilletje, you know better than that. The 'M' stands for 'Mamma.' They're all mine." She winked at us both, then asked Juffrouw [Miss] Liebowitz to wrap up three cookies for us to enjoy with tea later that day.

That night, as I lay on my side gazing at the light house and trying not to think about what Pappa said about recent events in Germany, I heard a noise.

"Sieglinde, did you hear that? I think I heard horse's hooves on the roof."

No answer. She was asleep. I ran down the dark stairs in my white nightgown. "Pappa! Mamma! I heard *klip-klop* on the roof! Did you?"

Pappa nodded. "I expect that's Sinterklaas on his horse making the rounds with his helper, Piet, just looking down the chimney to check if the children are being good or bad. Now, go back to bed, Spilletje."

I did, but couldn't sleep. How was it possible that Sinterklaas's horse could get onto a roof? The horses I saw on the streets couldn't fly—they didn't have wings. His horse must be magic! I thought about it all week, but did not come up with any answers.

It was Saturday again. Right after dinner, Mamma said, "Put your shoes in front of the stove, my drei Grazien. Sinterklaas may come tonight. Who knows? If you've been good, he may leave something for you."

After carefully lining my shoe up with those of my sisters, I stood lost in thought while chewing on my collar. Were the naughty things I'd done bad enough so I wouldn't get candy? I really, really liked candy. Would I get a delicious candy or a piece of coal? I asked Sieglinde.

"I don't know." Sieglinde narrowed her eyes and said, "I hope you've been good enough, but I really don't know. You're such a tomboy!" She shook her head, plopped into a chair, and once again buried her head in a book.

This worried me, but, as I opened my mouth to get Mamma's opinion on the matter, footsteps and a rustling sound originating from upstairs interrupted me.

"What do I hear?" Pappa cupped his ear with his hand. "I wonder if it's Piet?"

"I heard a noise, too!" I whispered, grasping Mamma's hand. Sieglinde looked up from her book. Corrie ignored all of us.

After another suspicious rustle from upstairs, Pappa got to his feet. "I'll just go check," he murmured before mounting the creaky stairs up to the bedrooms.

More noises. Sieglinde jumped up from her chair, sidled over to Mamma and clutched my other hand.

We heard Pappa's footsteps on the stairs before he came into the living room and looked sternly at each of us. Then his blue eyes began to twinkle and he grinned, first at Corrie, then at Sieglinde and finally at me, before drawing a large, heart-shaped, chocolate *borstplaat* out from behind his back. "I guess it was Piet. Look what he left behind."

I breathed a sigh of relief. It seemed that none of the Pieten had noticed all the bad things I'd done. (Traditionally, Sinterklaas's servants are all called by the same name: Piet. In prior days, they were dressed in a costume typical of the Moorish people.) Pappa broke the candy up into five equal, yes equal, pieces, and we all enjoyed the treat before going up to bed.

Early the next morning, I crept out of bed and shook Sieglinde's shoulder. "Let's go down and see if Sinterklaas came last night."

"Meta, it's still dark outside."

"Come on, Siegie! I can't wait!" I pulled on my sister's hand until she got up.

We sped down the stairs, rushed over to the *kachel*, peeped into our shoes and saw... candy! Yes! There was a fondant mouse coated in chocolate and wrapped in colored foil paper in my shoe and a candy frog in Sieglinde's.

Piet came around again on the remaining Saturday and Sunday evening before Sinterklaas, leaving *borstplaat,* candy and a little gift: a brightly colored red tin whistle for me and a green one for Sieglinde. I wondered how Sinterklaas knew red was my favorite. Clearly, he didn't think I was bad, even if others did!

On the evening before the feast of Sinterklaas, we all gathered around the dinner table a little earlier than usual. On each plate, Mamma dispensed a small pile of *hutspot*, a blend of onions, carrots and potatoes, made a hollow in the top, and carefully spooned in gravy. She put a small piece of smoked sausage right next to the *hutspot*. After a chorus of "*Eet smakelijk*," we got busy.

"Look, Sieglinde, I made a waterfall going down my *hutspot* mountain. I put the meat in the gravy lake at the bottom. It's a boat."

"I'm going to make a canal. The meat can be a house next to it."

This was one meal where we were allowed to play with our food.

Pappa pointed to his plate. "I made a whole city with criss-crossed roads."

Mamma rolled her eyes. "Cor, aren't you a little too old to play with your dinner?"

"I've been thinking. Sinterklaas has to go to all the homes in the Netherlands, and he only has tonight to do it. How? I wonder if he'll be able to make it to us." Corrie sneaked a sideways look at her younger siblings.

Mamma shrugged. "We'll have to wait and see. I'm sure he'll try."

She pushed herself up from the table to clear the dishes and make hot chocolate.

As soon as she was out-of-sight, Pappa winked at us and took a *banketletter* out of the buffet, putting it on her place. When Mamma returned carrying a tray of hot drinks, Pappa made a deep bow, with an expansive sweep of his arm. "Here you are, Guusje."

"Why Cor, *dank je wel!*" Mamma said, first setting the tray down and then dramatically throwing up her arms. "What a surprise!"

We giggled, because Pappa and Mamma did this every year.

Afterwards we all enjoyed a piece, Mamma and Pappa washed and put away the dishes, and we girls sat around the *kachel*, singing *Sinterklaas Kapoentje* and *Dag Sinterklaasje*. (One can hear these songs at www.youtube.com/watch?v=R9IufkAo3hc.)

Suddenly, there was a loud knocking that sounded like it originated from the back plate of the *kachel*. I clutched Sieglinde. What was it? Was Piet on the roof? Would he throw candy down the chimney like he did last year?

Pappa came walking in the room just as candy started falling from behind the *kachel*. We scrambled to pick it up, and even Corrie made sure that she got her share. No sooner had we taken our seats to survey our loot, than the front doorbell rang, loud and long. I caught my breath. Sinterklaas? Could it really be him?

"Well, open the door!" Pappa chuckled, leaning back to blow a smoke ring, his legs stretched out and crossed at the ankles.

I didn't dare, so I took my mother's hand and scooted close to her side. Sieglinde caught hold of her other hand. "Corrie, you go," I implored.

Corrie rose to her feet, strode into the hallway, turned on the stairway light, and peered down the stairs. I watched her breathlessly.

"Sinterklaas came! Look there, near the front door. He left a big pillowcase that's full to the brim!"

Sieglinde and I ran to look down the stairs.

Corrie turned to Pappa. "Can I go and get it, Pappa?"

"Of course, you can. Be careful, it may be heavy."

"Corrie, hurry! Maybe Sinterklaas is standing there waiting." I was hopping from excitement.

Corrie sedately made her way down the stairs, opened the door, and looked up and down the street. "He's gone. Probably didn't have time to stop."

Then she grabbed the pillowcase, pulled it up the stairs, and put it down on the living room rug. It was stuffed full.

I couldn't believe my eyes. "Mamma, Mamma, open the case, open the case! Let's see what's in it."

Mamma clapped her hands. "Calm down, *Kinderen*. Sit on your chairs and be quiet."

We all took our seats, and I held my breath and tried not to wriggle. After you could hear a pin drop, Mamma opened the pillowcase and passed each of us our gifts. Everyone received the initial of our first name in chocolate. I got the biggest letter, an "M." I figured that meant I had the most chocolate. Corrie had the least. Finally!

Sieglinde and I also got a set of doll clothes, a coloring book, and colored pencils. Corrie was given a pretty scarf, gloves and a nice-smelling soap. Pappa got leather gloves and Mamma a fur shawl. They both put them on immediately, spinning and prancing around to show them off.

After dressing Rietje and Grietje in their pretty new clothing, Sieglinde and I began to color while Mamma read, Corrie sang quietly, and Pappa puffed on a special Cuban cigar, filling the room with its fragrance. All too soon, the evening was over.

"Okay, Ukkies, time for bed."

By then, Sieglinde and I were so tired that we didn't even mind. We fell asleep with big smiles on our slightly candy-smeared, sticky faces. My hand was hanging out from under the covers resting on my gifts, which were piled next to my bed on the floor. It was to be the last Sinterklaas for a long time.

～

"Siegie, let's go look at the Christmas trees at the Belgisch Park. It's not raining today."

"Can we, Mamma?"

"Of course. Just be back by lunchtime."

Sieglinde and I raced down the two streets to get there and then slowed down to stroll through the tall trees. I inhaled deeply. "Do you smell them? It's like we're in a real forest. Let's pretend we are two ladies taking a vacation in the woods."

Both of us immediately started to take mincing steps, the way we imagined that chic women would walk, and talked with what we thought was a classy accent.

"Oh, my dear, how do you like my hat?"

"It's simply divine, my dear! How do you like my gloves?"

"Simply marvelous! Ideal for wiping your nose."

We dissolved in giggles.

I sighed deeply. "I wish Mamma and Pappa would buy the tree today. I want a tall one, just like this one here!"

"I don't think that any of the tall trees will be here by the time they buy a tree. All the people around here are rich, and they'll buy them before we can. Trees won't be cheaper until Christmas Eve." My down-to-earth sister led me to the smaller trees. "Maybe we'll get one of these. If we can afford a tree at all." She scuffed the toe of her shoe on the ground.

On Christmas Eve our family went to Catholic Mass but, when we got home, there was no tree. We drank a cup of hot milk with anise-flavored sugar by the stove and sang Christmas songs until Sieglinde and I were falling asleep. One at a time, Pappa carried us up to our beds. As I turned onto my side, I sleepily murmured, "Tree?"

Pappa stroked my hair, kissed me on the forehead and whispered, "Wait and see."

On Christmas morning as every morning, my parents went downstairs before we did. But on Christmas, we had to wait to come down until we were called. To my delight, when we were finally allowed to make our way down the stairs, and the door at the bottom swung open, there was a tree! Somehow, it had been smuggled in, decorated, and the room magnificently prepared, all while we slept.

My eyes shone as I inhaled the fresh pine scent and gazed reverently around the living room.

At breakfast, we celebrated what was after all a religious holiday quietly with special food and Christmas songs. I was unusually subdued, being busy scrutinizing, touching, and sometimes eating, the pretty ornaments. Those that were edible, anyway.

Mamma and Pappa's eyes met over the table. "Cor, what do you think we'll be doing next year?"

Pappa shook his head. "I have a bad feeling there. Things don't look good." He took a deep breath. "For now, we enjoy what we have."

I pressed my nose to our cold front window. Oh no! Was that der Stiefel standing there in the shadow of the garage across the street?

In January, I turned five. Mamma told me that, as the birthday girl, I was expected to bring treats for my class: sweets for the students, and because teachers are important, chocolates for them. I had big questions about this policy!

When I returned home, relatives and friends came over to celebrate. Mamma bent down and whispered, "Today, Meta, you are the important one, so I saved a chocolate for you. Only for you!"

After making tea for the visitors, Mamma brought out my birthday cake, a *Schneckenkuchen*, my favorite. I watched breathlessly as she sliced it into pieces. One wedge was definitely bigger than all the others—and it was passed to me! I leapt up from my chair and danced around the room, all the while holding the plate with cake.

"Meta, sit down. The cake will fall on the floor. Then you won't be able to eat it!"

I quickly dropped into my chair to enjoy my cake with a chocolate on the side. Meanwhile, I eavesdropped on the adults.

"I guess we better enjoy this now—it won't last. England has begun rationing food."

"Yes, I'm afraid our turn will come soon. The secret papers that Belgium found showed Germany plans on attacking the Netherlands, too."

"Guusta, you grew up in Germany, didn't you?"

Mamma turned red before raising her voice to respond. "Yes, but I'm as Dutch as you. I became a citizen even before I married. And I certainly don't agree with any of what's going on."

The questioner quickly became absorbed in stirring her tea.

"Did any of you hear Churchill's speech?" The political discussion continued and soon became incomprehensible to me. Sieglinde and I withdrew to play a board game.

For weeks we had rain, cold, wind, more rain, more cold, more wind. Having shivered my way down the stairs in my nightgown, I burst through the kitchen door while Pappa was shaving in his winter underwear.

He turned from the sink and dabbed shaving foam on my nose. "*Goedemorgen*, Spilletje. Hear the wind howling. It's *kolere* [low Dutch swear word] cold weather. Dress warmly. By the way, you have something on your nose."

I slipped out of the kitchen, giggling, to get dressed in my undershirt, underwear, slip, every-day winter dress, and long woolen stockings. It was still too cold to play outside.

"Mamma, I'm bored!" I complained.

"I'm busy right now, Spilletje. You'll have to figure it out."

So, I did. I got my wooden whirligig out of my cupboard and took it to the tiny room. The toy spun nicely on the linoleum, balancing on the metal button that had been screwed into its bottom. My sister soon joined me.

"Look Sieglinde, I can make the whirligig go faster by using this." I wound a piece of twine around the whirligig from the bottom to the top and threw it while still holding on to the twine.

It landed on the floor with a bang, but did twirl more satisfactorily—sometimes.

"Let me try!" Sieglinde carefully wound up the twine and threw the toy, making a very pleasing crash, even if it didn't twirl.

All too soon we heard Mevrouw den Dulk thumping on her

ceiling with her broom. Next, she would be knocking on our door, so that game was over.

We wandered back into the living room. Since he'd worked all night and was home today, Pappa looked up from *De Leugenaar*.

"Pappa, Mevrouw den Dulk doesn't want us to play with our whirligig."

Pappa chuckled as he put his cigarette out. "I wonder why. Well, how about playing hide and seek?"

"*Ja*, let's!" I was already dancing from foot to foot.

"Wouldn't that be too noisy, as well?" Sieglinde asked, hesitantly.

"Mevrouw den Dulk shouldn't be able to hear you guys hiding."

As we ran to find good hiding places, Mamma smiled dreamily. "Cor, they're having such a good time. You know I always hoped to have a family like this. *Ja*, they're active, but aren't they just so wonderful?"

"I always wanted the same thing. If only..." Pappa's face fell.

It was my turn to hide, but I was stuck. We'd used up all the hiding places.

"Come here, Meta," Pappa whispered as my sister was counting in the tiny room. I approached and stood by his knee expectantly. Pappa pointed at the kitchen, and I tiptoed with him to see what he meant. There was a shelf high over the stove that formed a kind of canopy. Pappa lifted me onto the kitchen counter and held up his hands to form two steps. I put one foot on each hand, reached up, and pulled myself up onto that shelf. Crouching down breathlessly, I peeked over the edge.

"Ready or not, here I come!" I could hear Sieglinde searching behind the divan, under the dining table, in the WC, behind the carpet hanging in the hall and under the kitchen table. Finally, with her right underneath me, I couldn't help giggling. I was found.

Mamma enjoyed our continued antics for a while, but then it became difficult to work in the kitchen with ukkies running everywhere.

"*Kindertjes*, it's time to settle down. Why don't you look at a book?" Sieglinde and I went to the living room, cuddled under a blanket on a chair near to the *kachel*, and discussed the pictures in a travel book.

64

We didn't even notice Pappa get up and wrap himself in his warm woolen cape. It was black on the outside, bright red on the inside and smelled of cigarette smoke.

An hour later, we heard the clatter of Pappa hanging his bicycle up and went to wait for him. He arrived at the top of the entry stairs with a swirl of cold air and a delicious smell. Pappa swept off his beautiful cape and hidden underneath, protected from the rain, was a paper bag full of freshly roasted peanuts. He deposited the warm bag into my outstretched hands.

Mamma removed the table rug and covered the dining table with old newspapers. As we sat together, cracked the shells, and ate peanuts, happy chatter filled the room.

"You know the best peanut shop in town!"

"You must have cycled fast to get them home while they're still hot."

"Oh, I rode one-handed and held them under the cape. They kept me *lekker* warm."

When we were finished with our peanut feast, the table looked like squirrels had visited. The shells were collected in the newspaper, and the mess was gone.

Memories like this sustained me during the coming years—even as it grew more and more difficult to believe such things had ever happened.

8

THE OCCUPATION BEGINS

For the next several months, my parents gathered around the radio every evening, anxiously listening to the news.

On April 9, 1940, we heard that Hitler invaded Denmark and Norway.

"Well, that's it, Guusje. It's only a matter of time until we're under attack, too. I wonder when it will happen."

"How would I know? Why are you telling me? What do you expect me to do about it? Perform a miracle?"

My parents became increasingly anxious, resulting in far too many heated arguments and tense silences. My teeth chattered and my stomach hurt. I wished that family life could return to normal. It didn't. It got worse.

Just before daybreak on May 10, 1940, the spine-chilling wail of sirens woke Sieglinde and me up. We ran out of our bedroom in our nighties and met our parents and Corrie in the hall. "What...?"

"Quick. Everyone. Go to the WC. It's the safest place in the house." Pappa pushed his confused and terrified children down the stairs.

He led Mamma to sit on the lid of the toilet with me on her lap. Corrie and Sieglinde crowded along the walls on either side of the toilet. After he closed the door, Pappa stood on top of the toilet behind Mamma, bending his head so it wouldn't hit the water tank.

"Pappa," I began. "Why, what..."

"Those sirens mean we're about to be bombed. From now on, every time you hear them, run to the WC."

"How long do we have to stay here? I don't like being in here like this." Sieglinde's eyes were huge in her pale face. She hid her face as we heard the whistle of the first bomb.

"Another siren will sound the all-clear. We can't leave until we hear it."

"Uh, it's very stuffy in here. Could I crack the door, *alsjeblieft*?" Corrie's hand was on the door handle.

"*Ja*, but only by a sliver."

My mouth felt like cotton as I listened to the repeated whistles and crashes of bombs being dropped. As we cowered in the bathroom, Germany bombed our entire coastline in a tactic called Blitzkrieg.

When the bombing finally stopped, and we heard the sustained sound of the all-clear, we tumbled out of the WC and made our way to the living room window. "Oh Cor, look. The entire row of houses right behind the sand dunes has been flattened. Those poor people!" Mamma had tears in her eyes.

Putting his arm around her shoulders, Pappa said, "They'll need our help. Let's do what we can, Guusje. It's all we can do now. Do we have any spare blankets?"

Left standing by the window, my sisters and I watched the smoke, visible against the still-burning homes, curling up from the devastation. Corrie muttered, "I doubt hiding in the WC helped any of those families."

People streamed out of the bombed houses, but that was not what drew my horrified attention. There in the shadows was der Stiefel, standing with his legs apart and his arms folded. Had he followed us from Germany?

His thin lips twisted into a vile smirk as he watched overwhelmed survivors standing motionless in the street. Some, after coming to themselves with a start, hurried away from their crumbling homes. As they turned back to watch from a distance while their possessions went up in flames, der Stiefel drew closer. Several people sat down right in the street and wailed, and his ice-blue eyes lit up in malicious pleasure, like he was enjoying the tastiest of meals.

"Corrie, what are those people doing? Why don't they get up? Why don't they run from der Stiefel?"

"I don't know who you're talking about with this der Stiefel business. But for the survivors, they're in shock. They probably just don't know what to do."

When I turned away from the window, people were everywhere in my house: some I knew and some I didn't. I was relieved that der Stiefel wasn't among them. Several survivors sat on our floor, just staring out into space. Others were weeping. And many clung to each other.

Pappa directed the continual influx of people, telling them where to sit and trying to provide what comfort he could. Mamma served endless cups of tea. Neither parent had the time to console their frightened children, so we kept out of the way, observing everything with pale faces.

Vera, one of Mamma's childhood friends from Germany, who had a daughter my age, came in holding her daughter's hand and carrying her baby boy Johann in her arms. The infant was completely wrapped in a blanket, even his face. Whimpering, Vera held him tightly to her chest. Mamma gently put her arm around her friend, carefully exposed Johann's face, gasped and covered him up again.

"Vera, where's Jan? Is he coming?"

"*Nee*, he was out fishing when the bombing started. Our house is flat! I don't know where he is—or if he's alive." She sank into a chair and buried her face in the baby's blanket.

Eventually, the other adults came to understand that Johann was dead, but Vera just couldn't let him go. She told Mamma that a shell fragment hit him in the head while he was sleeping in his crib. After several days, Vera reluctantly allowed Jan, who joined us a few hours after she did, to take the tiny body away.

I wasn't allowed outside, but stood at the front window watching the refugees in the street entering almost every home. The doors on our street all stood open.

For us, people kept on flooding in, and my parents welcomed them all. I overheard one lady whispering to another that she figured this was a safe house, since Mamma has such a thick German accent. No German would think of looking inside our house.

I turned to gaze at Mamma in surprise. German accent? I listened closely. Nope. She just sounded like Mamma to me, whether she was speaking German or Dutch.

The house was bursting at the seams. At night, strangers slept on the floors of the living room, the kitchen, the tiny room and the hallway. Pappa would not allow anyone to go upstairs where we slept. I felt secure knowing that, as long as Pappa was near, neither der Stiefel nor anyone else would be able to get to me.

Four days later I discovered my parents listening to the radio which they kept hidden at the back of clothes closet under the eaves in their bedroom. Sliding down the wall to sit on the floor outside their door, I peeked around the doorframe.

Pappa had his back towards me. "Guusje, I can hardly believe this. First, our ridiculous queen, Wilhelmientje, abandons us. Now, the Germans have flattened 25,000 homes in Rotterdam. And they are threatening to bomb still more houses. Those *schoften* [bastards] are targeting innocent civilians!"

Mamma made a cutting motion across her throat. "Watch your language, Cor. Little ears might be listening. Big ones, too." Lowering her voice to a whisper, she continued. "Do you think they'll keep bombing Scheveningen and the coastline, as well?"

"Possibly. I expect that Hitler will maintain the pressure, because he wants our government to surrender quickly. And they might, just to prevent more deaths. But the bombing may also mean supplies can't make it through from Rotterdam. I'm afraid that soon there'll be a food shortage for people from Den Haag."

Mamma sighed. "Just like before. It might be better for us to drown ourselves now."

"*Nee, nee.* We'll survive. Trust me. I'll figure out a way."

~

The following day, the Netherlands surrendered to Hitler and became an occupied country. Germany was in charge, and everything changed. Watchful German soldiers stood on every corner, tanks rumbled past our front window, barbed wire blocked access to my precious beach, and war planes droned overhead.

Pappa continued to drill us in saying "I don't know" in answer to every question asked by anybody. Our pretty little country and my formerly sheltered and familiar home were no longer safe. My perpetual stomachache grew worse.

Sometimes, a German greeted me, but Pappa had taught me well. I knew they were just pretending to be nice. He'd said that the Germans hoped they could fool Dutch people into agreeing with their side of the war. But we all could see the results of their bombing campaign. Just a glimpse of the trademark black jackboots made the hair on the back of my neck stand up. If I could avoid it, I never smiled at, or spoke to, any of them. I just ran away.

By listening to my parents' conversations, I learned that, if a person wasn't obedient to the orders that the Germans nailed to posts or dropped from airplanes, they could be shot. So, I was careful to read whatever I found, but often didn't understand the instructions. That worried me. Hopefully, my parents would tell me what we needed to do to stay safe. I didn't want to be shot.

Pappa was particularly incensed about a posting that said that the National Socialist Movement (NSB) political party was now the only legal one. "Guusje, if a person is discovered supporting another party, they'll be killed on the spot. Life has become very dangerous."

Mamma swallowed. "Well, the soldiers aren't everywhere. How would they find out about our political opinions? You're always so careful to comply—at least while they're looking."

Pappa looked around the room and dropped his voice. "NSBers."

My skinny knees knocked at his tone of voice, but I was too curious to leave the room. What I heard next was even more frightening.

"Yes, we can avoid the German soldiers. They're easy to recognize.

But the NSBers are hidden traitors, invisible enemies, *vuile rot schoften* [dirty rotten bastards]."

"Cor, they may think we're on their side because of my accent. They'll never suspect…"

Pappa shook his head quickly, and said, "Shhh!"

I elbowed Corrie, so she would ask him what he meant. I was considered too small to be included in such conversations.

Pappa took a deep breath. "NSBers are Dutch Nazis who believe Hitler's lies. They think having blue eyes and blond hair makes them better than anyone else. They hate Jews and think the war is a good thing." He went to our front window and being careful to remain invisible to anyone outside, pointed out a group of men loitering on the street corner cozily chatting with a couple of soldiers. "Stay far away from them."

The problem was that NSBers were so hard to recognize. Time and again, I overheard Pappa and his friends warning each other about a neighbor whom they'd heard was an informer. It was vital not to say anything anti-German in their hearing, because the NSBer would alert the occupiers, soldiers would come to that person's home in the night, and the outspoken person would disappear.

Sitting against the living room wall with my knees drawn up to my chest, I realized that absolutely nobody except my immediate family could be trusted. NSBers looked like us, spoke like us, lived near us, and even ate like us, but they weren't loyal Dutchmen. You just never knew. Pappa often said that he could drink their blood.

I grew absolutely petrified of most everyone whom I did not see my father confiding in. The little girl who used to stop to chat with anyone and everyone did so no longer.

~

"Why don't you go play outside, girls? It's a nice day. Just stay far away from any soldiers." Mamma blew a stray hair out of her face.

So, my sister and I went, hand-in-hand as usual to my favorite place, the sand dunes just behind the railway. We knew that we wouldn't be able to watch the *nettenboetsters*, because it was late in the day and very few men still went fishing, the coastline being a strategic place for fighting. But maybe we could pick some wild flowers and make a bouquet for Mamma. Nature was totally unaware of the disruption to our lives that the war was causing. But as we began to gather the prettiest blossoms, enjoying the smell of salt water and the wind in our hair, the war once again inserted itself into our lives. First we heard, and then we saw, airplanes roar in from over the land. Others flew in from over the water.

"What do you think they're going to do, Siegie?"

"I don't know, but I don't hear sirens. I don't think they'll bomb the sand dunes, anyway. Why would they?"

"Let's watch. This is a good place to sit." We dropped to our bottoms in the sand.

We soon heard bullets whining through the air, followed by crashes when they struck their target airplane. I put my fingers in my ears, but continued to stare at the spectacle, which I later learned was a dogfight. One by one almost all the airplanes flew off or disappeared until only two were left. One of those planes went down in a column of black smoke; the other flew off.

In the ensuing silence, broken only by the swish of the waves and call of the seagulls, I asked, "Sieglinde, why did the airplanes do that?"

"I think the planes from the land are flown by Germans— Germany is in that direction anyway—and the ones from the sea are probably flown by our friends. It looked to me like they were fighting."

I turned to gaze in the direction of the sea. What was that there in the distance? I squinted to see better.

"Do you see those men hanging from parachutes? I think those must be some of the pilots. What do you think will happen to them?"

"Meta, do I look like an encyclopedia? I don't know. Let's go home and ask Pappa."

Bursting through the door, I raced up the stairs, full of questions. "Pappa, we saw airplanes fight. Sieglinde said some were Germans, and some might have been our friends. Is she right? Also, we saw some people parachuting into the sea. They'll drown because of the undercurrent, right? So, why do they do that, if they know they'll die, anyway?"

My father gave a quick glance around the rather full room. "Let's go upstairs," he said, quietly.

Once Sieglinde and I were seated on my bed, Pappa answered my questions. "So, Spilletje, you're right that the sea is dangerous. You must never go in it unless I'm there. But for the pilots, they might be okay. The Dutch resistance is watching all the time. If they see someone fall from an airplane, they launch a boat to get him. If the pilot is our friend, they hide and keep him safe until he can be sent to England. If the pilot is a German, he'll be made a prisoner-of-war."

"Oh, so the men that sometimes stay here... that one downstairs..."

Pappa slammed his hand over my mouth. "No more talking. Never talk about that! Ever. Do you understand?"

I nodded, even as my stomach clenched. I also began to understand what was happening in our home. As the homeless people moved out, other people took their place, even though no more homes were bombed. Some of those men were moved from our house to another just down the street. Could those be rescued pilots who would end up at the Scheveningse harbor? I knew I must not talk about any of what I witnessed, so I never confirmed what I suspected and feared: Pappa was participating in the resistance. Mamma was his cover.

Nonetheless, the dogfights became fascinating to me, and I used to watch whenever Mamma allowed it. I sat and dreamt of the surviving pilot surprising his family when he arrived at home alive, all the while wondering if he would spend any time under our roof while on his way there.

Of course, Allied pilots weren't the only people who were shipped from Scheveningen to England.

"Mamma, where is Meneer Meijers? He made such amazingly good bread."

"He went to England, Spilletje. It wasn't safe for him and his family here."

"Will he come back? After, I mean."

"I don't know, but I hope so. Things are so different now..." Mamma sighed deeply.

I reflected that it wasn't fair that our Jewish neighbors would have to leave their homes and shops but, at that time, had no idea just how dangerous the circumstances were, and would become, for the Jews of the Netherlands. The ones who left the country were the most fortunate among them.

～

Our family was cozily seated next to the *kachel*, me snuggled on Mamma's lap with my head on her shoulder, when we heard pounding on our door. Friends knock; they don't pound. As if connected with invisible wires, my parents simultaneously jumped to their feet and stood with rigid bodies and rounded eyes. We girls, me now on the floor, instantly became motionless, almost not breathing.

Just recently, the occupying force had "invited" Dutch men to join the German army. Pappa was adamantly opposed to doing such a thing, but could the people at the door be soldiers coming for him? Mamma's German relatives had friends who'd become Nazis. Had one of those people betrayed her husband?

After exchanging a fear-filled glance with Pappa, Mamma took a deep breath and walked down the stairs. In earlier discussions, my parents had decided it would be safer for my mother to answer any time a German came to the door. Her speaking German couldn't help but be an advantage. Also, some of Pappa's features might give rise to questions about his heritage—that would definitely be bad.

Mamma doubtless pasted a smile on her face before opening the door. I crept into the upper hallway and peeked around the corner to see what would happen. Two German soldiers were leaning on the door frame, and they just said three words: "*Kupfer und Messing*," which means "copper and brass."

Mamma's shoulders sagged with relief upon hearing that they were after brass and copper and not my father. The soldiers then burst through the door, rudely pushed my mother aside, and ran up the stairs.

My heart jumped into my throat recognizing that one of them was der Stiefel. Now he was up close, I could better see his features: pale eyes with the blackest of pupils, immaculately coifed hair, and skin so tightly drawn across his prominent cheekbones that he resembled a corpse.

I quickly joined Sieglinde in a cozy chair, shrinking back to try and make myself invisible. Knowing now that they weren't after him, Pappa came forward to help—all the better to encourage the hated enemy to leave quickly.

The soldiers looked down their noses to survey our home. After dumping the contents of our brass coal pail onto the rug, they began replacing the coal with Pappa's large brass ashtray and the copper and brass ornaments that had filled the top of our buffet. I opened my mouth to protest; Mamma shook her head and frowned, and I was silent.

Der Stiefel spotted and grabbed Mamma's purse. My stomach clenched as she forcefully snatched it out of his hands, speaking German all the while. He barked an order, and Mamma emptied it onto the table herself: inside there was a lipstick, her comb, and a few pennies. The other soldier indicated that Pappa should put the contents of his pockets there, too: cigarettes, two guilders, a two-and-a-half guilder piece, and some square nickels. Finally, the contents of the housekeeping jar, even the half pennies, were tipped out onto the table, making a dreadful clatter in the silent room. Der Stiefel and his companion stuffed all the money and the cigarettes into their pockets before picking up the coal pail and leaving.

I stared down at my lap with my lips pressed together seething inside as the soldiers, having stolen so many of my family's possessions, went out the door, even picking up our tall brass umbrella stand on their way out.

I knew I was not allowed to speak until after they left, but nobody could stop me from thinking. The greedy pigs! It looked to me as if they'd taken all the money we had to live on. Would their theft mean we wouldn't be able to buy groceries and pay the rent?

"Who do those Nazis think they are?" Pappa stood with clenched fists, chest heaving. We waited, fearful of what more would ensue.

Not much. Pappa shrugged. "Well, that's it. Life goes on. Guusje, do we have anything for supper?"

Mamma, looking as if she'd aged 20 years, pushed herself off the table and went to the kitchen. We all knew that some of those ornaments had been extremely precious to her; they'd belonged to her now-deceased parents. Now, they were gone, going to be melted into bullets. There was nothing anyone could do. Resigned acceptance appeared to be the best response.

"Ha!" Pappa said with a grin on his face. "The soldiers were so focused on the money that they didn't notice my smoking table. It's still there. Greedy pigs!"

"Uh, Pappa? How can we buy food now?"

Pappa grinned as he messed up my hair. "Spilletje, I learned a long time ago that a person must always have reserves that nobody knows about. We'll be okay."

A few weeks later, Mamma and Pappa were talking over dinner. "Guusje, today at work I found out that Thijs and Karel are no longer there. They've been forced to join the German army. I haven't seen Sjaak for quite a while now, so I expect the same thing may have happened to him." He reached across the table to take her hand. "I'm afraid that soon the *Kleine Schilder's Jongen* [little painter's apprentice; Hitler] will call me!"

Mamma threw her hands up. "They just take and take and take! Maybe it'd be better if we all just went and drowned ourselves now."

Although my sisters and I were used to Mamma's drama, I felt my heart jump into my throat. Were things really as hopeless as all that? We weren't allowed to speak at meals, so I had to stuff my fears down inside, where they filled my belly and made eating impossible. I laid my knife and fork down.

Pappa, noticing my pale face, shook his head. "Let's not give up, Guusje. I'll figure something out. I always have, right?"

Mamma forced a smile. "Yes, I suppose you have. But can you

really win against all of them?" Turning to her silent children, she continued. "Eat, *Kindertjes,* while you still can."

All too soon the dreaded letter arrived. Pappa's lips stiffened into a sneer as he read it out. It was an order instructing my father to report for a physical with a German physician in a week. There they would determine his fitness to have the honor of serving das Reich.

"*Schijt* [sh*t]! It didn't take the *ellendelingen* [horrible people] long to call me. As if I would help Nazis!" Pappa's fist hit the table so hard that the vase of flowers jumped.

Mamma sunk into a chair, leaned forward and covered her face with her hands. "Cor, we need you here. I can't do this alone. Someone has to provide food and protection for our family. What can we do?"

Pappa paced the floor with his hands behind his back. "The Germans won't care at all about our family, and their soldiers have to obey their orders. But I'll figure something out. I have to."

The next evening, Pappa invited a few trusted friends to our house, and they all discussed the problem.

"Cor, the only way to avoid having to go is to fail the physical." Rainier shook his head. "The trouble is that you're a strong, vigorous man."

"Hmm, let's think. How can I fail it? There must be a way. I'll do anything!"

Luuk had been sitting silently, but now he perked up. "Anything?"

"Yes, of course!" Pappa stubbed out his cigarette and leaned forward. "What did you have in mind?"

"Well, I've heard of people who managed to fail their health exam by staying awake for a long time. After a few days without sleep, you'll look and feel absolutely terrible. Guaranteed!"

Rainier grinned. "Sounds like a great idea to me. Even better, when they ask you questions, your answers won't make any sense."

Pappa stroked his chin and nodded slowly. "It's worth a try. How long do you think I'll need to go without sleep, Luuk?"

"I think three days and three nights should do it. But it'll be very difficult. We promise to keep you awake, but you need to promise to do exactly as we tell you—no matter what. It's the only way you'll succeed."

"You have to make a solemn vow," Rainier added.

Pappa stood up in the middle of the group and formally promised: "I solemnly swear that, from the beginning of the three days and nights until the exam, I will obey you all without question." Then he shook hands with each of his friends, thanking them profusely for being willing to help.

Luuk chuckled. "Trust me, soon you won't be feeling very grateful at all."

On the evening of Day 1, some men who'd already gone through the exam and failed it came and gave Pappa advice on how to behave at the German military doctor's office. My father and his friends played cards all that night.

The next day, a different set of trusted colleagues kept Pappa awake at work by poking him every time his eyes drooped. In the evening, other men came home with him and kept Pappa awake all through the night.

During the third day at work, Pappa later told us that his friends were relentless in keeping him moving. That evening was worse. Cousin Joop and other friends came over after work, took Pappa's arms and made him walk up and down the living room so that he couldn't sleep. I felt sick, seeing my precious Pappa slumped between them, totally exhausted, with a thin stream of drool coming out of his mouth. Pappa pled with them to just let him sleep, but his friends were relentless.

Mamma, seeing the dark circles under her husband's red eyes, begged, "Just let him sleep for a few minutes! *Alsjeblieft!*"

"*Nee*, he can't rest. It's too close to the exam. Cor, remember you gave your word." The men kept him awake all night.

In the morning, Pappa was slurring his words; he couldn't even answer the simplest questions. He was a wreck. Mamma told us to stay out of his way.

At the right time, another set of friends picked him up to take him to his fitness exam. Pappa couldn't walk on his own. Mamma waited at home, vigorously cleaning everything—even things that were spotless. Corrie wrung her hands as she stood by the window watching for his return, and Sieglinde and I sat silently. My stomach was in knots. What would happen?

After a few hours, we heard the door open and Joop call to us. We rushed to the top of the stairs and watched as he supported/dragged Pappa up the stairs.

"What happened?" Mamma asked breathlessly.

Pappa looked up. "It's okay, Guusje," he slurred with bleary eyes.

Joop explained further. "He was disqualified due to ill health."

Joop and Mamma helped my exhausted Pappa up the stairs and into bed. He slept all night, all day and all night again. I kept creeping in to peek at him and make sure that he was still breathing. He didn't notice.

When he finally woke up, Pappa got up, washed, ate and went to work. He'd recovered completely and was just fine. So were we. Until we weren't.

9

LIFE IN THE MAUSOLEUM

"*Kinderen*, today your mother and I will need your help—we have to move. You'll need to pack your things."

I looked up from Sieglinde and my game of Ludo. "Why Pappa? Where are we going?" My voice rose. "I don't want to move!"

Pappa sighed. "Neither do Mamma and I, Spilletje. But Germany decreed that their soldiers need to live near the beach. The government gave us a place in Den Haag. We've been ordered to vacate tomorrow."

"Does everyone have to move?" Corrie got up and began to take those things the soldiers hadn't stolen out of the buffet.

Mamma walked over to help her. "Almost everyone. Mevrouw van Kruijsen told me that they have to stay in Scheveningen because her husband is a streetcar conductor, but I don't know of anyone else who is staying."

"Necessary to their cause," Pappa muttered. "Now Ukkies, go upstairs and put your things in the boxes we left on your beds."

The very next day we set off walking, Pappa pushing our belongings in a rented cart.

"Oh Mamma," I said, clapping my hands as we completed the six-kilometer journey to our new street. (This was about four miles.)

"Look how long the street is! And so many shops!" I loathed being the youngest child of the little postman living in a tiny home on the short street—now our street was long.

Mamma's shoulders were uncharacteristically rounded, and she did not answer.

"Here we are. Let's go in." Taking a deep breath, Pappa fitted the key to the lock in the door to the corner apartment above the butcher at the Weimarstraat 46c.

I pushed past my parents to be the first to race up the two flights of stairs and enter our new place. My breath made a quick exit from my lungs as I reared to a halt. I'd had visions of a cozy place similar to, but better than, our home in Scheveningen. Not this.

The living room floor was made of scratched and graying wood; there was no rug for warmth. Faded wallpaper that had once been patterned with pink roses covered the walls and the cupboard door. I stood in the entrance way and stared, tracing the ghostly roses with my forefinger. Perhaps it had been pretty a very long time ago, but no more. Now, the house just looked old and washed-out, lifeless. Something from the past that should no longer be there. Drained of my former enthusiasm, I sank onto the floor.

"Meta, get up. You're in the way. And we all have a lot of work to do." Corrie squeezed past me, suitcase in hand.

I disconsolately moved further into the room towards a dark, gaping fireplace that looked like it might swallow up the living room. Curious, I went over, stood inside the huge hole and peered upwards to see a pipe going up the chimney. It looked for all the world like the skeleton of the corpse that was disguised as our new house. There was no cozy *kachel*, and I shivered.

Now totally dejected and more than a little spooked, I wandered into the kitchen. It was no better. The walls and counters were dirty and discolored; it smelled like an elderly woman's breath.

Mamma bustled past me and switched on the stove burners. "Well, there's a mercy. They work. After everyone puts their things away, we can have a hot drink."

Sieglinde and I quickly put our few possessions in our new

bedroom, Pappa returned to the Leeuwardensestraat for his next load, and the rest of us sat on the yellowed kitchen floor to drink a coffee substitute, partially made with burnt beans.

This house wasn't home. There would be no church, no Sinterklaas, no Christmas. Nothing. But it was where we were.

~

Within a few months of our move, both the gas and the electricity were turned off. The house was darker than ever, and the stove was now useless, not that we had much to cook.

While we were still living in Scheveningen, we'd been able to take our tin bowls to a soup kitchen once a day and receive something to eat. But those had closed long ago.

"Cor, I took our ration cards all up and down the street, but the shops are almost empty. Even the butcher downstairs told me he has nothing."

"That's strange. I'm pretty sure I smell cooking when I pass his door."

"*Ja*, I suspect he has enough for him and his family. But not enough to sell."

"Well, if we can't get food from the shops, I'll have to go straight to the source."

So, Pappa joined the droves of other hungry people, going to various farms on his wooden-wheeled bicycle and asking them for help. He traded many of our towels, linens, his watch, and some clothing for food. One farmer from Friesland, after meeting Pappa only once, occasionally sent a loaf of bread through the mail. A virtual feast! But as the supplies of everything continued to diminish, my family began to learn what real deprivation was.

"Mamma, I'm hungry. My tummy hurts!"

"*Ja*, Spilletje, I know. We're all famished. But I can't pull dinner out of my elbow. *Alsjeblieft* don't make things worse by complaining."

Thus, I came to understand that I should keep my discomfort with regard to lack of food to myself.

The move to Den Haag negatively impacted me in more ways, as well. Obviously, I had to switch schools and make new friends. At first, I adjusted, but the changes were relentless. The place where school was held was relocated time and again as the Germans commandeered one building after another. Every time I had to muddle through getting to know a different group of students, understanding a change in curriculum and learning from unfamiliar, often stressed-out teachers.

It was too much. From someone who used to be extroverted, I became increasingly uncommunicative and fearful. From someone who used to do well at school, I lost virtually all interest in my studies. There was no point in even having friends. Nothing lasted.

"Mamma, Anna doesn't come to school anymore. Did she move, or does she just go to another school?"

"Spilletje, she's Jewish. The German soldiers won't let Jewish children go to school anymore."

"But how will she learn?" I stopped and thought for a minute. "Oh, did she leave the country, like Max Abbas? I miss him."

"I heard that the Abbas family moved to France before we left Scheveningen to avoid the war. I hope that somehow they do." She heaved a sigh. "But I think it's too late for Anna and her family. They won't be allowed to escape now."

"But Mamma..." I began to whine.

"Sshh! Keep your voices down! You don't know who's listening." Pappa had been growing increasingly anxious about the NSBers, who were ever vigilant in their spying. We had a German neighbor downstairs, Hildegunde, whom we didn't know yet, and the walls were not sound-proof. Could she be an NSBer?

I looked out of our window and broke into a sweat, recognizing der Stiefel leaning against a lamppost with his legs crossed at the ankles. He was joking with a group of uniformed and nonuniformed men. Why was he here? Was he following us? Did he suspect my father? I didn't share my worries with anyone. What would be the point?

My parents frequently spoke of crushing worries of their own: the increasing hostility of German soldiers towards Dutch citizens, diminishing food supplies, and no fuel at all. I was only six years old and already knew that there was no point in telling them about how I was feeling. Nobody could change the situation.

Often, attempting some kind of escape from my circumstances, I played hooky from school. Once alone, I withdrew into my own thoughts, telling myself stories of lands far away. Instead of interacting with my family, I day-dreamed of hiking through the woods or strolling by the sea.

The chatterbox fell silent. Nobody noticed.

I was so homesick for the sea. Den Haag had too little air, the towering buildings crowded out the sky, and I was suffocating. I needed to hear the raucous cries of the seagulls, feel the wind lifting my hair, and shiver from the icy waves washing over my toes.

Early one morning I reasoned, the beach is very long; the soldiers probably wouldn't notice me. I could just skip school again. Mamma never noticed before, and I'm pretty sure she wouldn't find out this time.

That same day, after glancing over my shoulder, I walked down my street in the opposite direction from school, continuing all the way from Den Haag to Scheveningen, through the Scheveningseweg and down the Neptunis Straat. Finally, I ran across the Boulevard, which is next to the beach.

Upon arrival, I screeched to a halt, dismayed to see immense rolls of barbed wire blocking my access to the beach. "*Vuile rot Moffen*," I muttered under my breath, feeling very proud of my bad language. "But if you get through to the beach somewhere, so can I."

I walked along the rolls until I found a place where I could slip through and come out onto the sand. There it was: the sea that I'd been missing so much and the long, long beach. It looked rather lonely; neither a sunbather nor a soldier in sight. I remained motionless for a time, feasting my eyes on the expansive view.

Taking a couple of steps forward, I then closed my eyes and tilted my head back. As I inhaled the salted air, listened to the rhythm of the waves, and felt the warm sun on my face, the emptiness inside me filled up. "Sooo wonderful," I whispered, sinking down into the soft sand.

"*Oi, geh vom Strand weg* ['Hey, get off the beach' in German]!" My eyes flew open, and I saw a soldier running towards me while waving his arms furiously. Because, before the war, my mother was as likely to address us in German as she was in Dutch, I knew what he was yelling. He wasn't welcoming.

Stopping directly in front of me, the soldier crossed his arms and demanded that I tell him my name. I remembered what my parents had instructed me to say, but it didn't seem to fit under these circumstances.

My knees were knocking and my heart pounding, but I flipped my messy braids back over my shoulders, looked directly into that enemy soldier's narrowed eyes, and answered in flawless German, "*Herr Soldat, ich bin* Meta!"

The soldier's face softened, possibly because he heard his mother tongue being lisped by a blue-eyed child. "Where do you live, little girl?"

Only then did I answer as I'd been instructed, "*Ich weiß es nicht.*"

The soldier raised his eyebrows, but pointed to the Boulevard. "Go home."

Another soldier, who appeared from outside the barbed wire, took me by the arm, and firmly escorted me off the beach. That soldier left me there on the street.

But now I had a problem. A big one. Going to the beach had been so easy; I'd just followed my nose. Returning was a whole different story. I'd lied about not knowing my address, but I genuinely had no clue how to get there.

Eventually, seemingly miraculously, after walking for many kilometers, I found myself in a street where one of my school friends lived. I knew the way home from there. When I finally fell through the door of my home, it was obvious that my mother hadn't noticed anything amiss.

I never went back to the beach again until the war was over. Just one more thing to hold within my aching heart.

~

"Mamma, the bakery windows are dark—they have been for over a week. Where are the Liebowitzes?"

"I don't know." Mamma sighed. "Maybe with the family who ran the linen shop. Don't ask..." Shaking her head, Mamma began to scrub the countertop.

I walked slowly into the living room, pulling my collar into my mouth. What could she mean? Could they be in France with the Abbas family? But France was also occupied.

A few days later, Pappa added to my worries. "Guusje, BBC Radio Oranje just broadcast something that may develop into a problem for us. Do you remember how the Nazis picked up hundreds of Jews to take them to Buchenwald?"

"Yes, some people protested by going on strike, didn't they?"

"*Ja,* and now the strike has spread all over the country. Lots of people are joining in."

"That's a good thing, isn't it? If some of the Dutch people don't stand up against the terrible things that the Nazis do, who will?" Mamma hung the tea towel up to dry.

Pappa shook his head and exhaled noisily. "I agree with you. They're doing what's right... but I'm sure it won't end well. The Nazis will retaliate; they always do. And if they're angry..."

Mamma put her hand over Pappa's mouth. "Let's not borrow trouble."

Trouble came anyway. My parents were whispering once again, and Mamma was in tears.

"Pappa, Mamma, what's going on?" My heart was in my throat. I could feel the arm that Corrie put around my shoulders trembling.

"The *vuile rot Moffen* killed all the people leading the strike, including Henk. Every one of them," Pappa groaned. "I doubt it'll stop there."

I swallowed hard and sank into a chair to hear more.

Mamma murmured, "They'll be after anyone they think is a part of the Resistance."

"If they find out who is, you know they'll kill every person in their village... or neighborhood."

Mamma twisted her apron between her fingers. "Cor, for goodness' sake, be careful!"

By now my collar was soaking wet. When my father discussed politics with his friends, he made no secret of his hatred for the Nazis. What if he was active in the resistance? What if one of his 'friends' was an informer? Would my family be the next target? When would it be our turn?

I couldn't ask; I didn't want to know the answer.

∽

In 1942 Jewish people in the Netherlands were forced to wear a yellow star.

"Pappa, today I played with Rita. She showed me her star. It looks pretty. I wish I could have one."

"Those stars are not pretty; they're evil. The star shows everybody that your friend is Jewish. She shouldn't be on the street. I'm so sorry for her and her family. If you see her again, tell her to stay home."

"Why?"

"The soldiers are now forcing Jewish people onto trains. They're taken to camps where there's almost no food and they'll have to work very hard. Rita's family would not want to go. They should hide. Now." Pappa's eyes fastened on mine. "Do you understand?"

Mamma added, "My brother wrote that their government has been sending people to camps since even before the war started. They're terrible places."

"Oh, I'll go and tell her!" I already had one arm in the sleeve of my coat.

"*Nee,* stay away from Rita," Pappa barked. "Her parents will look after her. Don't get involved."

Later, I overheard my father talking with his friends and learned more about the concentration camps, how most people there died: by illness, by starvation, through over-work, by being beaten, or shot. I realized that the stars were a target on a person's chest. They were worse than bad.

I never saw Rita again.

10

SURVIVAL TACTICS

"Meta, come here! Look! Do you want to learn to stand on your head like me?" Pappa proceeded to demonstrate, right in the middle of the living room.

I stood with my head tilted, waiting to see if he would fall over. He didn't. Seemed like it was worth the risk. "Oh *ja*, can you teach me? Come on, Sieglinde! You do it, too."

"*Nee, dank je*. I can do somersaults. That's enough for me. I'll read." Sieglinde buried her nose in her book again.

"Okay, Spilletje, it's just you and me. This is how you start. Put your head on the floor like this. Your hands go on either side. Got it? Now put your knees on your elbows." Pappa helped me to balance in that upside-down frog-like position.

"Now slowly and carefully straighten out your legs." My father assisted me with sticking my feet up in the air, holding me in that pose until I seemed balanced. He let go.

"Look, Siegie! I'm doing it!"

Oops. Not anymore. Pappa caught me so that I didn't get hurt. Sieglinde laughed.

"Okay, now do it by yourself," Pappa encouraged. "I think over by the wall is the best place."

I obediently put my head next to the living room wall and

carefully placed my hands on either side of my head. Pappa stepped over and adjusted them to be just so. Then I placed my knees on my elbows and balanced, only wobbling a little. Lastly, I kicked my feet up. Bang! My feet hit the wall.

There was a clatter in the kitchen, and Mamma came running. "Cor, be careful with that child!"

"She's fine. Too small to fall very far!"

Mamma didn't really approve of this game, but I continued to practice, determined to succeed. The already-faded and torn wallpaper became increasingly grimy. As he sat smoking, Pappa winced each time my feet hit the wall.

"Meta, how would you like to learn to roll cigarettes?"

I turned the right way up and walked, a little unsteadily, to his chair. That sounded like a useful skill. After all, Pappa started smoking at eight years old, and that was only just over a year away for me.

"This is how. Flatten out the cigarette paper. Work a pinch of tobacco until it's a thin roll and put it on the paper." Pappa carefully showed me each step of the process. "Next, lick the edge, roll the paper up with the tobacco inside, and stick it. Like this."

After watching closely, I tried it. "Pappa, look! It's a cigarette!"

Pappa chuckled as he inspected what I'd produced. "Good job, Spil. Now I think I better try what you made." My father lit the rather loosely packed cigarette and declared it wonderful.

A few days later, he came home from work with an ear-to-ear grin. Reaching under his cape, he produced a bundle of huge green leaves. "Look!"

"What are they, Cor? I don't recognize them." Mamma inspected the plant matter carefully. "I'm not sure how these would be cooked."

"They're not for eating, *Guusje*." Pappa chuckled. "Rainier somehow managed to get me some tobacco leaves! They're not ready for use; they need to dry first, but they are tobacco. The real deal."

I raised my eyebrows at Sieglinde. We both knew that tobacco does not grow in the Netherlands, but said nothing. By then, the war had taught us that it's often best not to ask, "how," or "from where."

Whistling while he worked, Pappa threaded a piece of rope,

usually reserved for hanging toilet paper, through the leaves and hung them up to dry.

Once the leaves were brown and crumbly, Pappa mixed the tobacco leaves with grass and other leaves that he'd dried on a plank. This was the concoction he used to make ersatz cigarettes. The German army had procured all of the real thing for their own use. Having watched him closely, I was pretty sure I could do it, too.

Pappa gave this special mixture away to his colleagues, so they too could make cigarettes. Those men, who were grateful to have anything at all to smoke, "acquired" and gave us an occasional potato, thereby helping us survive the war.

~

The war dragged on into its third year, and although it hardly seemed possible, food supplies continued to diminish. We suffered more hunger than some because we had no farming relatives who could help us. (By then, both Mamma and Pappa's parents were deceased. Mamma's relatives, except Agnes, lived in Germany. Pappa only had one living sister, and she was not wealthy.)

Pappa had now been gone for several days. He returned carrying a few of our remaining possessions in his arms. "Guusje, I've been to every farm anywhere near here. No one could share. Great long lines of people were begging. At one farm, probably a thousand. I didn't bother to ask." Pappa's shoulders were round, and his eyes were missing their usual sparkle.

Mamma took a deep breath. "I guess they're doing what we are. Taking care of their own families. But what can we do? Look how the children's ribs are showing!"

"I'll discuss it at work. Maybe the men will have some ideas."

They did. Pappa told us that their plan was to look around them and use everything they could find. Some farmers were sending food to their city relatives wrapped in brown paper and string. These packages often broke while the post office was handling them, and sometimes food was spilled. In prior days, the mess would be thrown away, so as not to attract rats and mice. No more.

Now the men cleaned the floor much more carefully than they handled the packages. The contents of the dustpan were scrutinized on a daily basis, and Pappa and his colleagues shared any morsel of any food, usually beans, between them. They fed their families with the floor sweepings.

Unfortunately, it wasn't enough to fill our bellies. Sieglinde and I often walked down the street searching for scraps of food that might have fallen off a cart or wagon. Our efforts were in vain.

"Oh Siegie, look! It that an onion?" My mouth watered as I imagined the aroma of onion fried together with potatoes. I ran across the street to pick it up, but it was a rock. My face fell.

That night, Pappa told us that the Dutch government had decided to release its stores of tulip bulbs so we could eat.

Mamma took the three bulbs that he produced from inside his cape, sliced up a potato, and fried everything together with a few beans.

"Dinner," she called.

We all came to sit at the table. My stomach growled, but I poked dubiously at the small pile on my plate. Pulling a face at Siegie, I cautiously took a bite.

"Yuck! Ugh! This is terrible!" The tulip bulbs were so bitter and dry that they sucked the spit right out of my mouth. I threw my fork down.

Mamma, who had been carefully arranging her napkin on her lap, picked up her knife and fork, pushed some of the unappetizing mush onto the fork with her knife, and put it into her mouth. As it touched her tongue, she inhaled sharply and pulled a face, but doggedly chewed and swallowed. Mamma prepared herself another forkful before saying, "It's all we have. Eat it."

We obeyed, but it didn't do us any good. Everyone threw up soon after dinner. Even though my tummy was now empty, I grew sweaty and breathless, and my heart pounded. But the worst was the ensuing pain. It was almost more dreadful than the hunger! Lying in my bed, I curled up, holding my stomach and crying. In the morning Mamma announced that our family would not be eating any more tulip bulbs. A month or two later, the government put out a proclamation: no more tulip bulbs would be provided, because they're poisonous.

~

Corrie had stars in her eyes as she passed the news on to her little sisters. "Have you heard? The government is going to be providing us with sugar beets. You know what those are, don't you? They make sugar out of sugar beets."

"Oh my goodness, how wonderful!" I exulted. "I bet that the beets taste like dessert. Or maybe, maybe even like candy!" We waited impatiently to receive our family's ration.

A few days later, Pappa brought home a sugar beet. Mamma turned it over and over in her hands. "Cor, I'm not sure how this should be cooked. Baked, boiled, fried? Any ideas?"

Pappa stroked his chin. "It's a beet, so let's boil it like we do with red beets."

Mamma gave a quick nod. She boiled the sugar beet, sliced it up carefully, and added a little salt. I sat at my place at the table the entire time she was cooking. I was totally ready for something yummy. Actually, I was ready for any food at all.

As soon as everyone had been served their slices of sugar beet, we'd said the Lord's prayer and "Eet smakelijk," I dived in and took a huge mouthful. After a couple chews, I stopped, and my nose wrinkled. The sugar beet did not taste like dessert. It didn't taste like candy. It wasn't bitter like tulip bulbs, but was bland and rather revolting. I exchanged a glance with Sieglinde, who was chewing slowly. "Mamma, this is disgusting!"

"Eat your dinner anyway. Every bite. At least, we know sugar beets aren't poisonous."

A few days later, Pappa came home with a liter bottle of eggnog flavoring stashed under his cape. We did not know how and where he got it. Mamma grated the sugar beets, cooked them in water, drained them, and mixed in a few drops of flavoring. It colored the sugar beets yellow and made them taste, well, perhaps a little disappointing, but not too bad. At least we could swallow them.

Sieglinde and I played imagining that we were eating a dessert. I held up a forkful of sugar beet and took a small nibble. "Oh, so delicious!"

Sieglinde tried hers, chewing delicately. "Like food for the gods!"

Corrie rolled her eyes at our antics, but Pappa smiled and winked. "Oh *ja*," he squeaked in a lady's voice. "Simply divine!" Then, he made a gagging noise and pointed his finger down his throat.

Even Mamma giggled.

Soon afterwards, Mamma discovered that raw, grated sugar beets taste better than cooked ones. We ate those with eggnog flavoring, too. That flavoring lasted for almost as long as sugar beets were available.

The sugar beets didn't provide enough nutrition for growing children, but it was all we had—until we had less.

It was finally my birthday, and today I was the important one. I put on my Sunday dress, combed my hair, and strutted around before breakfast. "Today, everyone is going to visit me—not you," I informed my sisters, my hand jauntily placed on my bony hip.

I wondered if, it being my special day, I might get a gift. I knew that wasn't likely, because we had so little, but I still hoped. We all sat down to drink tea for breakfast. There was no food. But after giving me a quick kiss on the cheek, Mamma produced two presents from behind her back: a coloring book and a couple of crayons.

"*Dank je wel*, Mamma!"

Sieglinde and I began coloring immediately, quickly, if temporarily, forgetting about our empty stomachs.

The doorbell rang, and I ran to open the door.

"*Van harte gefeliciteerd met je verjaardag,* Meta!" [Many congratulations on your birthday]. It was Tante Agnes and my cousin Albertine.

I shouted, "*Van harte gefeliciteerd met uw verjaardag,* Tante Agnes!" while giggling. My aunt and I shared our birthday.

Tante Agnes pinched my cheek and came in to the living room and, as is the Dutch custom, congratulated Mamma, Pappa, and my sisters on my birthday. Everyone congratulated her and Albertine, as well. It was a lot of congratulating.

Traditionally, the birthday person or their family offers some kind of treat to everyone who comes to visit. We had some weak tea with leaves that had been used before, and each of us enjoyed a *zuurtje* that Mamma had been saving specially for the occasion.

Then, Tante Agnes carefully put her cup on its saucer on the table and reached into her bag. Surely not! Could it be possible that I would receive more than the two gifts I'd already been given? I tore the newspaper off the present and found a lovely dress for Grietje that my aunt had sewn from scraps of cloth. Dressing my doll in her new clothing, I knew that she looked even more beautiful than Rietje. She was certainly better dressed than Siegie and me.

Mamma gathered us around. "Girls, remember this. Always celebrate what you can, when you can, with whom you can. Even a little is better than nothing."

~

Pappa arrived home after work with rounded shoulders and shaking hands. "Guusje," he called in a strained voice. "Where are you?" He didn't even look at me sitting in the corner playing with Grietje.

Mamma came out of the kitchen, drying her hands on a towel. "I'm here, of course. Where else would..." She stopped abruptly when she caught sight of her husband's grim expression. "Cor? What's wrong?"

"My friend Geert is dead."

"What?" Mamma crossed the room to take his hands in hers.

"They told me that German soldiers came to his home. They asked for him. His wife lied and said he was already fighting." Pappa took a deep breath and wiped the cold sweat off his forehead. "The soldiers just barged in past her. They said, 'Well then, this doesn't matter, does it?' and shot into the floors, cupboards, and ceiling. Right in front of his children! They got him. The blood began dripping down from the ceiling onto the floor. He was hiding in their bedroom under the bed."

Sieglinde sidled over and reached out to grip my hand. We were breathless with horror at the mental picture.

Mamma sank into a chair, her face pale. "That's horrible! Poor Frieda! Their poor children! How will they bear to live in that home? And who'll provide for them now?"

Jumping to my feet, I began to sob out my fear. "Pappa, are they going to come here? Will they kill you? Mamma?"

Corrie, who'd been listening from the kitchen, came into the room and stood trembling like a leaf. As I watched her, I decided that I would be different. I swiped away my tears, closed my mouth, and lifted my chin. I was going to be brave, even if it killed me.

"Now, don't worry. I'll be fine. We'll just figure something out," Pappa assured all of us.

The next day Mamma invited Hildegunde, the young German lady who lived downstairs, to join her and Pappa for a cup of ersatz tea. "Hildie, we need your help."

Hildegunde's husband Ben had already been conscripted and was fighting in Germany, so Pappa often shared our meager food supplies with her and her daughter Maria. She leaned forward to learn how she could repay this kindness. "What can I do for you?"

Pappa explained. "You know the German army is running out of men, right? And that now the soldiers are going house-to-house searching for males of any age? Well, it's likely that one day very soon soldiers will come here to draft me. I absolutely do not want to go. But we found out what happens to those who refuse or hide."

Hildegunde nodded solemnly.

Mamma joined in. "We've been thinking. When the soldiers came for our copper and brass, I found they loved to speak with one of their countrymen in their own language. Maybe you and I can deflect them that way."

"It's worth a try." Hildegunde pursed her lips as she considered. "We have everything to gain, and the situation can't be made worse than it is already."

Pappa jumped up and shook her hand. "Great! *Dank je wel*! When we hear soldiers at the door, we'll let you know by tapping the floor with the broom. Guusta will answer the door, and I'll stay out of sight. Then, it'll be up to the two of you."

A few days later, Sieglinde and I were outside playing catch when we saw two German soldiers ring our doorbell; one was der Stiefel. I felt sick to my stomach, but stood behind them to watch what would happen.

Mamma opened our door, pasted on her finest pretend-smile and greeted the soldiers warmly in German. "*Guten Tag, meine Herren*! How can I help you?"

The soldiers came in and Mamma turned to regally ascend the stairs, her hand floating above the banister until she just before she reached the first landing. The mesmerized soldiers followed her closely. Hildegunde was standing at the entrance to her own home, also feigning a radiant smile while adjusting her blond curls. Mamma introduced our neighbor to the soldiers, in German, of course.

Sieglinde gripped my hand as we stood unnoticed, now just outside the doorway at the bottom of the stairs, with our hearts in our mouths.

The soldiers gruffly informed both our beautiful mother and pretty, young Hildegunde that they were seeking men to recruit into the German army.

The women batted their eyelashes and smoothed their hair, and Hildegunde warmly reassured the soldiers. "Our husbands are already in Germany fighting in the defense of the *Heimat* ['homeland' in German]."

The younger soldier glanced at der Stiefel, who shrugged and nodded his head.

Mamma continued, "So, tell us, how's it going there? And how are you all coping? This war is so hard for all of us!"

Hildegunde, her blue eyes sparkling, eagerly added, "Is there any way you can find news of our husbands for us? We would be so, so grateful!"

Sieglinde and I held our breath and our tongues. To my amazement, der Stiefel's companion relaxed his defensive posture, even lounging against the wall.

"No, I'm afraid we have no way to get that information for you both, Ladies. Everything is so difficult. We're in chaos and aren't enjoying this war any more than you are. We have to fight and fight, and there's no food. Even worse, so many of us have been killed that now we're recruiting old men and teenage boys."

"Oh, but surely you're well on the way to winning now, aren't you?" Mamma tilted her head and twirled a lock of her hair around her finger.

"We wish. Honestly, we desperately need help from the Dutch in order to even continue the war effort."

Der Stiefel inhaled audibly and glared at the younger soldier, who turned red and grew silent.

I was sure, if he could hear from where I expected he was sitting at the top of the stairs just out of sight, Pappa was pumping his fist in glee. He would be ecstatic to know the German army was losing strength.

Mamma looked straight into der Stiefel's icy eyes. "Oh, I feel so bad for you all. I do hope things will turn and go well for you now."

"They will—they are." Der Stiefel clicked his heels together, and both soldiers gave them the Nazi salute. "*Heil Hitler*."

Mamma and Hildegunde duly returned the vile gesture, and the soldiers turned to leave, passing by Sieglinde and me on their way out. I closed my eyes tightly and looked down, hoping that der Stiefel would not recognize me.

Pulling us in, Mamma firmly closed the door behind us, and we all mounted the stairs to our home. Both Hildegunde and Mamma were trembling. When she reached Pappa, my mother threw herself into his arms, and he embraced her tightly. Then, Pappa stepped back and tenderly wiped the tears from Mamma's cheeks. "It's over. You both did a great job. Now, go, sit down and rest, Guusje. I'll make you and Hildie a nice cup of tea."

For the entire time my family lived in Den Haag, although I often saw der Stiefel with his shiny black boots lurking in the shadows, no German soldiers ever searched our home.

"Mamma, look. What are all those people doing?"

My mother pushed the curtain aside to gawk at the long queue of people waiting on the sidewalk. Opening the window, she leaned out and called down, "What's going on?"

One of the ladies standing with her shopping basket in hand looked up. "The butcher has meat."

Mamma quickly pulled her head in. "Meta and Sieglinde, go wait in the line. Quick! You heard her. My goodness, I don't even know what meat looks like anymore! Here are the ration cards; don't lose them. I'll be there before you reach the shop door."

Sieglinde and I grabbed our coats, my sister stuffed the cards in her pocket, and we ran down the stairs. The line to the butcher's shop right below our home snaked down the Weimarstraat all the way until the Regentesseplein. It seemed everyone had heard about the meat before Mamma, and those people had definitely arrived first. We dutifully went to the end of the queue.

"Meta, do you think he'll have anything left by the time we get to the front?"

I shook my head. "I don't want to think about it. Let's just hope so."

And so we waited. And waited. And waited. I hopped from one foot to the other, trying to stay warm. I distracted myself from the boredom, and the cold wind blowing through my threadbare coat, by eavesdropping on the conversations around me.

I heard about one lady's husband and another woman's baby. Then a couple of ladies standing just ahead of us began to discuss me. Me!

"Watch out for the little girl behind us. She's absolutely skeletal. I wouldn't be surprised if she were the next to drop dead."

Her friend sniffed. "I'm afraid you may be right. This horrible war! I never expected to see the day when people dying from hunger would become commonplace. Poor little thing!"

Both women turned to look at me with pity in their eyes.

I raised my chin, filled my cheeks with air so that I would look fatter, narrowed my eyes and stared defiantly at the two women. I knew, just knew, that they were wrong. I had no intention of dying. If I could've, I would've stuck out my tongue, too! But that would have let the air out.

Sieglinde quickly put an end to my charade. "Meta, stop. You're not fooling anyone. Everybody knows that you're just puffing up your cheeks!"

I didn't answer her, but resisted letting the tears pricking at the back of my eyes fall. I thought, putting on a brave face is good. If nobody can see how they hurt me, then at least I can feel proud of myself. Looking down, I was delighted to notice how shiny my shoes were. The realization that nobody could see the holes in their soles gave me a little jolt of pleasure.

After we had waited in that queue for two cold, long hours, a message was passed from the front down the line. "There's no meat left."

I was pleased to note that the two women didn't get any meat either. Served them right!

Sieglinde and I walked home, her lips trembling and feet dragging. We were both bitterly disappointed, and my stomach hurt. But I remembered my new vow to keep up appearances and marched home with my back straight and chin up. I was still hungry, but at least no one knew.

"Siegie, Corrie is sunbathing on the roof. Let's go up and join her."

Mamma was busy repairing clothes, and Pappa was at work, so neither one was watching us. We mounted the stairs that led to the attic. At the top of those stairs, there was a window. I looked at Sieglinde, and she looked at me. I gave a quick nod. It was decided. We opened the little window and squeezed through to climb out onto the roof.

"What are the two of you doing here? You know you're not allowed." Corrie pushed her windblown hair out of her face.

"We're going to get a suntan, just like you." I narrowed my eyes to show her that she would lose this fight.

Corrie sighed, leaned back, closed her eyes and lifted her face to the sun. Sieglinde sat next to her and did the same.

I was not about to close my eyes; there was too much to see. The roofs were flat, so it was possible to overlook much of what was happening. I didn't dare to go to the very edge of the roof, but stood close to the window out of which we'd climbed, turning my head in every direction.

"Sieglinde, Corrie, look! There's an airplane stuck in the church tower over there."

Corrie stood up and shielded her eyes from the sun. "So there is. How strange! I wonder why it doesn't fall down. It looks so precarious."

Sieglinde and I ran downstairs to tell Mamma; Corrie was close behind. Mamma looked, but couldn't see anything out of the front window.

"Mamma, you can see it from the roof. Come on!" I tugged on her hand.

"Spilletje, mothers don't climb on roofs. Let's walk over to the church to have a look. But if you run ahead, don't go too close in case the airplane falls or the steeple breaks."

We walked down the sunny street and eventually joined a crowd of people, all standing near to the church and gazing upwards.

"Well, I never!" Mamma exclaimed. "That airplane doesn't look like it's coming down. I wonder where the pilot is."

After gawking for a while longer, we turned to go home. That adventure being over, Sieglinde and I were again at a loose end.

"We could read," Sieglinde suggested, hopefully.

"*Nee,* let's go up to the attic again. I really, really want to see what's in all the rooms up there. Maybe today the doors will be open."

Again, we mounted the stairs, but this time we passed by the window and entered the attic proper, which consisted of three rooms off a central hallway. The room in the middle was ours, but we had nothing to store. It was empty and the door open. The room on the left was assigned to Hildegunde. The door was unlocked, so we went in. It was empty, too.

Just then we heard a rustling. I jumped, and Sieglinde clutched my sleeve. "What was that?"

Silence answered us. We crept out of Hildegunde's room and made our way towards the door on the right.

I remembered that Pappa had warned us about that room when we moved in. "Don't touch this door. Don't go anywhere near it."

When I asked him why, he said, "No questions. Do as you're told."

Despite Siegie's protests, I tried the door. It was locked. Truthfully, I'd tried it before, and it always was.

"Siegie," I whispered, "I wonder if that room is haunted. I've heard noises before, but I've never seen anyone go in or come out." I rattled the doorknob again.

"You're going to get us in trouble. Let's just go." My sister tried to pull me away, but I resisted.

The sound of a groan changed my mind. "Let's get out of here, Siegie!"

We both bolted down the stairs, only slowing down when we came within sight of Mamma. It was vital that she never know what we'd done.

On April 11, 1944, Mamma peered out of the window. "It looks quiet outside today. Why don't you guys play at the playground for a while? You've been cooped up in here for too long. But remember, if airplanes come and swoop low, the Allies are getting ready to drop bombs. Go and lie down in a ditch until the bombing stops."

Sieglinde and I nodded our understanding. "Yes, Mamma," we chorused, grinning at each other.

After racing down the stairs and out the door, we ran down our street to the playground. It was empty. My favorite piece of equipment was the seesaw, so I suggested that we start there. As always, Sieglinde agreed. I took one end, and my sister plonked herself on the other.

No sooner had we commenced going up and down than we heard the deafening rumble of airplane engines. We peered up into the cloudy, and now drizzly, sky and saw a squadron of six airplanes flying in our direction. Straight towards us. Bombers.

One airplane swooped down, right near to the playground. It looked for all the world as if it were aiming for us! Remembering

Mamma's instructions, I jumped off the seesaw. In my panic, I didn't even notice that Sieglinde was at the top, and I'd just dropped her.

Sieglinde rubbed her bottom and scolded, "You could have warned me!" Just then another airplane swooped in our direction. My sister's eyes grew round. "Let's get out of here!" She didn't even wait for me, but darted left towards the exit of the playground.

I gazed in fear at the airplanes, each of which was making a pass right near to the playground. What were they doing? I knew I was very fast, but there was no way even I could outrun an airplane or a bomb. Nearby, on my right, was a creek. That would do. I sprinted over to it and flattened myself onto the embankment.

As I lay there, I heard the screech of the planes continuing to dive, one after another, each plunge followed by an explosion as they dropped their bomb. Every bomber made several passes. The hair on the back of my neck stood on end; I'd seen up close what bombs do. Tucking my head into my chest, I screwed my eyes tightly closed, put my arms over my head as I'd been taught, held my breath, and prayed that they'd soon stop.

Eventually, I heard the airplanes flying away. Even before I got to my feet, I became aware that people were screaming, I could hear the crackling of fire, and the air was filled with smoke.

Standing up, I looked in the direction of the dreadful noise. The bombs had fallen on the Kleykamp building, which was now on fire and still collapsing. Evidently, the screams were coming from people who were trapped inside. In the haze, I could just make out der Stiefel. With his hands clasped behind his back, it looked as if he were watching to make sure no one escaped.

I took off for home with my hands over my ears, trying to escape the awful sound. Flinging myself through the front door, I pelted up our stairs. Sieglinde was already there, telling Mamma about how I'd dropped her. Seeing me, Mamma pushed her aside and pulled me into her arms. "Thank goodness you're home!"

I took a moment to catch my breath. "Mamma, there were... I saw... I heard... oh... all those people screaming..." I collapsed in anguish, even unable to cry.

I was now nine years old, but Mamma picked me up, sat down

and held me on her lap while she stroked my hair and wiped my tears. "Shh, shh, Meta, it's over and you're here, alive. It's okay. Rest."

I couldn't. She put me on the couch and I sat dry-eyed with my knees drawn up into my chest, trying not to hear the screaming. Mamma brought me a hot cup of tea and pressed a *zuurtje* that she'd been hoarding into my hand. My hands were shaking too much for me to hold the cup, and the candy tasted like dust.

When Pappa got home from work, I tried to tell my parents what I'd experienced.

"The airplanes—six of them—kept circling and circling, dropping more bombs. And the building was burning—so much smoke! But the screams... I just ran away—I couldn't look."

"Yes, I passed by the building on my way home. It was still burning."

"Were the people still screaming? Did you see der Stiefel?"

Pappa glanced at Mamma before answering me. "*Nee*, I only heard the sound of the fire. I didn't see anyone."

Eventually, Pappa learned more about the incident. Radio Oranje reported that the Kleykamp building had contained identity papers for Dutch people and other important documents. The Germans having access to those papers made it impossible for the Dutch Resistance to forge new ones. The Allies bombed the building to destroy the papers.

Pappa paced the room with tight lips. "The German soldiers were more focused on rescuing the documents than the people who were trapped inside. As the building burned to the ground, about 300 people died."

History records that only 62 people died: five of them were NSBers and the rest innocent Dutch civil servants. I don't know which version is the truth. But I heard them screaming and saw der Stiefel keeping them from leaving.

11

THE HUNGER WINTER

My parents had been huddled by the radio for what seemed like hours, all of their attention focused on what the announcer was saying.

I listened carefully. Could it be true? "Mamma..." I began. I was shooed away. I tried my father, saying "Pappa, Pappa!" most insistently.

"Don't interrupt! Sshh!" Pappa's fists were clenched on his lap as he leaned forward so as not to miss a word.

By now Corrie wasn't very well at all with flushed cheeks and a troublesome cough. Nonetheless, she took Sieglinde and me by the hands and pulled us away from our parents. We all sat down in one easy chair, so emaciated that the three of us fit with room to spare.

"Corrie, will the war be over soon? Is that what they were saying? Will we get food? When?"

Corrie stroked my thinning hair back from my face. "The news seems to be good, at least to me, but I don't know about when we'll get food. The announcer said that yesterday soldiers from three of the Allied countries landed on the beach in Normandy. Now the Allies are marching towards Paris."

"Ha! They did it on Pappa's birthday. It's a present!" I covered my mouth with my hand, hardly daring to hope.

Sieglinde looked cautiously hopeful. "Does that mean the war will finally end?"

"Perhaps. If things keep going well for the Allies, maybe they'll be able to reach and conquer Germany. If they do, it really will be over."

Having turned the radio off, Pappa overheard our conversation. "We don't know when it'll end. But at last, it looks very likely that Germany will lose." He pumped his fist.

Every day for the next several months, my parents listened closely to their illegal radio, marking the progress of the Allies. First, they reached Rome, then France was liberated, then they won part of Belgium, and finally some of the Netherlands was freed.

"Guusje, did you hear that? The Allies reached the border of Germany. Maybe the fighting will finally end."

"Not before time, either! This war has lasted far too long."

"Pappa, with the Allies in the Netherlands, will we now get something to eat?" I was dreaming of freedom and food. Mostly food.

"Oh, I would think so. It should be soon. But we have to wait and see. Meanwhile, don't go outside. The German soldiers are furious. My colleagues said they're killing anyone they see."

I nodded slowly as my stomach clenched.

It was now September of 1944, and we three girls huddled together under a threadbare blanket while sharing a chair in the living room. Mamma, who was pregnant, was lying on the couch. Pappa came in from work, laid his warm black cape over Mamma and sat at her feet while he related the day's bad news. "It looks like now we'll be getting even less of our rations. The Allies asked the railways to go on strike to stop the Germans from getting any supplies. But of course, that also means no food for us." Pappa's shoulders were rounded.

"Well, how long will the strike have to be? I think we could probably manage for a few days, especially if it helps us win." Mamma's weak voice belied her words, and she struggled to sit up and take Pappa's hand in her bony claw.

"I would hope that a week will be enough, but who knows how long it'll take for the Germans to give in?"

Corrie, coughing as usual, looked up and gasping for breath, asked, "Can't the government... get food to us... by truck? Or what... about... canals?"

I glanced at my sister's hands, which she was endlessly wringing, and noticed her handkerchief was stained with blood. "Uh, Mamma..." I began. Corrie shook her head at me.

"You need a doctor," I muttered under my breath, knowing full well that it was not going to happen.

Pappa shook his head sadly. "The Germans are very angry about the strike. They banned all transport of food to our part of the country."

I thought about this. "But that means the German soldiers won't get food either, doesn't it?"

"*Ja*, it does. Let's hope they quickly become hungry enough to back down."

The stand-off continued for six long weeks.

Winter came early that year. When the block on shipments was partially lifted, the situation could no longer be reversed. The canals stayed frozen until February; no boats could pass. The Germans bombed the docks and bridges, so food couldn't be transported by canal, sea or land. If anything did get through, the Allies destroyed it, because they wanted to starve the Germans out.

We got nothing at all. Nothing.

Shops and schools were closed. Some homes were empty, and most had broken windows. Many areas of Den Haag had been flattened, and Allied bombing continued relentlessly. Numerous people were homeless. Death was common place. Desolation was everywhere. This was the Hunger Winter.

～

"Guusje, I hate this! This damn war! I detest seeing my family like this!" Pappa furiously dashed the tears from his eyes. "Look at the *kindertjes* with their bones showing. What can I do? What can I do?"

"Oh, Cor, don't upset yourself. None of us can help this. Maybe there'll be an end soon… if not to the war, to us." Mamma hesitated briefly before continuing. "But I think it's high time we figured out something to end the children's suffering."

A jolt of fear passed through my body. Was Mamma really suggesting that they should kill their children?

Pappa paced the room with clenched fists. "No! No, that's not an option! When I was only a child washing windows to earn money for my mother and sisters, I promised myself I would always provide for my family. We're not going to die and we'll not be 'ending any suffering'. I'm going to figure something out."

A few days later, Pappa shared his plan. Being a mailman, he was allowed to break curfew, so he went out way before daylight. He'd stayed away all day, and my mother sat on the couch, her eyes unfocused while her fingers twisted her apron. As evening drew near, Mamma progressed to weakly shuffling up and down the room. "Where's your father? He should have been home an hour ago!"

"Maybe he stopped off to see his friend, Harry. Why are you so worried? Sit down. He'll be home soon." Sieglinde led Mamma back to the couch, plumped up a pillow, and slid it behind her back.

Corrie said nothing. She couldn't.

"You don't understand. He was going to try to get us food from the Malieveld.

"Um, that's where the Germans grow their potatoes, right?" Sieglinde frowned at me and rolled her eyes towards Mamma.

I stopped playing my imagination game, the one where I pretended to be a doctor who could heal my big sister, and took Mamma's other hand.

"Yes! What if he got caught? Maybe he's already on the way to Germany. Or, maybe they shot him! They do that. He might be dead, and we'll have to cope without him." Mamma's voice rose, and she pulled her hands free to again begin her endless apron twisting.

My stomach turned over, but I raised my chin. "We'll be fine, Mamma. I'll…"

Just then, we heard the front door open. Pappa came in with a big grin on his face and a bundle of flowers in his hand which he presented to Mamma with a flourish. "Guusje, you could almost have put those on my grave!"

I gasped. What could he mean?

Pappa strode into the kitchen and proudly emptied his mail bag onto the counter. There were a few potatoes. "Look! I stole them. I even got enough to give one to Harry and his family!"

Next my father placed his uniform cap beside the potatoes, arranging it carefully while winking at me. I was the first to spot them: two perfectly round bullet holes—one in the front and one in the back of the cap.

I looked at Pappa with wide eyes. With a mischievous grin on his face, my father bent down and showed us the top of his head. Our mouths dropped open. There was a line of singed hair going from the front of Pappa's head all the way to the back. We could see his pink scalp peeking through the smelly blackened hair.

Mamma traced her finger along the line of missing hair. "Cor, what happened?"

"As I was filling my bag with potatoes, I noticed a German soldier watching me. He looked about 12 years old, but he had a gun. I jumped on my bicycle and began pedaling like crazy. Just then, I heard a shot. I went even faster. Who'd have thought a bicycle with wooden wheels could go like the wind? It sure did give me a rough ride!" Pappa rubbed his bottom as he laughed.

Patting his head, Pappa said, "It's a very good thing that I'm not a tall man. He got my cap, but he missed me."

I remembered the jackboots covered in the blood of another man on a wooden-wheeled bicycle, and the blood drained from my face. "Pappa, *alsjeblieft*, don't do that again. We're not that hungry."

"Cor, where did you get these?" Mamma asked, fingering the flowers. "Oh, never mind. I'm pretty sure I don't want to know."

Although it hardly seemed possible, a few weeks later the icy winter weather took a turn for the worse.

"Cor, we need some heat," my mother shivered violently. "I can't even boil water!" The cold wind howled down the gaping fireplace into the dark living room.

"It's much too cold for you and the *kinderen*. Tomorrow I'll talk the problem over with Rainier and Luuk. Between us, we may come up with some good ideas." Pappa tenderly covered Mamma's lap with his cape.

"I may have an idea." Mamma pursed her lips and frowned. "Let me see if I can remember. Oh yes!" The cold and starvation had impeded the function of our brains, as well as our bodies. "You know Henk, my friend's eldest son? When he stopped by the other day, he told me about a garbage can heater he made for his mother. Maybe he'd do that for us..." Mamma shrugged. "Oh, yes. Forget I spoke. We don't have a garbage can."

Pappa tilted his head to one side, pondered for some time, put one finger in the air, said "Aha!" picked up his cape, and left the house. We exchanged bewildered glances.

My father returned about an hour later with a silver-colored garbage can hidden within the folds of his snow-covered cape. It was approximately 60 cm high, 45 cm across and made of metal.

The next day Henk came home with Pappa. After he shook the sleet out of his hair, he knelt down to mortar red bricks on the insides of the garbage can. We all drew near to watch. When he was finished, the garbage can was a miniature stove. Pappa put it inside the empty fireplace, where the floor was made of stone, and we all giggled at the silly, but very practical, new stove.

Examining the stove from all angles, I grew very enthusiastic. Sieglinde and I no longer had the energy to keep ourselves warm by jumping up and down, and Corrie was too sick. Sometimes, if our fingers were turning blue, Pappa allowed us to burn two or three matches. But I thought to myself, a stove would be way better than a match. Better yet, with a little stove, we could boil water and cook our meager quantities of food, instead of eating things raw.

Pappa crossed his arms as he joined me in my inspection. "It's small, which is a good thing. It won't need much fuel."

I took a deep breath. "But Pappa, we don't have any fuel. Sieglinde and I tried collecting sticks. We couldn't find any. None at all."

"*Ja*, I know. People stripped the forest bare of sticks. I'm going to look in empty houses again. Maybe there's something I missed."

"May I come?"

"*Nee*, it's too dangerous. We could be caught. You stay here where you're safe."

Pappa searched all day and all night, but didn't find anything that could be burnt, not even manure. All the horses had been eaten a long time ago.

Mamma again began to talk about drowning herself.

Time for action. I decided to emulate what I'd so recently witnessed Pappa doing. First, I thought about where the Germans obtained their fuel; the trains which they used still needed coal to run. I said nothing to my family, but the first chance I got, I walked to the train tracks by the gas factory. Keeping a sharp eye out for der Stiefel, I scavenged fragments of coal from the ground, collecting them in the folded-over edge of my skirt.

Once I had a handful, I hurried home, the fear of the zing of a bullet and the memory of blood-smeared boots giving wings to my feet. There was our door. With a quick look over my shoulder, I opened it and went in, slamming the door behind me.

The adrenaline rush had by then passed, so I struggled up the stairs. "Mamma, Pappa, look what I have," I panted as pieces of coal spilled from my skirt onto the fireplace floor. "We can light our stove!"

"Where did you get those?" Pappa bit out.

"On the railway tracks..." I had been pretty sure he'd be delighted I'd outwitted the Germans and just as successfully as he did. The look on his face told me I was wrong.

The blood drained from Mamma's face as she struggled to sit up and look at the coal. "*Dank je wel*, Spilletje, but..." Her shoulders sagged, and she lay back down.

Pappa stalked over and grasped me by the shoulders. "Don't you ever, ever do that again. You could've been shot." He gave me a little shake. "Do you understand? Never do that again!" He said a lot more than that. He may have been proud of me, but if he was, he hid it well.

12

NOT OF STRATEGIC IMPORTANCE

"Cor, I think it's time. The baby's coming. Take me to the hospital."

Pappa jumped to his feet and hurried over to the couch to lay his hand on her swollen abdomen. "It can't be. It's too soon. The baby isn't due for another two months."

"Well, I'm not feeling well and am pretty sure I'm in labor. *Alsjeblieft* hurry, Cor!" Mamma's weak voice rose.

Pappa ran to pack the little brown suitcase with a clean nightgown and clothing for the baby, all of them sewn by Aunt Agnes and laid ready by Sieglinde and me.

I helped Mamma struggle to her feet, and Sieglinde assisted her into her coat and hat.

We knew that my parents would have to walk against the howling wind through icy streets for almost two kilometers to reach Ziekenhuis Westeinde [Westend Hospital], doubtless stopping so Mamma could rest.

Pappa told us that, once he delivered Mamma into the care of a nurse, he would wait in the hallway of the hospital until he heard the baby was born and she was safe.

My sisters and I huddled together in one bed waiting. We heard the door open. Pappa stopped in our room. "Girls, you have a little brother."

"Is Mamma okay, and is he healthy?" I was worried, having discussed the risk of a premature birth with Corrie.

"Yes, both are fine." Pappa left us, probably to collapse into his own bed.

In the morning, awaking before Pappa, I crept into his room. I had a very important question. "Pappa, what's my brother's name? Corrie is named after you and Mamma already, but he's your first son."

Pappa sat up and his eyes crinkled at the corners. "Always the curious one, aren't you? We will call him Ronald Alexander, both good English names, since a German name would be pretty unpopular. Now, I need to get up and go register his birth. Hand me my shirt, *alsjeblieft*."

By the time Sieglinde awoke, Pappa was bundled up and gone. The jobs of helping Corrie get up and heating her a cup of weak tea fell to Siegie and me. As I pulled off her nightgown to replace it with her dress, I noticed that, despite the frosty bedroom, Corrie's cheeks were flushed and her skin was radiating heat. "Oh Corrie," I murmured, "you really need a doctor." How I wished I were a doctor already!

Corrie coughed into her handkerchief and quickly hid it under the sheets. "Don't... tell. Pappa and Mamma have enough... to worry."

Soon afterwards, Pappa arrived home with his nose red, his fingers blue, and his eyes twinkling.

"Look here at what I have, Girls." He drew a tea cup-sized cube out of the folds of his cape. "This is honey, through and through. The government gives one of these to every family where a baby is born."

My eyes grew round as Pappa removed the wax paper and took a great big bite. We all knew that him becoming weak with starvation was not an option, so nobody said a word. Someone had to remain strong enough to take care of the family. However, we did watch every movement of his jaws with our mouths watering. After swallowing with his eyes closed in ecstasy, Pappa winked at us. "Your mother gets food at the hospital. Here, all of you, have some."

Sieglinde and I each took a delicious mouthful of the cube of honey. I tried to keep the sweet treat in my mouth for as long as possible, savoring the amazing taste. It made my mouth water so badly that my cheeks hurt.

Sieglinde gave Corrie a bite and then took the leftover honey into the kitchen, wrapped it carefully, and gave it to Pappa to take to Mamma the following day. She was so weak that she had to remain in the hospital for two more weeks. Ronald, being very premature, had to stay longer.

Mamma had been home for about a week when Vera, the friend who'd lost her infant to the Blitzkrieg, rang our doorbell. Mamma leaned out of the window and saw that Vera was proudly carrying a new baby in her arms. "Vera, come in! I'm so glad to see you. Show me that beautiful baby boy!"

Vera walked up the stairs, laid her baby on the couch and unwrapped him. Seeing his mamma, Karel broke out into a gummy smile. Vera's eyes danced as she enthused, "Gusti, he's an absolute miracle. Of course, nobody can replace little Johann, but Karel has brought laughter back into our home."

Mamma's eyes filled with tears of joy as she picked the infant up and gently stroked his downy hair. "Oh, he's so wonderful. I do hope that Ronald will grow quickly so we can bring him home from the hospital. Maybe they'll become best friends, just like we are." Mamma placed a tender kiss on Karel's forehead.

Only a month later, when Pappa arrived home from work, he led Mamma to the couch. His face was drawn. "Guusje, sit down. I have very bad news."

Mamma gripped her apron between her bony, now trembling, fingers. "All the *kinderen* are here. We're hungry and cold, but alive. What could be wrong?"

"The Allies bombed the Bezuidenhout neighborhood in Den Haag. I'm told it was an accident. Some idiot turned the negatives of the bombing target the wrong way up while they were being printed."

"Wait, that's where Vera lives..."

"Yes, that's what I was going to say. Vera and Jan's home was destroyed. I heard they and their daughter escaped, but little Karel was killed."

Mamma threw her apron over her face and wailed out loud. "How is it possible? Bombs killed both her baby boys! I can't imagine what she's going through!"

A few days after this, my parents were told that Ronald was ready to come home. He'd been in the hospital for three months and there, was given milk. When my parents picked him up, the nurse pressed a bag with a few days-worth of formula and ration cards for more into Pappa's hand. But the stores were empty. Mamma was unable to nurse her baby: she was too skinny, and he'd been in the hospital too long. All too soon, there was nothing for Ronald to eat.

Poor Ronald was screaming with hunger. Mamma tried to comfort him by offering a bottle with water in it, but her efforts were in vain. He kept crying. When the doorbell rang, Mamma deposited Ronald into Sieglinde's arms and looked out of the window. Seeing it was Vera, she flew down the stairs to enfold her good friend in her arms. "Oh, Vera, it's so wonderful to see you. How are you doing, *meisje* [girl]?"

I stood at the top of our stairs, watching as Vera burst into tears. "We're doing the best we can, Gusti. Jan's family is good to us, but it's not the same as being home. The loss of Karel devastated us. Let's go up. I want to see your little man." She forced a smile. "He obviously has an excellent set of lungs."

The women came up the stairs, and Mamma took Ronald back to show him to Vera. Immediately, Ronald stopped crying and began rooting at Mamma's breast, desperately searching for food. Mamma's eyes filled as she whispered to her son, "There's nothing there, little man."

She again offered the bottle of water, but it wasn't what he wanted. Ronald began to wail in earnest. Tears dripped onto his head as Mamma walked the floor trying to comfort her hungry infant.

Vera, also weeping, stood watching for a while and then silently took Ronald from Mamma's arms. She sat down. Then my mother's German best friend opened her dress and nursed my baby brother. I drew near to watch in wonder.

As Ronald guzzled hungrily, Mamma began to sob aloud. Between gulps, she tried to express her gratitude to Vera, but the words would not come. They weren't needed.

When Vera left that day, Mamma gave her an extra-long hug. Vera smiled through her tears and promised, "I'll be back tomorrow."

After that, once a day, Vera made her way through the icy streets to our house and nursed Ronald. She explained that it couldn't be more often because, being undernourished, that was all the milk she had.

"Cor, I'm so very thankful for what Vera is doing, but once-a-day milk isn't enough for Ronald. He's becoming so very pale and listless. What can we do? The stores are still empty. I'm checking every day."

"Hmm, I'll discuss the problem with my colleagues."

The very next day, the men agreed to help Ronald by shaking the few parcels that reached the post office and listening for a telltale rattle. It wasn't harvest time, but they were persistent and found one. Inside, there was a handful of beans. Possibly just enough to feed a baby.

Pappa brought the carefully wrapped beans home. Mamma washed them thoroughly and cooked them until they were soft. Pappa pushed them through a sieve to get rid of the peels, and Mamma diluted the mushed-up mess with water. Finally, she sat down and fed her hungry baby with a bottle of sloppy beans. As his tummy filled, Ronald closed his eyes and slept peacefully.

After that, Pappa and his colleagues spent even more time 'shaking' parcels and more beans were 'found'. They chewed on a few of the raw beans, and Pappa brought the rest home. Thus, baby Ronald was fed a diet of Vera's milk and brown beans. The beans did ease Ronald's hunger and were much better than nothing, but beans aren't really baby food, and Ronald often spit them up. What's more, Mamma noticed that in the mornings after Ronald threw up during the night there were holes in the necklines of his clothing.

"Cor, look here at Ronald's shirt."

"Strange. I expect the sour spit-up is dissolving the fabric."

"Hmm, I don't remember that happening with the other *kinderen*. But then, they weren't fed with beans."

The following night, when she heard Ronald stir, Mamma got up to comfort him immediately. As she bent over his little bed, she noticed something moving on his chest. Looking closer, she saw a rat happily eating Ronald's vomit—and his shirt.

Mamma screamed loud enough to wake me up. I peered into the room as Mamma snatched her baby out of his crib while muttering about mice and rats. The rat, of course, had scampered.

I followed to watch as she climbed into her own bed while clutching Ronald. Mamma shook Pappa's shoulder and gasped out, "Cor, there was something on Ronald, and it was eating his spit up. I'm pretty sure the holes in his clothes are caused by rodents. When there's no vomit, maybe the rats and mice will eat him!"

Pappa sat up suddenly. "Light a candle. Is he okay?"

Both my parents inspected their tiny son. "Thank goodness he's unharmed, but from now on, Ronald sleeps with us." Pappa tucked his son under his arm protectively, and turned to me. "And you, Spilletje, back to bed before you freeze. We'll handle this."

"But Pappa, will the rats hurt m... I mean, Sieglinde?"

"*Nee*, you and she are too big. They're scared of you. Go to bed."

I raised my chin. "Well, I'm not scared of a little critter." Nonetheless, I checked under my covers before crawling into bed.

Gazing at the reflection in the window as I clutched Grietje, I barely recognized myself. My hair hung limply, my eyes were sunken, and my clothes swamped my skinny frame. Listlessly, I gazed at my doll. Her ribs weren't showing, her tummy wasn't protruding, and her hair was still thick. Oh, to be a doll! I sighed.

What had changed the most, however, was way down deep inside. Whereas, before, I'd been determined to survive, now I really didn't care if I did. Whereas, before, I'd been careful to put on a brave face, now I had no interest in impressing anyone. I lived in an empty fog: no action, no awareness, no singing, no playing, no interests. All-consuming hunger was all that was left, and death no longer seemed like such a bad prospect. I dropped Grietje on the floor, where she lay with her legs and arms inelegantly sprawled.

Lying in my cold bed, I tried to escape into my imagination. "I think that I see a loaf of bread under your bed, Siegie. Mmm, I smell it. It's still warm. Let's take a bite."

"Ooo yes. The crust is crunchy, but the inside is so soft. It's making my mouth water." Sieglinde's trembling voice as she fought tears belied her words.

I sighed deeply. "Never mind. This is making it worse. My tummy hurts." I turned over and curled into the shape of a roly-poly bug, too miserable to move.

The government-provided sugar beets had run out; Pappa couldn't obtain anything at all for his family to eat, no matter how many parcels he shook. Once in a great while, if it was a particularly good day, we found a potato in the doorway, left by friends who had been successful on Malieveld. Mamma would mix it with a little tree bark or weeds, and the entire family would share in the 'meal'.

One day, I crawled through our kitchen cabinets, hoping to find a kernel or two of rice. "I found some! There are three here!"

"Well done, Spil. I'll cook them, and you can each have one."

The Germans had been pushed out of the southern part of the Netherlands, and now the Allied soldiers liberated the eastern and northern regions of our country. Maybe... maybe...

Pappa was glued to the radio. "Oh no," he groaned. "The Allies lost at Arnhem, so they'll go straight to Germany. They won't care about us in Den Haag."

"What? What about us?"

Pappa stroked my cheek gently. "Our area is not of strategic importance. We in the west will have to wait."

"But, but... we're starving!"

He sighed, shook his head and repeated the same devastating phrase. "We're not of strategic importance."

"Cor," Mamma rasped. "Where will we be when we're finally liberated? Will we even be alive?"

"I don't know, Guusje. Let's not lose hope. It can't be too much longer."

Mamma plucked listlessly at the ragged shawl she wore around her bony shoulders.

I wondered if our home in Scheveningen was still standing. We were far too weak to walk and see. But maybe, when and if we could move, we could catch fish. A fish would taste so good!

Meanwhile we waited, shivering, with empty stomachs, hollow cheeks and spindly legs while sitting in our dark house.

Making everything worse was the fact that there was also no soap. Even if we'd had the energy to do it, any cleaning of people, clothes, or houses was impossible.

Lying on my back, I looked down at myself. "Siegie, look how my tummy is sticking out. How can I be so hungry and also so fat?"

Sieglinde silently shook her head and turned over on her bed. I leant over the side of my bed and tried to throw up in the bowl next to it, but there was nothing to come up.

By now, Mamma was too weak to get up and did nothing but lie in her bed. Ronald had stopped crying for food. He just dozed next to her.

Now we all knew that Corrie had tuberculosis (TB). She was so ill that she also couldn't get up, even if she wanted to. There were neither TB clinics nor medicine.

At times Sieglinde and I shivered with fever until our teeth rattled. We tried curling up into a ball to ease the stomach ache, but it didn't help. Sometimes, we just stumbled around the house in a daze, too miserable to even know what we were doing.

"Pappa, I feel so yucky. Why do I throw up and have diarrhea all the time when my tummy is empty?"

"Schatje, I think we have dysentery. Maybe because we don't have soap to wash our towels and sheets, let alone ourselves."

Even Pappa got sick, but not as badly as we did. He ate a little of the food that was on occasion provided at the post office.

I overheard him discussing his situation with Mamma. "Guusje, I hate eating when I know the *kinderen* and you need much more than you're receiving."

Mamma pressed her hand over Pappa's mouth. "We discussed this. You have to eat, so you can take care of us."

"But the family is starving!"

Mamma sighed. "I guess we should just go drown ourselves. Not that we have the strength to walk to the sea."

~

On May 5, 1945, I awoke to the raucous sound of a cheering crowd. The bedroom floor shook from the rumble of tanks.

I tottered on shaky legs to the same window from which I'd witnessed my first murder, grasping the sill tightly to keep myself upright. There, just outside my home, tanks were parading down the street from my left to my right as if in formation. Allied soldiers with friendly, smiling faces were strolling beside and sitting on top of the tanks. They were handing out chocolate bars and cigarettes to those skeletal, but exultant, neighbors who were gathered in the street.

I made my way to my parents' room, holding onto the wall for support. "Mamma, Pappa! Wake up! Can you hear? Can you hear?"

Pappa climbed out of the bed and accompanied me to their bedroom window. His face lit up as he took in the joyful scene. Turning, he gave me a tight hug and then, breathless with excitement, told Mamma what was happening. "Guusje, the war's over! Canada liberated us! We're free! Even us, who are of no strategic importance."

Mamma, whose sunken eyes looked huge in her bony face, tried to stifle her sobs in her pillow. Pappa sat and leaned down to gently hold his fragile wife. "Don't cry, Guusje. It's over. It's over. And we all survived."

Watching them, tears flowed down my own skinny cheeks. I turned to wake Sieglinde with the news.

"What? Is it possible?" Siegie hugged me, and her tears poured out.

"I sure wish I could go down and get some of that chocolate, but..."

Starvation meant I did not consider myself to be part of the living —I'd already left the world I could see downstairs. Moreover, I was far too weak from *hongerziekte* [starvation sickness] to venture outside.

~

I still cry when I remember that day. We'd waited so long. We'd helplessly watched as we and so many friends grew more and more emaciated. We'd given away everything of value in exchange for food and burned much of our furniture for heat. We'd witnessed homes being bombed, friends taken away to concentration camps, babies being killed, and far too many people dying.

I'd completely lost my trust in people, my innate exuberance, and even my brave face. The war was finally over for the Netherlands; on May 8, 1945, Germany surrendered. I was ten years old, but the size of someone much younger. Nonetheless, a glimmer of hope began to flicker in my soul.

13

LIFE'S NOT FAIR

Finally, we were no longer occupied, but food supplies remained extremely minimal for us who were not of strategic importance. Many of the farms were littered with mines. Repairs to the roadways, bridges and railway would take years. Pappa told us food parcels were being dropped from airplanes, but they never reached us. Occasionally we received a loaf of bread from flour sent by the Swedish Red Cross. It was devoured with gusto. That meant we were now strong enough to go outside—but only just.

"Pappa, don't they know we're hungry? Why don't the Allies or the government send more food to our area of the Netherlands?"

"Some German soldiers are hiding in the countryside, because they don't want to be taken as prisoners-of-war. That's why you have to stay near home—they shoot anyone who walks nearby. The government wants to make sure they don't get food." He shrugged. "So neither do we."

I wondered if der Stiefel had remained behind, and my shoulders began to sag, but then I remembered my brave face. I gave Pappa a bright smile. "That's okay. I have enough."

A few days later, Mamma came home in great excitement. "Agnes said that the Red Cross just air-dropped healthy cookies. They'll be issued alphabetically; as Bisschops, we should get ours soon!"

Pappa went out immediately so he would be in the front of the line at the distribution center. Sieglinde and I chattered like magpies, joyfully dreaming of tasting the cookies. We stood with our noses pressed to the window to watch for Pappa coming home. There he was! We flew to greet him.

Pappa's step was heavy as he slowly mounted the stairs. "Sorry, *Kinderen*. No cookies. They told me our letter hasn't come up yet, and that it won't today. I really don't understand it. In my alphabet, 'B' comes right after 'A'."

Mamma sighed. "Life is never fair."

Just then, the doorbell rang. It was Mamma's friend, Mevrouw Hijenga. She'd already received her cookies, a whopping great silver-colored tin of them which was poking up out of her carpet bag.

Mamma invited her up for a cup of ersatz tea, and as she settled into a chair with Ronald on her lap, Mevrouw Hijenga asked us how we liked our cookies.

My shoulders slumped. "We didn't get any."

Pappa added, "It would seem that, for us, 'B' comes after 'H'. We're just not that important, I guess."

My eyes narrowed as I pondered the issue. Could it be that we didn't get our cookies because my mother was an immigrant from Germany? I shrugged. There was no point in even suggesting the possibility.

While Mamma made tea, we just sat and stared at Mevrouw Hijenga's tin longingly.

At first, Mevrouw Hijenga appeared to be strangely fascinated by our faded rose wallpaper, but then she nodded her head just once. The kindly woman then bent over, took the tin out of her carpet bag, and opened it.

Sieglinde and I went stiff with excitement. We'd lost hope that we would ever taste the cookies for ourselves, but couldn't help drawing nearer to look. I inhaled deeply. The cookies smelled so good that my mouth watered.

My eyes grew round as Mevrouw Hijenga gave little Ronald a cookie. Then while he happily sucked on the now-soggy mess, she generously offered a cookie to everyone in our family!

I accepted and held a precious cookie carefully, almost too overwhelmed to try it. I touched it tentatively with my tongue and then nibbled a little bit from an edge. *Lekker!* The cookie just melted in my mouth. I ate it all with tiny bites, so the heavenly experience lasted as long as possible.

Of course, one cookie didn't fill me up. Sieglinde and I could still smell the rest of them, but asking for another was out of the question.

Just then, our family again heard the sounds of singing and celebration outside our window. Mevrouw Hijenga exclaimed about how much she loved to watch men in uniform, so she and Mamma went over to the window to watch the Canadian soldiers. Mevrouw Hijenga put her carpet bag with the tin of cookies in it down between her feet and leaned out, resting her stomach on the windowsill. Her dress ballooned behind her nearly covering the tin—but not quite.

Sieglinde and I eyed that tin longingly, and my sister pulled me into the hallway, where there was less chance of being overheard. "Meta, look, the tin of cookies!" she whispered.

"Shall I get us one each? She's not looking." I was ready! I began to creep closer.

Sieglinde caught me by the arm and pulled me back. "*Nee!* What if you get caught? I don't want Pappa to punish you," she worried. "But, oh, don't they smell wonderful!" Sieglinde inhaled deeply.

I lifted up my bony chin and whispered fiercely, "If I get caught, it'd be worth it. I'd shove it in my mouth and eat the entire cookie before being punished. They wouldn't be able to get it back!"

Sieglinde closed her eyes tightly, but she gave me a little nod.

I made my move. I figured Mevrouw Hijenga wouldn't notice a skinny little girl crawling under her dress, if I was very careful. Sieglinde peered around the corner of the living room and held her breath as I tiptoed until I was right behind the ladies. I bent down, quietly opened the tin, and helped myself to two cookies. One for Siegie and one for me!

After all, if life isn't fair, a person can't be blamed for doing all they can to remedy the situation.

～

"Hey, Siegie, it's a nice day. Let's go out on the balcony."

We leaned over, enjoying the sunshine and watching the people below. "Look at that lady. How do you think she gets her hair that color? It's as red as a flame!"

"What about that man in the raincoat and hat who's just coming around the corner? His nose is so long that a person could slide down it onto the ground."

I giggled. "I wonder if we could get his hat." Since we were now receiving at least a little bit of food, our playful natures were beginning to return.

"Whatever do you mean?" Sieglinde frowned.

I clarified. "If we were to spit, could we hit his hat?" Before my cautious sister could stop me, I gathered up my spit and tried.

"You missed! Your spit fell way behind the man. You need to spit before the person gets to where you're aiming. It takes a long time for it to fall three stories. Let's both try on the next person."

Soon, we spied another lady, this one wearing a scarf on her head. Both Sieglinde and I stood ready. When she was where we each thought our spit would hit her, we launched.

"Sieglinde, you nearly hit her! Good work! Mine was nowhere near. I need to spit sooner. Let's try again."

The next woman was hatless and dragging a toddler by the hand. We saw her little girl look up at us, but the lady didn't notice the two girls on the balcony overhead. Both Sieglinde and I leaned over the railing and at the right time, let fly.

The lady flinched and raised her hand to her head to investigate what she'd felt. We got her! Sieglinde and I ducked down quickly so she wouldn't see us, hoping she would blame a bird. From there we snuck inside for what dinner there was.

It was windy when we woke up, but we decided to try again. The challenge was calculating the factors that influenced whether our spit would hit our victim. How fast the person was walking, how hard and in which direction the wind was blowing, and how much spit we could produce were all important considerations.

Sieglinde and I practiced the spit bomb game until we became very proficient: champion spitters.

~

Finally, in the summer of 1945, our family was granted permission to move back to Scheveningen.

"Guusje, the council said we may choose from any of the empty homes. Where do you think would be good?"

My mother pushed herself out of her chair. "Let's go and see the different places."

My parents, Sieglinde and I walked back to our old neighborhood, pushing Ronald in his pram, discussing which houses might be available. Corrie was too sick to walk that far, so she stayed at home.

I skipped along, the prospect of moving where der Stiefel couldn't find me giving wings to my feet. "I don't care where we live as long as we leave that tomb! And if it's near to the beach. And I really want a downstairs house with a garden. Hmm, lying back in soft grass surrounded by beautiful tulips and daffodils just watching the clouds float by. Maybe also munching on some chocolate. Heavenly!"

Pappa pulled my hair with a grin. "Sounds good to me, Meta."

Mamma joined in. "Maybe we could have a huge garden. I grew up with a big backyard and lots of space, even chickens and a pig. I don't like chicken, but still enjoy pork. So, space is good."

Pappa's eyes twinkled. "I don't think we'll find a backyard big enough for livestock in Scheveningen, but you never know. Let's investigate the houses at the end of the Leeuwardensestraat where there's the most grass in the back."

We walked to the Leeuwardensestraat 5, which was under number 3 and number 1, where we used to live. The house was empty, so we went through it into the backyard.

"Guusje, what do you think? It's smaller than the house we used to have upstairs, but there is a little garden in the back."

Mamma stood with her head back, looking at the balconies overshadowing us. "How low do you think the laundry of the upstairs neighbors would hang? I think it would cover our windows." She pressed her lips together and narrowed her eyes.

"Also, if we're on the bottom, when the neighbors beat their rugs and mattresses out, it'll be over my clean, wet laundry." With a decided shake of the head, Mamma proclaimed, "No way! Sientje will never live above me."

It was decided. We would move back to the upstairs home where we'd lived before the war.

Sieglinde and I packed our few possessions while Pappa and Mamma did the rest. The bedroom being cleared, I ventured up to the attic just to check that I hadn't left Grietje on the windowsill. To my amazement, the third door, the one that was always locked, was ajar. After pushing it open, I cautiously peeked in. There I saw a table covered in dirty dishes, papers on the table and the floor, a chair and several unmade beds. It looked as if whoever had been there left in a great hurry.

Narrowing my eyes, I considered. This room belonged to the butcher who, while he always seemed to have some food, never shared with us. Could it be he had nothing to share because he was feeding the people living up here?

I found Grietje, with her still-plump cheeks and elegant clothing, under my own bed.

On the following morning, moving day, my wiry father rented a wooden cart with two wheels and two handles. He carefully carried our family's belongings down the two flights of stairs and piled them in the handcart. While Pappa worked, I stood outside guarding the cart so nobody stole our few, and rather shabby, personal effects.

Pappa pulled the fully laden cart to the house where we would again live. Then, he and I carried everything up the steep, narrow, and heartwarmingly familiar stairs. Leeuwardensestraat was empty; there was no need to watch the handcart.

As Pappa did the heavy labor, I ran my hand over the living room wallpaper and stood in front of the window, looking at the street where I used to play. Making my way upstairs to my former bedroom, I gazed out over the red rooftops towards where I used to watch the light coming from my old friend, the lighthouse which stands near the harbor. I took a deep cleansing breath. I was home!

Pappa walked back and forth from Den Haag to Scheveningen three times that day, a total of 36 kilometers. It took him all day! I accompanied him on two of the trips, but was too tired to join him for the third. Maybe it was good that we'd traded many of our possessions for food and burnt some of the furniture for warmth. There was less to carry.

~

Finally, we were in our old house, our old street, and our old town. We even had the same family living below us—the den Dulks with their five children. It was all very familiar, but so much had changed. Before the war, many of our neighbors were Jewish. Now, those people were gone and the inhabitants of their houses were strangers to us.

With her shopping basket on her arm and me skipping alongside, my mother set out to pick up milk at the shop on our corner, Boogaard's. Mevrouw van Kruijsen was busy cleaning her front step, so Mamma stopped for a chat. After the usual pleasantries, Mamma asked, "Do you know what happened to the Goldbergs? Sientje doesn't know, but perhaps you do, having lived here all during the war."

Mevrouw van Kruijsen leant on her broom as she shook her head sadly. "I'm afraid they aren't coming back. They disappeared early on, and German soldiers lived in their house. They made a dreadful mess and stole everything of value, even the beautiful silver coffee set she inherited from her mother. Do you remember it? Now the Germans are gone, other people live there."

"I was afraid something like that had happened. I always enjoyed spending time with her but, with everything that was going on, we lost touch." A tear made its way down Mamma's cheek, and I slipped my hand into hers.

Mevrouw van Kruijsen awkwardly patted Mamma on the shoulder. "The same thing happened to almost all of the Jews who lived around here. They were forced onto trains and then died, or were killed, in the camps. Their lives ended, and ours go on." She sighed. "It isn't right, but it is how it is. Anyway, do you have time to come in for a cup of coffee?"

Mamma shook her head. "*Nee, dank je.* I have to get back to feed Ronald."

I looked up at her in surprise. She'd done that before we left. Perhaps small talk wouldn't mix well with tears.

Later that evening, Mamma told Pappa about what she'd learned. "I knew from my relatives that very few people survived the camps, but this about the Goldbergs makes it all too real. I don't even want to think about that whole family probably having perished and others, who didn't even know them, living in their house."

I jumped to my feet, shocked as I finally realized what I'd been hearing. "What about if someone were to have survived the camps and somehow make their way home? Would they no longer have a house because strangers live there? And oh Pappa, we burnt their furniture!"

Pappa sighed, "We had no choice. But, don't worry, Spilletje. Most of those who went won't return. They'll never know."

Thoughts about unfairness of the war kept me awake that night. Why should my family have survived, when so many died? Why should we have gotten our own home back, when some survivors might end up with no home at all?

Our daily trips to the shops rubbed the changes in. Before the war, many of the shop-keepers were Jewish. Now, almost none of the merchants were. In fact, the only person that I recognized from before the war was Meneer Abbas, who owned the dry goods store. I'd always found his little hat and long forelocks interesting, but didn't much like his long beard. I knew that he and his family fled our country early on.

"Mamma, I'm so much looking forward to seeing Max again. I can hardly wait for school to start." Max Abbas had been a good friend before the war began.

"Spilletje, much has changed. Max might have, too."

Four months after the war ended, after more than a year of no school at all, the government decreed that everyone should go to the grade that matched their age. I landed in fifth grade, even though I'd never completed the third.

It was a little strange to go back to school after so much time off, but it was a welcome strange. I adored my teachers; I relished the learning; I was deeply grateful that changing buildings to make room for Nazis was now a thing of the past. And I loved making lots of friends. My naturally outgoing and cheerful disposition slowly began to return.

A few weeks after school started, Max Abbas came back. Because he was the only Jewish child who both survived and returned to our school, the headmaster introduced him to our class. We welcomed him with applause; Max didn't even lift his face. I peered at him in shock. What a disappointment! The cute happy child I'd so fondly remembered had grown into a scrawny, awkward pre-teen. My crush evaporated instantly.

~

Hannie, a petite Jewish girl with shiny black hair, was new to the school and soon became my close friend. Hannie neither talked about her birth family nor the war years. I wondered whether she'd lived in hiding, maybe like the people in our attic, or survived the camps, but I knew I should not ask. Mamma had schooled me well.

Hannie did tell me that Dutch Jewish people had adopted her and her new brother. Privately, I thought her new parents must be very wealthy, because they bought both floors of a row house on the Stevinstraat. I wondered what it would be like to go from having nobody to having parents and a brother you'd never met before moving in with them.

"Meta, I want to show you my room and all the things my parents gave me. Can you come over after school tomorrow?"

"Sure. If my mother says it's okay, I'll walk home with you."

The next day Hannie and I skipped along the sidewalks to her home. She threw open the front door, hollered, "Hello, Mother, I'm home!" and turned to me. "Come on, Meta!"

With my eyes nearly popping out of my head, I followed my friend down the carpeted hallway past the open door to their living room. "Oh, how beautiful," I breathed, admiring the plush furniture and dainty ornaments.

Hannie grabbed my hand and pulled. "Come on, Slowpoke!"

We went upstairs to her pretty pink-and-white bedroom, and I gasped. The shelves were full of toys, and the walls were covered with beautiful pictures. Even the bedding had ruffles. I was shocked to think that these things were available in the stores. We could barely get food! Of course, I wouldn't dream of trading my family for a beautiful bedroom, but thought it would be great to have both.

Hannie threw open her cupboard. Once I tore my eyes away from the rest of the room, I noticed that it was full to the hilt with clothing. Hannie picked up an outfit and held it in front of her, swaying to and fro to make the skirt swing.

"So pretty! It really suits you." Slightly befuddled, I forced a smile.

"Do you like it? Take it!" Hannie threw the outfit on the pink-carpeted floor in front of me. I hastily picked it up and placed it on the bed.

"Now, look at this one! Mother bought me this last week." Hannie held up another.

"That's just lovely," I ventured hesitantly while stroking the silky fabric.

"Take it! My mother said it would be okay to give you clothing." Hannie thrust the outfit into my hands. I carefully placed it with the other outfit.

Hannie continued to show and offer me several more outfits, repeating, "I have so much more than I need," again and again.

I grew more and more confused and uncomfortable. Backing away, I held out my hands to stop her. "*Nee, nee, dank je.* I really don't need them. I have enough clothing."

Hannie's eyes rested on my faded and threadbare dress. "Hmm, okay. What about this one? It would really go with your blue eyes."

My hand was on the doorknob. "Um, I think I should go now. Mamma told me I shouldn't be too long."

Slipping on my shabby coat, I turned and ran home, leaving all the pretty outfits behind. There I cornered my mother, telling her all about my visit. "Mamma, why did Hannie do that? It was weird! I was so embarrassed."

Mamma pursed her lips. "There are a lot of unanswered

questions here, but I suspect Hannie may be experiencing 'survivor's guilt.' That's when people who lived through the war feel guilty that they survived when so many didn't." Mamma sighed and touched my cheek. "Hannie's birth family all died. Now she's even being spoiled. I expect she feels she doesn't deserve what she has. Who can blame her for trying to give some of the surplus away?" Mamma shrugged.

I crossed my arms. "Well, I didn't take anything. There's no way I'm accepting charity!"

"Oh Meta, sometimes it's kinder to accept a gift than keep a brave face."

I didn't answer. The friendship with Hannie ended.

~

Mounting the stairs in a hurry, I dropped my bag and hung up my coat while calling for Mamma. She was in the kitchen preparing broth for Corrie.

"Hello, Spilletje. How was your day?" Mamma stroked my hair. "Sit down. I managed to get some little cakes. Let's have one with a nice cup of tea."

"Oh Mamma, that's perfect today. I have such news! My teacher says that on the anniversary of Liberation Day all the fifth-graders in all of the Netherlands will be leading all of the people in all the celebrations!" I stopped to catch my breath.

"That sounds wonderful, but why the fifth-graders?" Mamma poured me some tea. "Sit down, Schatje."

I couldn't and continued to pace. "Because the war was five years long! Isn't that cool? We'll stand on bridges, all on the same day, all at the same time. We'll even sing all the same songs, all in the same order, ending with *Het Wilhelmus* (the national anthem)!"

"And Pappa and I will be there to hear you." Mamma pulled me to a chair. "Now, drink your tea!"

A few days later my teacher announced, "Class, I have a big surprise for you. The fifth graders in the USA will celebrate Liberation Day together with us; each child there sent something for each child here. Come forward in a line to receive your package."

We filed to the front of the class, and the teacher handed me a shoebox-sized parcel from a boy in Ohio. Sitting down at my desk, my hands trembled so much that I had a hard time undoing the tape. I started with unwrapping the smallest gift; it was a gorgeous blue brooch that looked like a sailor. Next, there was a package of Bazooka bubble gum. I set it aside. The white facecloth wasn't so amazing, but my favorite gift followed: a big, green bar of Dial soap. We could only get Sunlight soap in our part of the Netherlands; this soap from America smelled beautiful.

As soon as the bell rang, I grabbed my wonderful gifts and ran all the way home. Racing up the stairs, I called out, "Mamma, guess who has the nicest smelling soap, you or me?"

Mamma grinned. "Me of course, because you don't have any soap!"

"Nope, you're wrong. Smell this!" I thrust the soap under her nose.

Mamma inhaled deeply. "How did you get this? Where did it come from?" She turned the soap over and over in her hands as she walked towards the living room.

"From America. The American Red Cross had fifth graders in the United States send packages to the fifth graders here."

Mamma sank down onto a chair, still holding the soap. "I can't believe it! I'm seeing, touching, and smelling soap that came all the way from across the ocean!" She sighed. "America!"

"Hey Mamma, let's wash Ronald with this soap!"

"Good idea!" Mamma filled a tub in front of the stove while I undressed my little brother. Then, with Siegie and Corrie watching, Mamma gently sat him in the water.

Ronald splashed happily as Mamma lathered him up with the beautiful American soap. "Oh Ronald," I giggled. "You're getting me wet!"

After Ronald had been rinsed, dried and dressed, I proudly carried the soap and facecloth into the kitchen to be shared with rest of my family. I could hardly wait for Pappa to come home; he was such a fan of fragrant soap.

Then I showed Mamma the brooch. "Where do you think this should go, Mamma?"

"It's yours. It's up to you."

I looked around and spotted Ronald's tiny brown coat hanging in the hall. "There!" I pinned it on, pleased as punch that I could.

It was time to sample the chewing gum. Sieglinde and I sat by Corrie, who was lying on the divan, and I passed each of them a piece. What would it be like? I smelled it, then popped it in my mouth and chewed cautiously. It was peppermint flavored, but became unexpectedly slimy. It accidently slipped down my throat.

"Meta, you're not supposed to swallow! Gum is for chewing and blowing bubbles." Sieglinde chewed industriously.

Corrie spat it out immediately. "That's disgusting!"

Sieglinde's eyes met mine, and I grinned, knowing what she was thinking. She pushed the gum to the front of her mouth and tried to blow a bubble to match the picture on the wrapping. It didn't work. Sieglinde's gum joined Corrie's, and I threw the remaining pieces away.

Finally, the day of celebration arrived. I dressed in my Sunday clothing to go to school, and together the children in my class walked to the canal bridge assigned to our school. I stood up as tall as possible and belted out the songs at the top of my lungs.

Even though many had not, we had survived the war. I hoped that if I avoided thinking about what had happened to so many, maybe the pain would go away. It didn't work.

14

CONTINUING CHALLENGES

I walked home slowly while chewing on my collar. What should I do? Tell or not? My father was sitting at the kitchen table peeling potatoes when I arrived. Seeing him who had always been my security, I couldn't hold it in anymore. "Pappa, I'm very worried about something," I hesitated before continuing. "But I don't know if I should tell you."

Pappa put the knife down and drew me to his side. "You can talk to me about anything. You know that. What's up?"

"Umm, you know how Sieglinde often goes straight upstairs after school? Well, there's a reason. She doesn't want you and Mamma to know. She says it's a secret. But I hate how miserable she is. I think maybe this is the kind of secret I shouldn't keep."

"Sounds like it. Go on."

"Pappa, when she's alone with me, she cries. I just don't know what I should do."

"You're doing the right thing in coming to me. Tell me, Meta. What's going on?"

"Siegie says the boys at school keep pestering her. They call her a *mof* and tease and try to hit her. They laugh when she runs away. I haven't seen it myself, because I hang out with friends after school. If

I did, I'd probably punch those guys right in their noses! But what can I do, really?"

"She needs to learn to defend herself." Pappa got up and walked to the bottom of the stairs to the bedrooms. "Sieglinde," he called. "Come here, please."

Sieglinde came downstairs with reddened eyes, and we all sat in the chairs by the *kachel,* Sieglinde and I sharing one chair. "What is it, Pappa?"

"Your sister tells me you're being bullied at school. Is that true?"

Sieglinde gave me a dirty look and then hung her head. "Yes, some of the boys pester me. They tease me about anything: my curly hair, my German mother, and about being shy. Anything really. Some of them even pull my hair and kick me. I try not to cry, but..." Her blue eyes filled with tears.

Pappa leaned forward. "*Kindje, kindje toch*, why did you keep this a secret? You need to defend yourself. Do you remember what I taught you? Show me how you can hit me." Pappa stood and opened his arms.

Sieglinde got to her feet and swung at him feebly.

"Harder! That wouldn't hurt a fly."

"I can't, Pappa! I can't hit you—I don't want to hurt you. Also, the boys are so big! I'm scared. Please don't make me..." She started to sob in earnest, and Pappa enfolded her in his arms.

Looking at me over my sister's shoulder, Pappa said, "Meta, I think she needs your help. This has to stop, so let's practice some of the tricks I taught you earlier." He put Sieglinde aside. "Come on. First the uppercut and then the left hook."

I was more than willing. And as Sieglinde watched in horror, I punched my father as hard as I could in his stomach. He didn't react. I took a deep breath and threw all my weight into the next blow. No reaction. No matter how hard I hit him, he didn't seem to feel it. We practiced all weekend, and I learned the moves.

On Monday, I was fully prepared and on the lookout. There they were. Coming around the corner, I saw those vicious boys: they were stalking my sister! As she, glancing over her shoulder, increased her speed, the pack of savages ran faster. The war taught me that sometimes it's better to be quiet. But not this time.

I saw red. I was both much smaller and two years younger than the boys, but immediately bawled at the top of my lungs, "Hey bullies, stop that. Leave her alone!" I sprinted towards them at full tilt.

Hearing my war cry, the bullies screeched to a halt. I kept running, and to my astonishment some fled before I could even get near. Others remained stock still, goggle-eyed at the pint-sized girl who was threatening them so passionately. My fists were flying and my feet kicking as I screamed, "Stay away from my sister!"

That evening, Sieglinde told my parents what had happened. "You should have seen Meta. All the boys were scared stiff of her and ran away!"

I puffed out my chest.

Pappa gave me a grin and a thumbs up.

Mamma frowned and shook her head at him. "Oh Meta, you know that's not the way nice girls behave. Was it really necessary to hurt them? Couldn't you have talked it out? You'll have to apologize. The Bisschop family does not settle their arguments with fists."

In the morning, I dragged my feet to school, not looking forward to apologizing. Fortunately, when the bullies saw me, they *ran*. Even better, they left my sister in peace. I smirked at them and strutted around like I owned that school.

On my 11th birthday just after dinner, I glanced outside and forgot to breathe. There, in the gentle light of the street lantern, snowflakes were dancing. Twinkling, floating, swirling, twirling, and falling. As I watched with stars in my eyes, the snow began to fall faster, forming a pillowy blanket on the ground. I turned from the window.

"It's like a fairy tale outside! So beautiful! May we go outside, *alsjeblieft*?"

My parents smiled and gave permission, even though it was now quite dark. Sieglinde and I quickly put on our coats, hats and mittens. We didn't own boots, so I stuffed newspaper in the toes and along the bottom of my father's old boots and wore those. Siegie wore Mamma's. We clomped down the long, steep staircase and burst out the door. I inhaled the fresh, white scent with my head tilted back.

In no time, several other children joined us, and everyone danced around the lantern in the snow. Even Sjors Wieringa, a dark-eyed, curly-haired tyke who was much younger than we were, was allowed outside to enjoy the antics of the big kids.

"Hey Sjors, look at me. I'm catching snowflakes in my mouth!" The kids stopped to watch and then joined me in standing with their mouths open and their eyes shut. We remained outside until our fingers and toes were numb.

"Meta, Siegie, time to come in!" Mamma called from the window.

"Is it okay if I first take Sjors home?" I called up.

"Of course."

After dropping off the little guy, we reluctantly obeyed Mamma, leaving our snowy outerwear hanging on a hook and going into the living room to warm up. There another surprise greeted me. While we were out, my parents had decorated the table with the first birthday cake we'd had since the war and two gifts!

"Sit down, everyone," Mamma invited. Pappa made hot chocolate, and everyone joined in celebrating the birthday girl—me. I opened my presents and was grateful to receive a sketchbook with a red cover and a drawing pencil that was red on one end and blue on the other.

"Class, take out your dip pen and ink. We're going to practice cursive writing."

I dipped my pen in the ink kept in the little glass container fitted into the hole in the top of my desk and concentrated so hard that my tongue stuck out a bit. This was my least favorite class, penmanship, but I was determined to do well. "There. That looks great," I muttered, pressing my work with blotting paper.

I turned it in and held my breath while the teacher assessed what I'd produced. Was it good enough? She shook her head slightly, but I tossed my hair back as I made my way to my desk.

Next, the teacher beckoned for Nellie, an attractive girl with long, straight, brown hair, to bring her work forward. The teacher took a quick look, nodded, and then held her sheet of paper up to show us all. Her writing was the best in the class. Nellie's hazel eyes met mine as she walked back to her seat. Blinking back tears, I smiled bravely at her.

In that class every day a pupil filled the container in each student's desk with dark blue ink from a liter bottle with a silver-colored spout. But if someone wrote very beautifully, the teacher gave that person a tiny bottle of red ink, and their next penmanship assignment could be written in red! I looked on slightly enviously as Nellie was given red ink.

I was proud of her. After all, Nellie was my best friend. We enjoyed similar activities: running, climbing, jumping rope and playing ball. But I was better at all of these than she was; I liked that. In writing, however, Nellie surpassed me. She left me in the dust.

There was a level higher than red ink—green. In all the time I was in that class, only one student wrote so well that she was allowed to use green ink, and she only achieved it once. Nellie.

When I told Mamma about it, she gave me a little bottle of red ink. I bought myself a bottle of green. I used those bottles to practice my penmanship at home, but it wasn't the same. I wanted to win.

Nellie and I strolled from school towards her home over the dry goods store.

"Geography was so interesting today—just imagine what it would be like to live in an igloo!"

"Is it even possible for anywhere to be colder than Holland in the winter?"

Nellie shook her head and chuckled. "You wouldn't think so. Anyway, guess what I did yesterday: I climbed over the rail of my balcony and into the pear tree that's in the store's backyard. The pears are ripe, so I picked one and ate it. It was *echt lekker!*"

"Lucky!" I sighed. "My sister, Corrie, gets to eat soft fruit, like peaches and grapes, because she's sick. But the rest of us..." I caught myself before I spilled out the shameful fact that my family couldn't afford special fruit for everyone. I smiled brightly. "I'd love a pear!" My mouth was watering at the very idea.

"Well, let's get one!" Nellie skipped away.

"How did you do it?" I asked, running after her. "I thought the trees were too far from your balcony. Weren't you afraid to fall?"

Nellie stopped, putting her hands on her hips. "It was easy. I just climbed over the railing, reached for a branch, and swung myself over."

Hmm, I thought, if she can do it, it'll be easy for me. Out loud I said, "I'm willing to try."

Arriving at Nellie's house, we shouted a hasty greeting to her mother, who was busy in the living room. Then we proceeded into the kitchen and through the door onto the balcony. With a quick glance over our shoulders to make sure that Nellie's mother hadn't followed us, we climbed into the pear tree.

There we sat, each blissfully eating an entire pear. The juice ran down our chins, onto our fingers, and down to our elbows. We licked up all the juice and even ate the core!

A few days after this, Sieglinde and I were passing the greengrocer. I admired the pears, remembering my adventure, but then caught sight of the blushing peaches. Their aroma filled the air. Slowing down so my strait-laced sister was in front of me, I hastily grabbed a small peach and popped the entire thing into my mouth.

I intended to swallow the juicy, sweet flesh and spit out the pit, but being worried about being caught, I was in too much of a hurry. I choked on the stone. I sprinted to catch up to the self-same sister I'd been hiding from, coughing desperately. The pit flew out just before I reached her. I never told Sieglinde what I'd done, and I never stole fruit again.

"Meta," Sieglinde whispered. "Come on! You'll get in trouble again!"

Low down on the wall, at the top of the stairs to the bedrooms, was a triangular sink with a brass tap. Like all the faucets in our home, it dispensed rainwater that the sand dunes had filtered.

Mamma had forbidden drinking straight from the faucet, but I was bent over with my mouth wide open, just letting the water run in. Delicious!

Sieglinde pulled me into the bedroom, and gasping we slid into our icy beds with their crisp white sheets and scratchy woolen blankets. On very frosty nights, Mamma put a stone gin bottle filled with hot water in a sock at the foot of each bed to pre-warm it. She hadn't had time tonight, so we curled up like roly-poly bugs.

Once in bed, Sieglinde and I began discussing the next instalment of our made-up story series. The imagined adventures kind-of helped me to forget about how thirsty I was.

I'd been given nothing to drink with dinner, nor afterwards, in hopes that I might not wet the bed. Mamma always got me up at night to go, but I still had accidents. My bedwetting caused a lot of work, not to mention embarrassment. Even the mattress got wet and had to be dried by hanging it out of the window. There, everyone on the street below could see it.

As I lay with my legs crossed, my stomach clenched. I knew that, when I was asleep, the pee might just come out. I might dream that I had to pee, was sitting on the toilet, and could finally let go. Only, I wouldn't be on the toilet. And I would wake up in the morning in a dreadful, uncomfortable, and embarrassing puddle. I turned over, trying to think about something else.

Soon, I heard soft snores coming from the other bed. My bed was near to the window, so I rolled over and looked out at the light from the lighthouse. Knowing that it was there, warning the boats and fishermen, I felt safe. My bed was toasty now, and my pillow felt oh so soft. Finally, breathing in the salty air that always blew in around the window frame, I fell asleep to the rhythmic sounds of the waves.

Watery sunshine broke through our lightweight white curtains, alerting Sieglinde and me to the arrival of morning. We jumped out of our cozy beds into an icy room, where even the inside of the window was frosted over. Sieglinde's teeth were chattering as she grabbed her clothes, slid back under the covers and quickly dressed. It wasn't a simple process, but it was preferable to goosebumps as high as mountains!

I couldn't slip into day clothes in similar comfort, because my bed was wet. Again. I cleaned myself with a wet cloth at the brass tap while my teeth chattered, and shivered into my clean clothing. Grietje, who was perched on my dresser, caught my eye. Ha! She never had to deal with anything like this. Once day, I determined, I would be like her. Elegant. Clean. Unaffected.

My parents never made a big deal of my bedwetting, but it was excruciatingly embarrassing for someone who desperately needed to be admired. I outgrew it at Hemalie.

15

HEMALIE

Zonnelicht schijnt overal
Op ons huis bovenal
Wat zal Hemalie zijn
Zonder die zonneschijn

Zonnelicht schijnt overal
Op ons huis bovenal
Geeft ons weer nieuwe moed
En doet ons goed

Sunlight shines everywhere
Especially on our house
What would Hemalie be
Without that sunshine?

Sunlight shines everywhere
Especially on our house
It gives us new courage
And is good for us.

"Class, when I call your name, proceed to the nurse's office. Your parents will be waiting for you there."

It was my turn. When I arrived at the office, the nurse weighed me. She clucked her tongue as she recorded the number, and I noticed my mother exchanging a look with my father. I was now 12 years old, and my clothing still swamped my emaciated frame.

The nurse indicated that my parents and I should go into the next room. There a government official in a suit and tie and the school doctor in his white coat were seated behind a table. I knew why we were there, so just in case it helped I rubbed my shoes on the back of my socks and stood up very straight.

Both men sat silently while they reviewed my file. After several excruciating moments, the government official frowned, turned to the doctor, and shook his head, murmuring. "Much too thin. It's been more than two years since the war. At this point, I think it's unlikely she'll ever recover." My heart sank—I hadn't fooled him for one minute.

"Hold on a minute. My records show she had *hongerziekte* for a year, which is why she's so thin. But she recovered. Just look at her."

A grin split my face, and I puffed out my chest.

The doctor winked at me and continued. "You know, spirit sometimes makes all the difference. She has a whole lot of that. Her teacher says she's very active. Personally, I think this child is a good candidate."

"Well, you're the doctor; you may be right," the official mused while stroking his beard. "What's your first name, Bisschop?"

My mother had told me the children who were selected for this government program would be sent on a vacation with lots of food, and now I could see I had a real chance. I raised my chin, looked him in the eye, and announced. "I am Meta!"

The official duly wrote my name on his paper, but then brought up a potential difficulty with my parents. When this plan was conceived, the government knew that there were far too many undernourished children for it to be possible to send them all for special treatment. Therefore, in order to qualify for the program, the children had to show they had a good chance of surviving and were suffering from some infirmity in addition to plain old starvation.

"Perhaps we could say she needs a simple operation—one that carries minimal risk." The government official raised his eyebrows as he turned to the doctor.

The doctor nodded thoughtfully. "A tonsillectomy would do the trick. Her chart shows she suffers a lot with earaches."

It was agreed. A few days later, my parents took me to the Westeinde hospital for my totally unnecessary surgical procedure. I sat in a special chair, they put me to sleep, and I woke up still in the chair with a sore throat, but without tonsils. I watched carefully as medical personnel scurried around the ward. One day, I thought, I'll be a doctor and help children who want to go on vacation.

Recovery was pretty rough, but it was worth it. I now qualified to go for special treatment in a forest in the middle of the country, at Hemalie near Soesterberg. I was an 'official' *bleekneusje* [pale nose]!

"Cor, I must go shopping. Meta needs clothing for Hemalie. Look at this list they gave me; she doesn't have most of what's on it."

Pappa scratched his head. "Guusje, we just don't have any extra money. The loan we had to take out for Corrie's TB treatment takes a chunk out of my weekly pay. Is there nothing you could alter for her?"

"*Nee,* but perhaps I can pick up some inexpensive fabric somewhere. It'll be cheaper to have the undergarments made than to buy them."

Soon afterwards, Mamma came home with a large piece of turquoise cotton that Tante Agnes had obtained at a discount. Then, because Mamma wasn't good at sewing, she made a bargain with Mevrouw van Kruijsen's eldest daughter. Cornelia made me an underslip, two undershirts, two pair of underpants, and a nightgown. She was allowed to use the leftover fabric for herself.

Carefully folding and packing my turquoise clothes into Mamma's little brown suitcase, I felt extremely wealthy. I hadn't possessed that much clothing for a long, long time. Actually never. I was quaking inside at the idea of leaving my loving family and living far away, but put on my brave face and smiled gaily.

It was time to go. My parents walked me to the train station, and I found myself with a group of children who were all traveling from Den Haag to Hemalie. Once I arrived, I was assigned to an upstairs dorm room, which I shared with 23 other girls. The little boys, some as young as six, also had an upper-level room and those boys that were my age were downstairs. A supervisor slept in a bedroom right next to each of the dorm rooms. Even though people surrounded me, a few lonely tears slipped out that first night.

It was morning when things always look better. I cautiously felt my sheets—dry! Surreptitiously taking stock of the potential friends all around, I jumped out of bed, splashed water on my face, dressed, and ran down to the dining hall. Everyone was seated at a long table. I quickly joined a table of children who were my own age, smiling sunnily at the girl next to me, Lottie. There in front of us was a tall glass of milk and a plate with a knife and fork on either side of it. The kitchen staff brought out serving dishes piled high with fresh whole wheat bread spread with creamy yellow butter. My eyes widened as I watched Lottie consume eight slices, one after another. I couldn't manage more than five, but resolved that, by the time I left Hemalie, I would outdo her.

The matron stood to speak, and we all grew quiet. "*Kinderen*, welcome to Hemalie, where you will grow healthy. Every morning we will take a brisk walk in the fresh air. Since this home is near to a runway, be sure that, if you see an airplane, you fall down on the grass. They fly low. We may meet one or more this morning, so we'll show you what to do then."

Remembering my experience with the bombers, my stomach clenched. I glanced at the big eater next to me. What did Lottie think? She licked the butter off her fingers with relish. Evidently, she wasn't too worried.

"Time to get your coats on. Let's go." The teacher in charge of our group led us out of the forest onto the heath. No sooner had we arrived than we heard the roar of an engine. I inhaled sharply.

"Down!" our teacher shouted, diving for the ground.

Everyone dropped onto the heather bushes. The plane flew over our heads, we got up, dusted ourselves off, and carried on with our walk. Ducking airplanes near Hemalie wasn't a big deal—apparently.

After our constitutional, it was lunchtime. Sitting down between Lottie and my other new friend, Elise, I couldn't believe my eyes when the food-laden trays emerged from the kitchen. Meat, potatoes, vegetables, gravy, and milk. A Sunday meal on Monday! I feasted until I couldn't swallow another bite. The white-coated kitchen staff cleared our plates, and I tried to get up, but Elise pulled me back down.

Then I saw them. Desserts! On a weekday! I was served the same amount of chocolate pudding as everyone else, even the children who were taller than me. It appeared to me that Hemalie, which sounds a bit like "heaven" in Dutch, really was heavenly.

After lunch, we were led to cots that had been lined up in a building with three walls so we were protected from wind and rain while enjoying the benefits of fresh air. The smaller children slept for the hour while the older ones rested and looked at books. I whispered with Elise, telling her about my family and learning about hers. Later on, during our free time outside, Elise and I played tag together, until several other children joined in. All my concerns about living away from my family faded; I was loving this!

At dinner time, we again had more food than we could eat. Each child was given milk with two *boterhammen* with butter and Edam cheese. I was still hungry, so the person who was serving our table also gave me bread with butter and jam. I managed three slices that first night, but soon worked my way up to more.

After dinner came my least favorite activity of the day: the mandatory cod liver oil and two vitamin C tablets.

As the weeks flew by, my clothes grew slightly tighter as my face, arms and legs filled out. The weekly weight check confirmed what I could see in the mirror. Even my hair began to shine. I had lots of energy to sing, giggle, and play all kinds of games. The Hemalie treatment regimen was working.

~

The boys at my table were up to their usual tricks. "Hey Guys, look what I can do!" Thomas threw a piece of potato into the air and caught it in his mouth.

He'd been spotted. "Tom, stop that! Eat your food; don't play with it."

I exchanged a covert grin with him, planning to try this myself when the kitchen staff were elsewhere occupied.

"I can eat ten *boterhammen*—way more than any girl!" bragged Bernhard, who was sitting directly across from me and next to Tom.

My chewing slowed down, and my eyes narrowed. There was no way that I was going to let a boy, a mere male, beat me. "You're on! Tomorrow morning we'll have a contest. Me against all of you! I'll wipe the floor with you." I pointed to every boy at the table to emphasize my point.

The challenge was accepted, and word about the competition soon spread.

"Meta, are you crazy? There's no way you can eat more than any of the boys. Look at the size of you and the size of them." Elise's cautious attitude reminded me of Sieglinde.

Lottie clapped me on the back. "Well, I believe in you. I think you can do it."

"I know I can. With one hand tied behind my back!"

Bernhard overheard my boast and snorted. "We'll see about that!"

The next morning, everyone watched breathlessly as the boys at my table and I ate and ate and ate. Even the kitchen staff were intrigued, tolerantly observing our activities. Each contestant was assigned a monitor who was responsible for keeping count of how many slices had been consumed.

"1, 2, 3, 4, 5, 6, 7, 8, 9, 10, 11..." I looked up from my frantic gobbling and noticed that all the boys had dropped out of the contest. Except Bernhard. He had matched me slice per slice, until he had eaten 12 slices of bread and butter. I stared him right in the eyes, chewing methodically with my mouth open. He turned a little green and held his hands up to indicate that he was done.

I slowly and deliberately looked around at my spectators and then, holding Bernard's eyes with my own, I stuffed another slice of bread and butter into my mouth. I nearly choked, but I chewed and chewed and swallowed.

I'd won! My stomach ached, but I pumped my fist in victory. I had eaten more than any boy at Hemalie. Someone started to clap, and soon the whole room was applauding me, even the kitchen staff. I stood on my chair and proudly took a bow, reveling in the glory of my accomplishment. I did it, in my mind indisputably proving that girls are indeed better than boys.

A few days later, at mail call in the morning, I received a parcel. I danced back to my seat. What would it contain? After breakfast, I carried my package to a private place and opened it with baited breath. A long letter from my mother, one from Pappa, one from Sieglinde, one from Corrie, a scribble from Ronald, a hair ribbon, and walnuts! I opened the letter from Sieglinde first.

Dear Meta,

How are you? I hope you're enjoying Hemalie. I'm so jealous! Meat and dessert every day must be amazing.

Yesterday, Mamma and I went shopping, and I held Ronald's hand so he wouldn't run off. I think he's grown even since you left! Because it's nearly December, they had walnuts at the greengrocers. Mamma bought some to send to you. She also bought some for us, so I know they're good.

I miss you. The house isn't the same without your off-key singing.
Love, Sieglinde

I carefully opened the paper sack with the walnuts in it. One of the rules at Hemalie was that "All food received from home must be shared with everyone." I eyed my precious walnuts. I knew that, with 75 kids in residence, if I shared them, I would only get a sliver of one. And they were mine. Fair and square! I also knew walnuts were expensive and a luxury

—a sacrifice of love from my parents. I nodded my head and decided to ignore this very inconvenient rule. Any consequences were worth it.

"Meta, what do you have there?" Elise sidled over to my hiding place.

"Walnuts," I whispered. "But not enough to share with everyone. Trouble is they're still in their shells. How can I open them? I don't have a nutcracker, and I can't ask the teacher, because she'll make me follow that dumb rule." I smiled winsomely at Elise. "I only want to share with my friends."

My new partner in crime pursed her lips, considering the possibilities. "You know, Leo received walnuts last week. The boys were talking about how they snuck into the kitchen and cracked the walnuts open in the door. Let's ask Leo to help us."

Accompanied by two friends, I approached Leo and a couple of other boys.

Leo stroked his chin, even though he had no beard. "I'll show you. Meet us in the central hall at midnight. But you'll need to share with us guys, too."

So it was that my friends and I snuck out of our beds and made our way down the stairs to the central hall. We were very careful to be quiet as we passed the open door of the room where our staff member slept. I pressed my hand to my mouth, stifling a giggle at the sound of her snore.

The three boys met us in the central hall and led us to the kitchen. Leo authoritatively took a walnut from my sack and placed it in between the kitchen door and the frame. Carefully, but with enough force to break the shell, he closed the door. Crraacck! The sound echoed into the large central hall. We all jumped. I looked around to see if any adult had heard and would appear. No. Whew!

Leo bowed as he presented me with the first nut. *Lekker!* We all took turns cracking and eating a walnut until only one was left. Everyone else got three; I helped myself to the last one.

Strangely, nobody woke up, and apparently not a single person found us out. It seemed that no one even noticed the small pieces of walnut shell that were left all around the door.

Lottie woke me up before light. She was bouncing up and down on her cot. "Hey Meta! Wake up!"

"Whaa? Were we spotted? Are we in trouble?"

"No, Silly. I just wanted to know if you also heard that we'll be putting on a play for our parents when they come to pick us up."

"*Ja*, I overheard the boys talking about it. I'm so excited! They said it has two lead roles. One is for a bad girl, and the other is for a good one. I'm gonna try out. What about you?"

By this time, Elise was awake, too. She bit her lip and murmured, "Honestly, I don't want a lead role." She took a deep breath. "I don't even know if I want to be in it. Maybe I could help make the costumes."

"I really want to be in the play," I sighed, looking into the distance. "Even more, I'd love to be the good girl. But since the kids have a say in who gets what role…"

Lottie smirked. "They know you way too well. If you get voted to be anything, it'll be the bad girl."

I shrugged, pretending not to mind very much. "Well, let's practice and try out together."

The day came when we would find out who had been assigned to which role. I crossed my fingers on both hands, crossed my arms, and, just in case, crossed my legs. Even though it was hard to balance, I hoped this would bring me luck.

The teacher began with the smaller parts. Elise got to be a person in a crowd. She gave me a thumbs up. I held my breath, hoping not to be called. Not yet. One after the other, children were called forward to be assigned their role.

Finally, only two parts were left to be allocated. Lottie and I had not yet been called on, which meant I was either the bad girl or the good girl. We held hands as we waited for the announcement to come. "I'll be the bad girl. I just know it," I whispered.

"Meta will be the good girl, and Lottie is the bad one. Congratulations! Come here and stand next to me, Girls." A shock wave went through me, and I stood stock still with my mouth hanging open.

Lottie shoved me forwards. "Meta, she called us. Move!"

Coming to myself, I strutted and swayed to the front of the room, looking around to be sure everyone saw me.

We practiced the play every day for a week, memorizing our lines and learning to project our voices. "Hey Meta," Lottie nudged me. "You should be a natural at this, because you're a loudmouth!"

"Ha!" I nudged her back. "And you're a natural at being bad!"

At the end of the week, Elise and I sat on the stairs in the big hall, keeping our eye on the front door while waiting for our parents to arrive. Elise's brown eyes filled with tears. "I'm going to miss you so much!"

"Yeah, I'll miss you, too, but we can write." I clasped my hands around my knees. "It'll be great to see my sisters and little brother again—and Christmas is coming!"

Finally, the teacher opened the door, and our parents streamed in; they'd all arrived at the railroad station and been driven to Hemalie in a bus. I spotted Pappa and Mamma immediately and pelted across the room to enfold them in a hug.

"Who's this?" Pappa asked, holding me away from himself so he could look me over. "I don't know this girl."

"Oh, you know," I giggled. "It's me, Meta!"

"*Nee,* I know Meta; she's skinny and pale. You're rosy and so healthy. Your eyes sparkle and your hair is shining. What did you do with my little Spilletje?"

"Pappa, that's her—she's just full of food and life!" Mamma's eyes danced.

I proudly showed my parents to their seats and went backstage. The curtains opened for the first scene, where the smaller children were performing in their pajama-costumes.

I stood anxiously in the wings, waiting for my cue, and fussing over my prop. I was supposed to pretend to pick strawberries in the shrubs, but it was winter. So, I put straw in the bottom of a basket and placed pieces of red apple on top. Those were the "strawberries," but the red part needed to show. I smoothed down my costume, which consisted of a blue-striped wrap-around apron. There was the signal. I was on!

Remembering every one of my lines, I thought I gave a wonderful performance being the good girl. After all, as the curtain closed, the applause was almost deafening. The curtain drew back again to reveal all the children, but Lottie and I got to stand in front. My grin was ear-to-ear as I made a beautiful curtsy, just like Mamma had taught me.

Finally, the good girl and the bad girl were allowed to introduce themselves to the audience. I announced, "I am Meta," and couldn't wipe the smile off my face for hours. Because I was the good girl.

16

HOPES, DREAMS AND FEARS

I was curled up in a chair by the *kachel*, engrossed in my newest library book and feasting my eyes on photographs of the Red Square in Moscow, Niagara Falls in Canada, the holy places of Rome, the icebergs of Alaska, and the pyramids in Egypt. Pappa's work at the post office offered lessons about geography to their employees, and he had taught me much by showing me stamps highlighting the special features of foreign countries. I longed to be like the mail and travel to each and every place! I couldn't—not physically, not yet. So, I did what was possible and visited in my imagination, reading books and collecting pictures that I found in magazines and on stamps, writing about the places and pasting pictures in a notebook.

"Sieglinde, look at this!" I exclaimed, pointing at a photo of Niagara Falls. "Imagine how loud all that water must be. I wonder if you get wet just standing nearby and how close to the water you can get." My eyes were shining. I'd never seen a real waterfall.

Sieglinde, who was reading about life in the 1800s, hit her forehead and rolled her eyes. "Meta, you're driving me crazy. Think of all the beautiful things we see here. But look here at these amazing hoop skirts. Do you think women in 1850 could even sit down?"

"Don't know. Don't care," I muttered.

My friend, Jenny de Haas, was totally different from my sister.

Hearing me talking about my foreign country scrapbook, she invited me to bring it over to her house. The next day, Jenny and I sat at her dining table, looking through my scrapbook.

"And here we have the Red Square in Russia. See St. Basil's Cathedral and the Kremlin? The cathedral is actually made of lots of separate round rooms, each under one of the towers."

Mevrouw de Haas was busy in the kitchen while Meneer de Haas sat nearby with a book on his lap. He wasn't looking at it, but at me, his haunted brown eyes becoming increasingly unfocused. Jenny's father was a tall, slim Jewish man who'd been gone for several years during the war. I'd seen and heard enough so I could guess where he'd been.

All too soon, it was time to go home. Jenny walked with me for part of the way. "How ever did you manage to visit all these places? We had the war, and you're still so young!" Jenny's head was cocked to one side as we walked.

I giggled. "I didn't go to any of them. I just want to, so I read about them."

"What? My dad thinks you've actually been to America, Russia, and Egypt! You talk about them as if you had."

I grimaced. "No, but I sure hope that one day I will."

~

Sieglinde looked up from her book. "Listen to that noise outside, Meta. Let's go see what it is. I need to stretch my legs, anyway."

Pappa joined Sieglinde and me to investigate the source of the roaring sound. Huge, smoke-belching machines were digging a deep hole on a vacant lot on the Harstenhoekweg.

My father surveyed their work with interest. "Ah, now I remember reading that they're going to erect an office building here. I didn't realize it'd be so close to our home."

This provided me with months of free entertainment. I watched as the basement was excavated and concrete poured around the edges of the rectangular pit. Eventually, workmen constructed brick partitions, which formed a network and came all the way up to street level. While the men were at lunch, I skipped along the walls from one end of the yawning cavity to the other.

"Meta, stop. You could fall!" Bram, a boy who was a year older than me, came running from his home on the Harstenhoekweg.

I placed my hands on my hips while balanced over the middle of the pit. "I'm not scared. I dare you to try it!"

Tim, who lived below Bram and had strolled over to join in watching, cocked his head. "That looks dangerous to me."

I gave a little jump. "No, it's not. The walls are as wide as two bricks. It's super easy to walk on them. Try it for yourselves. If you dare..."

Tim gingerly stepped onto the closest wall and walked across with cautious steps, arms extended to either side. Bram hung back, but after seeing Tim survive, he followed suit. Soon a whole group of my friends were promenading on the walls.

"Hey, get off there!" boomed a voice.

We hadn't noticed the workman who came around the corner after his break. Until then I also had not seen little Sjors, the sweet neighbor boy who followed me like a puppy, preparing to copy us. This game was definitely too dangerous for him.

"Hey everyone, let's play tag, Guys. Come on, Sjors, you be "it" first."

After dropping Sjors off at his house, I burst into our living room just as it was getting dark. "Pappa, you're home! You should see the office building now! They're now building walls in the basement. It's going to be massive!"

Pappa frowned. "You better have seen all this from a distance! It's not safe to play near to construction sites."

I scuffed my toe on the rug and didn't answer.

From our house, my parents could only see one outer edge of the coming office building, so when I next had the opportunity, I again joined the boys in our rather perilous pastime. Unfortunately, their parents could see us from their front windows.

"What do you think you're doing? Come down from there!" shouted Tim's mother. All the boys scampered away to their homes. I, on the other hand, continued my journey across those walls, all the while whistling a jaunty tune. When I reached the end of the hole, I jumped off, took a deep bow, and leisurely moseyed home. I knew the boys were watching admiringly.

~

The wind was howling, but that was not why Sieglinde and I awoke before dawn. We lifted Ronald out of his crib, and sat, cuddling our warm little brother, at the top of the stairs. We could hear our parents downstairs, but had been given strict instructions not to leave the upper landing until we were called.

Mamma opened the door at the bottom of the stairs and popped her head around. "*Kinderen*, you can come down now."

We flew down the stairs, Siegie carrying Ronald, but stopped short at the bottom. Mamma had closed the door again. That was a little strange.

"Mamma?"

Hearing us, Mamma dramatically opened the door to the living room. "*Gelukkig Kerstfeest, Allemaal* [Merry Christmas, all of you]!"

We tumbled into the room, and what I saw stopped me in my tracks. I forgot to breathe and was totally robbed of speech. The room was like something out of a fairy tale! As I gazed with stars in my eyes, I was transported into a magical place—but it was real. I could see, smell, and feel it all. The Christmas tree was lit with white wax candles, the yellow flames gently flickering and giving a warm light to the room. They were reflected in shiny, delicate glass ornaments, tinsel, and different kinds of *kerstkransjes* [edible Christmas wreaths]. Candles were also lit all over the room, and Christmas branches decorated the pictures on the walls, the mantel, and stood in vases everywhere. The entire living room shimmered and glowed.

"*Gelukkig Kerstfeest*, Pappa," we chorused, spotting him sitting right next to the tree with a bucket of water and a sponge within reach in case the tree caught fire.

"Come, my drei Grazien and my sweet boy, join us at the breakfast table," Mamma invited with a wave of her arm. We took our places, and I filled my eyes with the wonder of Christmas. A white sheet adorned with red, shiny ribbons placed in a windowpane pattern covered the table. Next to each breakfast plate, there was a paper plate cut into the form of a star and hand-decorated by Mamma with a Christmas scene.

Every plate boasted an orange, a shiny red apple, a handful of walnuts, and a small gift. Oranges don't grow in the Netherlands, so these were a very special treat. We took our time, carefully sucking the juice from each piece of the orange before popping the section into our mouths and chewing.

For breakfast itself, we feasted on bread with *muisjes*, cheese, ham, or eggs; Christmas bread loaded with golden raisins and lemon peel; and marble pound cake with confectioner's sugar on top.

Sitting in that beautiful room eating a breakfast fit for royalty felt like a dream. I was too overwhelmed to talk. I just ate and gazed at the wonderful trappings of our first post-war Christmas celebration.

It got even better. After we were finished eating, everyone was allowed to open their present. I received what I really wanted: an imitation pearl necklace.

"Oh, Pappa and Mamma, this is the best gift ever! *Dank je wel!*" I immediately put it on, right over my nightgown, and danced around the living room.

"Sieglinde, come look!" It was December 31, and I was standing by our living room window, holding Ronald up so he could see out. "The men are heaping their Christmas trees up, right there on the corner."

"Yes, Mamma told me all the families on our street and the Assensestraat will be celebrating New Year's Eve together with a huge bonfire."

As Mamma started making the traditional New Year's Eve cuisine: *oliebollen*, a bit like deep-fried donuts with raisins, and *appelflappen*, deep-fried apple slices dipped in batter, the house filled with delicious smells.

Twilight drew in while we finished our evening meal. The celebrations were about to begin. "Sieglinde, are you ready? Let's go to Dickie's house. We've been invited to a game of *sjoelbak* [a table game with wooden disks]."

"Sure. Let me just run upstairs and grab the socks that we're knitting so Mevrouw Heesterman can show us how to do the heels."

I followed her up to our room. "What? Knitting on New Year's Eve? You're crazy!"

"It has to be done, so why not? You could do with learning some responsibility!"

"Ha!" I snapped my fingers in her face. "That's what I think of that!"

Siegie giggled, and we raced down the stairs again. "You would!"

As we left the house, we passed our parents and their group of friends who were chatting while sitting by the *kachel* with an *olliebol* in one hand and a drink in the other.

Braving the wind to walk next door, we found the Heesterman door ajar. It was open season tonight, so we just went in, climbed the stairs, and enjoyed a lively game of *sjoelbak* with the eldest six Heesterman children. I won, of course.

When it was nearly midnight, Sieglinde suggested that we go outside.

We joined what seemed like all the people in the neighborhood, most of whom left their front doors open so we could hear the chiming of their clocks. "1, 2, 3, 4, 5, 6, 7, 8, 9, 10, 11, 12. *Gelukkig Nieuwjaar!*" we all shouted together, just as the fathers lit the trees.

The hot, bright flames shot high into the air, and the crackling of the trees was deafening. I'd been standing with my family and now backed away anxiously. "Mamma, my face feels so hot. I don't think I like this."

I closed my eyes tightly. The fire reminded me of the burning Kleykamp building and the chatter of excited neighbors of the screams of the people trapped inside it. I was pretty sure I'd seen der Stiefel in the smoke, and he was watching me.

My mother put her arm around my shoulders. "Spilletje, don't be afraid. You're safe here next to me and far from the fire."

I threw my shoulders back. "I'm not scared. Why would I be?"

I didn't sleep much that night.

159

~

"Hey, Siegie, it's such a beautiful day. Let's go to the beach."

"Okay, but first let me finish this chapter." Sieglinde didn't even lift her eyes from the page.

I put my hand over the part she was looking at. "You're always reading. Can't you put the book aside until we get back?"

Sieglinde pursed her lips. "It'd be good for you if you were to read a little more!"

"I read enough—at least my teachers think so. But today, even though it's cold, it's sunny. Let's leave the reading for when it's raining."

"Oh, all right then. Let's go." Sieglinde uncurled from her favorite chair.

As we skipped through the sand dunes, we saw what had become a very familiar sight: Queen Wilhelmina with her lady-in-waiting. No security people accompanied them. Both women were riding shiny black bicycles with metal wheels and rubber tires. The queen was living near to us at her home, De Ruijgenhoek, while the war damage to the royal palace was being repaired.

We waved cheerily at the small, plump grandmother, who was wearing a black coat and a foxtail fur around her neck. Queen Wilhelmina had neither a crown nor a royal robe, but her upright posture betrayed the training that came with her noble birth. She regally waved hello, smiled graciously, and bicycled on.

After she passed us, I turned to my sister. "Wouldn't it be nice if she were to stop for a chat? I'd love to hear about all the great things she did in the resistance during the war."

"Yeah, and I'd love to hear about what it was like to be a queen when you're only ten. Do you think she got to boss people around?"

"Well, we all know she didn't actually reign until she was 18." I raised my chin. "I expect that I could do it when I get to be that old."

"As if you'd ever get the chance!"

"No, and I'll be too busy being a doctor. But I sure would like to follow in her footsteps and be a billionaire. Did you know that she's only the second lady in the whole world who became a billionaire?"

Sieglinde frowned. "Meta," she worried. "You do know that girls don't become doctors, don't you?"

"Ha. Just watch me. I will."

After spending some time at the beach, we returned home and told our parents about who we'd seen. Pappa snorted. "The queen is just a person. She's no better than you or me. She goes to the toilet just as we do."

I nudged Sieglinde with a grin, noticing that we'd interrupted Pappa in his frequent pastime, drawing mustaches on the photos of "important" people that he found in *De Leugenaar*. The queen's appearance was quite altered and not for the better.

17

FIGURING IT OUT

It was my favorite time of year. On the way home from the Catholic church down the Harstenhoekweg, I dawdled to admire any flower I caught sight of. "Oooh, look at that. Sooo beautiful!" I spoke aloud as I noticed hyacinths blooming outside Mevrouw Van den Berg's living room window. I bent over the front wall, blew all the air out of my lungs, and then inhaled as deeply and slowly as I could.

Gazing at the waxy pink, purple, and white cone-shaped blossoms, I mused, "Wouldn't it be great to have one of these of my very own? Then I could smell it all the time. And Mevrouw Van den Berg has way more hyacinths than she needs. She probably wouldn't miss just one." Her front gate was ajar, and I couldn't resist.

I grasped the thick stem of the largest blue-purple hyacinth and yanked. Oh no! The bulb with roots came out along with the flower. I glanced at the house.

The lady of the house's furious eyes met mine through the window. Her face was the color of a tomato, but her lips were white.

I turned and ran like the wind. I peeked over my shoulder, only to see and hear Mevrouw Van den Berg, her face purple by now, bellowing like a charging bull. And she was gaining on me! My legs pumped even more furiously; I thought I'd be caught for sure.

Gasping for breath, I screeched around the corner onto the Leeuwardensestraat.

Mevrouw Streefland, who lived across the street from us, was standing at her front door when she spotted me with my wild eyes executing my panicked dash for safety. "Quick, come in." She further opened her front door and motioned me inside.

I slipped in through the doorway, and together we went into the front room. When Mevrouw Van den Berg reached the corner, it probably looked to her as if I'd just disappeared into thin air.

Hiding behind the net curtain, Mevrouw Streefland and I watched Mevrouw Van den Berg stop to catch her breath. Unfortunately, everybody knew where I lived, her included. When she pounded on the door of my house, Mamma opened the window and leaned out to see who was making such a racket. Mevrouw Van den Berg shook her fist as she shouted up, "Is that scoundrel here? She stole my hyacinth!"

It took no time at all for Mamma to realize who she was talking about. "*Nee,* Meta isn't here. But I promise you, when she gets home, I'll ask her what happened. If she did as you say, she'll have to apologize to you. You can be sure of that."

Mevrouw Van den Berg snorted and indignantly folded her arms across her bony chest. "What about my hyacinth? She took it."

"If that's true, she'll bring it back when she comes to say sorry."

"You'd better beat her, as well. She needs some sorting out, that girl of yours!"

Mamma shook her head and closed the window, a little more forcefully than was necessary. I knew she'd be murmuring, "I'll raise my children as I think best, thank you very much." She always did.

I lingered in the neighbor's house until Mevrouw Streefland told me I had to go and face the music. I wasn't looking forward to this part.

As I dragged my feet home, clutching my guilty evidence, I pondered how this caper had misfired. Normally, I thought about whether my crimes were worth the punishment, but, this time, I'd definitely been too impulsive. Maybe because I wanted the flower so much.

As expected, Mamma was lying in wait at the door. "So, what happened with the hyacinth, Meta?"

With the fragrant evidence in my hand, I couldn't lie.

Mamma listened with a solemn face, but she didn't beat me. She did something worse. "I'm glad you told me. You'll have to give the flower back and tell Mevrouw Van den Berg you're sorry. I'll come with you. And you'll have to promise her that you'll never steal again."

"I always have to apologize! I hate it! I hate it!" I stamped my foot.

"Well, if you don't do anything wrong, you won't have to apologize. Now, come on. Let's get this over with right now."

Mamma marched me to Mevrouw Van den Berg's home, and I mumbled an apology to that horrid lady while trying not to look at the tuft of hair sticking right out of the mole on her cheek. All the while my mother was breathing down my neck.

Stealing flowers wasn't worth the punishment. I'd just have to get them another way.

Leaning on our balcony railing, I breathed in the aroma of evening and admired the Golden Rain and Lilac trees growing in the garden behind our home. I wished I had a patch of ground where I could plant a garden. That way I could get flowers of my very own without even having to steal them.

Plans needed to be formulated. We lived in an upstairs home, so how could my imaginary garden become reality? I fleetingly considered having a secret patch in the sand dunes, but quickly realized that the native vegetation would overgrow anything I planted. The Scheveningse *bosjes* were also bad option. They were too busy with people; tender new plants would be trampled.

Then I identified the solution to my problem. Every balcony, ours included, had a storage shed with a bin for coal, hooks for brooms, and a shelf for cleaning materials. At about 50 by 100 centimeters, the leaded roof of the shed would be an excellent place to plant a small garden.

The second hurdle was gaining access to the roof, which was two meters off the ground. Clambering onto the kitchen counter, I reached my leg around the balcony door over the first broken tile to precariously balance on the outside kitchen window ledge. From there, if I stretched, I could just reach the top of the shed. I looked the roof over carefully. It was, indeed, a perfect place for growing plants.

"Mamma, Pappa, come out here. I found a great place for my garden. What do you think?" I pointed to the top of the shed.

"Actually, that's not bad, Spilletje." Even though I was nearly a teenager, Pappa messed up my hair.

"Well, may I do it? Plant a garden there?"

"Go ahead. Just be careful not to get any dirt on the neighbor's shed." That shed backed onto ours.

The third hurdle to surmount was finding rich dirt for growing plants. Borrowing a couple of my mother's grocery bags and a large serving spoon, I went to the Scheveningse *bosjes*, where I figured the lush growth attested to the quality of the soil. I scooped and collected, scooped and collected until both sacks were full. Then, I half-carried and half-dragged the bags of wet dirt the whole kilometer back to my house, sometimes stopping to take a little breather. I lugged them up the stairs and into the kitchen.

"Pappa," I panted. "I don't think I can get this soil onto the roof. *Alsjeblieft*, I need your help."

My father got his ladder out of the shed, climbed up, and emptied the bags on the roof. "You need more dirt, Meta. It isn't quite deep enough. Aim for at least ten centimeters."

So, I went back for more dirt and again hauled myself home dragging the precious but very heavy soil.

Pappa again assisted me. "I think this should be enough, Spilletje."

I climbed the ladder, spread it out nicely, and led my father and Sieglinde outside to admire my work. Pappa climbed up, looked it over critically, and approved. "Come, look at what she's done, Guusje. We should be proud of her determination and hard work."

Mamma looked and then backed away. "I'll take your word for it, Cor. No way am I climbing on that thing."

Sieglinde agreed, "Neither am I!"

Just then, we heard a voice from the garden below us. "You'd better not spill any of that dirt on my clean laundry!"

Mamma leaned over to look down at our difficult neighbor. "Oh, mind your own business!" Turning to Pappa, she exclaimed, "Honestly, you'd think that woman had nothing better to do than eavesdrop."

"I heard that!"

"Then, you know I'm right!"

Pappa winked at me.

Next, I needed seeds. That problem was easily solved. I asked Pappa, he gave me money, and I bought seeds for watercress, radishes, and marigolds. The frequent rain watered my little garden, the infrequent sunshine warmed it, and the watercress and radishes grew beautifully. The marigolds didn't grow at all.

"Pappa, what's wrong with the marigolds?"

"That dirt is too shallow for flowers. Just stick with growing watercress and radishes."

"But I want flowers. Just wait. I'll figure it out."

My father chuckled and pulled my hair. "I'm sure you'll find a solution. You always do. Just like me—determined."

I thought hard about how I could overcome the last hurdle to realizing my dream of growing flowers. I reasoned, the soil in clay flowerpots can be deep. The pots can't go on top of the shed, but maybe there's another place for them.

I looked at the balcony floor. The balcony walls were made of red bricks; it was too dark for flowers to grow there.

"Perhaps I could balance these pots on the railing. The sun could reach them there." I was nearly dancing in my eagerness as I carefully steadied a rather precariously placed pot.

Mamma, who'd seen me through the kitchen window, came out and looked at me in disbelief. "What are you doing? Are you kidding? Have you thought about what would happen if those heavy pots full of dirt fall on Sientje's laundry or, heaven forbid, her head?"

"They'd better not!" Evidently, Mevrouw den Dulk had her kitchen door open.

"Oh, that woman! Deaf when it matters, but nosy when it doesn't!"

I left Mamma and Sientje to their sparring. I had work to do. Which flowers would grow tall enough to reach their heads over the shadow of the balcony? Sunflowers. I planted sunflower seeds in three pots and placed them on the kitchen floor where it was sunny in the afternoons. Once they were tall enough to catch the sun, I moved them outside to the floor of the balcony. The plants grew and grew until they made huge, beautiful, radiant yellow sunflowers. I felt proud, like I'd performed a miracle.

Evidently, the seagulls agreed with me. They also thought growing sunflowers on a balcony was a good idea. They loved the seeds. I enjoyed watching them fly and listening to their harsh cries. My mother did not enjoy it when they pooped on her clean laundry. At least she acted mad. I suspected it might be pretense, because Mamma left cheese rinds out for the seagulls to eat, even after I'd collected the sunflower seeds for next summer's garden. Maybe she was hoping they'd bomb Sientje's laundry instead.

"Hey Guys, let's play soccer! The kids who live on my street are on my team, and the ones on the Zutphensestraat are on yours, Daan." My soccer ball was tucked under my arm.

"That's not fair! The kids on your street are faster, and they catch better!"

"Yeah, but you've got some good goalies. Sjors, come here, you're on my team."

"Why do we have to have him?" Luuk whined. "He's doesn't live on our street, and he's too small to be good at anything!"

"He's on my team. He always will be. Get over it." I put my arm around Sjors's little shoulders and gave him an encouraging smile as I fibbed. "He's really good at running fast."

By then, there was no doubt that Sjors with his sunny smile was my favorite not-brother little kid.

The game began, and I kicked the ball towards Sjors.

Unfortunately, he was waving at his parents, who were standing on their balcony watching the game. The ball rolled right past him. "Sjors, get the ball!" I called. "Kick it to me!"

The rest of my team groaned. "Back off, Guys! Give him a chance," I shouted.

One day, Sjors didn't join us for the neighborhood games. This lasted for several days. When I looked up at his home, the curtains were closed.

That night over dinner I asked my mother if she knew where he was.

"He's sick. His parents sent him away for a few weeks. Hopefully, that way his health will improve."

This news worried me. After all, when I was unwell, my parents didn't send me away, and it never took me weeks to get better. Well, not since I'd been to Hemalie, anyway. On the other hand, Corrie was taking an extremely long time to recover from TB; despite having received treatment, she was still exceedingly weak.

"Does he have TB, Mamma?"

"No, I don't know what's wrong. Don't worry. I'm sure he'll be fine."

Playing neighborhood ball games without Sjors was not the same. I missed seeing his infectious grin and his skinny legs pumping as fast as they could when he ran.

"Mamma, Sjors hasn't been outside for weeks now. I'm worried. Is he in the hospital? Why isn't he better yet?" I bit my lip anxiously.

Mamma pulled me down onto her lap. I was now a teenager, but I still liked sitting there. Stroking my hair back, she gently told me, "Schatje, Sjors won't be coming back to play. He was very, very sick with leukemia, and just yesterday, he breathed his last. His funeral will be in a couple of days."

My stomach plummeted to the ground, and I burst into tears. "He's dead? How can that be? He was just a little kid!" I buried my head in my mother's chest and sobbed until my head ached.

Once I'd quieted down, Mamma gently dried my tears with her fingers. "Why don't you go lie down for a bit? I'll bring you some nice, warm milk with an anise cube in it."

I threw myself down on the divan and stared at the wall, totally devastated; I didn't drink the milk.

On the day of Sjors's funeral, Sieglinde put on her coat and turned to me where I was sitting in a chair staring into the air. "Get ready, Meta. Aren't you coming?"

I shook my head and mumbled, "*Nee*. I can't. I can't do that. There's nothing in me; I can't go... You go."

After the family left, I lay on the divan with tears streaming down my cheeks. Ever since I heard he was sick, I'd prayed daily. Where was God when children die? Where was He when bombs killed both of Vera's baby boys? Where was he when der Stiefel haunted my recurrent nightmares? There were no answers.

Eventually, I rejoined my friends playing ball, but nothing was ever the same again. Always, in the back of my mind, I saw the shadow of a sweet boy running after the ball while his parents looked on lovingly.

~

"I'll wash. You dry and put away." I relished sticking my hands in warm, soapy water while standing in the rather chilly kitchen with its ever-open door.

"Okay, I'm used to that routine." Sieglinde shrugged as she picked up the tea towel and began to sing in her lovely alto voice. I joined in.

Pappa wandered into the kitchen to make a pot of coffee. He ground the coffee beans, holding the mill between his knees while he waited for the water to boil and joined his booming bass voice to ours. Then, Pappa fitted the enameled filter to the top of the coffee pot and put the freshly ground coffee in the filter. Finally, he slowly poured the hot water through the filter, waiting until it had gone through the grounds before he added more.

Corrie and Mamma, attracted by the delicious aroma, came in and sat at the little table. They harmonized with us, being as they were in a choir and had beautiful soprano voices. Ronald piped away as best he could. My voice, well, even though I could not carry a tune, it was enthusiastic.

The dishes were clean, dry, and put away in no time at all, and everyone moved into the living room. After Mamma put Ronald to bed, we ladies took out our knitting needles and wool. Pappa boiled some milk, whipped it into a froth, and brought everyone a cup of very strong coffee sweetened with lots of milk and a spoonful of special unrefined sugar. Our knitting needles clicked busily as together we listened to a radio show.

The previous day, Sieglinde and I had gone to the shop in the Gentsestraat that sold all kinds and colors of yarn. We'd chosen colors that we thought would coordinate to form a great outfit for Ronald.

"This is lovely yarn. Well-chosen, Girls! Corrie and I have the same hand of knitting, so we'll knit his top out of the sunshine-yellow yarn."

I picked up the warm-brown yarn. "I'll do his shorts in this color."

"That leaves the socks for me. Here's some thinner cotton for those."

"Great plan! You're very good at socks, Siegie. Maybe because of all the time you spend at the Heestermans'." I poked my sister in her side.

After only three evenings of knitting, Ronald's outfit was finished. My little brother wore the clothing that we'd made to church that week.

Looking around, I boasted, "He's the best dressed boy here."

Sieglinde smiled. "He's certainly the most loved."

"And the most challenging!"

I nodded. Explanations were not needed.

It happened on the very next Saturday.

Mamma came into the living room. "Sieglinde and Meta, *alsjeblieft* call Ronald for lunch. I think he's playing with Harry."

"Oh, Mamma," I sighed. My least favorite chore was to find Ronald at mealtimes.

I walked across the street to the Streefland house, where Harry, Ronald's little friend, lived. "Mevrouw Streefland, is Ronald here?"

"*Nee,* the boys left an hour ago. I thought they were headed to your house." Her forehead puckered.

"*Nee,* there aren't there. I haven't seen them all morning. Maybe they went to Tommy's."

"I don't know. They didn't say anything about that to me. Would you go check?"

I walked over and asked Tommy's mother, but they weren't there either. Scanning the street, I could see no sign of the two little boys and began to get annoyed. It often took an hour or more to find my little brother. Time to call in reinforcements.

I stopped at home to pick up my sweater and my sister. "Sieglinde, *alsjeblieft* help me find Ronald. The little monkey is gone again. You take the Zutphensestraat, and I'll take the Hasseltsestraat. Let's meet on the Harstenhoekweg."

After searching for 30 minutes, we met, but neither of us had found Ronald and his friend. "Where could those little scamps be?" I asked, worry beginning to sound in my voice.

"Well, it's a decently warm day. Let's go search the beach."

The blood drained from my face. "I hope he didn't..."

Sieglinde's eyes met mine. "Let's go!"

As we rushed over the Zwarte Pad towards the sea, Sieglinde formulated a plan of action. "Look out at the sand dunes in case they're playing there. You look right; I'll look left."

I sped up while looking right, frightened Ronald might have gone into the water without permission—like I used to.

There was no sign of the boys, neither in the dunes nor on the beach.

"Could they be playing in or around the German bunker?"

We checked. No. I looked at Sieglinde, and my panic was magnified by what I read on her face. "We'd better get some help in searching."

We hastened down the path, and I grasped desperately at a sliver of hope. "Maybe they're at home already."

They weren't. We told Mamma where we'd already searched. "Did you go to all of their friends' houses to see if they're there?"

"Ja, more than once. They're nowhere!" My voice grew frantic. "We need help!" I wailed.

It was lunchtime, but nobody could eat. Instead, my parents went over the Streeflands to request their assistance in getting the local community involved in the search. Mevrouw Streefland called the police, who also began searching for the lost boys. The fathers went out searching the wider neighborhood.

I fretted, "What if Ronald and Harry went to the beach and drowned? What if they wandered too far and are lost?"

"Let's go look again." Sieglinde and I called Ronald's name until our throats hurt, scanning the fearsome swells for little blond heads. There was no sign of Ronald or Harry.

We returned home to find Mamma white-faced while she paced the room and twisted her apron between her fingers. We didn't need to tell her that we'd found no one.

It was nearly dinner time when our doorbell rang. I flew to open the door, revealing two policemen, each firmly holding a little boy by the hand. Meneer Streefland and my father were right behind them.

Mamma ran down the stairs and held her arms out for Ronald. As she stroked his head, arms, and back, she sobbed, "Where did you find them?"

"Ma'am, they were found at a railway station in Rotterdam." The taller policeman folded his arms across his chest.

Pappa added, "I suspect that the boys were playing at the railway station here in Scheveningen, boarded a train when it stopped, and got off in Rotterdam. It's good they didn't leave that station."

Ronald tugged on Mamma's skirt. "I told a nice man our address, just like you taught me. He phoned someone, and these policemen came and took us on a train again. We did everything right!"

I exchanged a look with Sieglinde. We'd not been taught to give our address, but to say, "I don't know." Life had changed—for the better.

Meneer Streefland frowned. "The boys need to be spanked, so

they never do this again." He took Harry's hand and pulled him home.

My parents thanked the policemen and the neighbors who'd been searching, and Pappa carried Ronald up the stairs. Placing him on Mamma's lap, they praised him for knowing his address, but explained that we'd all been very frightened.

"The rules are going to change. Until you're ten years old, you won't be allowed to play outside our street. And if you go into a friend's house, you need to tell us first."

He did, but that night, and during many nights throughout my life, I had nightmares about losing children.

~

"Sieglinde, it seems like it's going to be really hot out today. 28 degrees! (This is about 82°F.) A beautiful afternoon to go to the beach and sunbathe."

"Oh yes! If it's not too windy, it'll even be warm enough to go swimming. If only we had bathing suits!"

Mamma overheard our conversation. "I have a couple of dresses you could use to make bathing suits. They're worn, but I think the fabric is still usable." She went upstairs, brought them down, and held them out for our inspection.

"Oh, they're so pretty," I clapped my hands.

One dress had a pattern of blue flowers on a white background, and the other had yellow flowers on a green background. "I think they look just right."

"Meta, you take the blue and white one. I know that's your favorite. I'll have the other."

We set to work immediately, cutting the dresses into the right shapes to sew into bathing suits.

I decided to sew my suit with a running stitch, in and out, so I could finish it quickly. The side seams completed, I glanced over at my sister. Sieglinde hunched over her fabric, carefully sewing with teeny tiny stitches, her tongue sticking out of the corner of her mouth.

"Sieglinde, what are you doing? Your stitches are microscopic! The sun will set, and you'll still be working!"

Sieglinde smiled placidly. "I want my suit to be perfect. Your seams won't last, because you're not doing it right. If it's worth doing, it's worth doing well."

I rolled my eyes. "Bla-di-bla bla bla. They'll work well enough, and at least I'll be able to swim while it's still day."

Sieglinde ignored me and persisted in her painstakingly slow stitching.

I glanced at the clock. In the summer, it stayed light until 10 pm, but got cold after 8 pm. I continued to sew with huge stitches, and in no time at all my bathing suit was ready.

"Sieglinde, I'm done. Hurry up!"

"*Rustig aan.* I'm going as fast as I can while still doing a nice job." Sieglinde held her suit up to admire the beautiful stitching.

The minutes ticked at a snail's pace as I tapped my toe and sighed repeatedly.

"Oh, just go already!" Sieglinde exploded. "If you stay at the bottom of the stairs at the Zwarte Pad, I'll find you easily."

I quickly donned my new bathing suit, put my dress over it, and ran to the beach enjoying the hot sun and the wind in my hair.

I was just coming out of the water, when I saw Sieglinde at the top of the long staircase leading to the beach. Her smile lit up her face as she gracefully hurried down the steps, flung down her towel, and took off her dress, revealing her exquisitely sewn bathing suit.

Finally, we were both in the sea, running from and jumping over the waves. I laughed as a wave pushed me over with its force.

"Meta, help!" Sieglinde's voice was panicked.

Scrambling to my feet and shaking the water out of my hair, I looked over to see that my sister was submerged in water up to her neck. Had she stepped into a pit? Or had a jellyfish stung her?

"Hold on. I'm coming. I'm coming as fast as I can."

I reached my sister as quickly as possible and found her, not flailing in the waves, but red-faced with embarrassment. "Meta, *alsjeblieft* get my dress. I don't know what happened to my bathing suit. It fell off."

"So, you're not drowning or stung? Just standing with your knees bent because you're naked?" After I stopped laughing, I waded to the beach, grabbed Sieglinde's dress, and brought it to her.

Once she was decent, we walked home, me wearing my bathing suit with my dress over it, and Sieglinde wearing a very wet dress with her towel wrapped around her waist. The waves had carried the bathing suit scraps away.

Giggling as we mounted the stairs, we discussed what could have happened. It seemed that the old material Mamma had provided was too weak. My big stitches didn't stress the dress fabric as much as Sieglinde's tiny ones did. Very old fabric requires big stitches.

18

HAUNTED BY THE PAST

My mother looked up from *De Leugenaar*. "Cor, it says here that the government will finally allow us to visit Germany. I miss my family so much. It's nearly been ten years! We just have to go."

"We really don't have the money. But I guess we could if I work some more overtime. That should make it possible to save enough to go when the summer holidays start."

"Yes, and I'll see if I can get more hours at the salon." Now that we were older, Mamma had a parttime job at a beauty parlor.

After a flurry of letters back and forth to and from Germany, the visit was arranged, and the preparations began in earnest.

"Siegie, what should we wear to meet the family? Wouldn't it be fun to surprise them with how fashionable we are, now we're so much older?" I did a little twirl, belying my grown-up status.

"Ooo *ja*. Have you seen those pictures of Christian Dior's "New Look" in France? Wouldn't it be great to have an outfit like that?" Sieglinde's eyes shone, and she joined me in a little dance around the room.

Mid-twirl, I caught sight of Pappa, who looked so tired after his extra shift. "It would, but I think we can fix up something we have to look almost as nice."

Sieglinde followed my eyes. "Of course, we can. We have enough."

Evidently, our parents did not agree. Only a few days later, Mamma pulled three parcels out from behind her back with a flourish and a bow. "Here you are, drei Grazien!"

"What? What's in those?"

"Open them and see!" Mamma smiled at Pappa.

I tore the wrapping off my package while Sieglinde carefully unpicked the tape. Corrie, who seemed to have recovered from TB, but was still weak, sedately carried hers to the divan and stroked the fabric. There was a pleated, red plaid skirt in my parcel. I turned to Sieglinde. Hers was green. Squealing, we held them in front of us and admired ourselves in the mirror.

I flung myself into Pappa's arms, and Sieglinde hugged Mamma. "Oh, thank you!"

That afternoon, Tante Agnes came over and gave each of us a glass necklace: mine was red, and Sieglinde's was green. Then, Mamma presented us with soft white wool so that we could knit ourselves lovely sweaters to go with our gorgeous skirts.

Once, I'd finished, I held my sweater in front of me and swayed in front of the mirror. "I look just incredible, if I say so myself!"

Sieglinde did the same. "So do I. We're two beautiful ladies, no doubt about it."

Pappa joined in and struck a dapper pose in his white flannel trousers and a white cap, which sat jauntily on his dark hair. "And I am a very handsome man!" he squeaked, imitating our voices.

After dressing Ronald in the sailor suit that we knitted as a joint project, Mamma and Corrie pranced around the living room in their sophisticated store-bought New Look dresses.

I giggled. "Our relatives will be so impressed!"

"Cor, listen to this." Mamma was reading a letter that had just arrived from her sister. "Ciska writes that the food they're rationed isn't even enough to feed their family."

Pappa looked over her shoulder, but reading German wasn't easy for him. "Will they be able to cope with the two weeks we're there? Does she say anything about that?"

"Well, she says they aren't going hungry, because they have livestock for milk, eggs, and meat, and Wilhelm contributes dry goods from his shop. On the other hand, they're short of coffee, tea and tobacco. They still can't buy those. Is it legal for us to bring those things into Germany?"

"*Ja*, but the allowance per person is small. We have six people in our family, so could probably take quite a bit, but you know we don't have much of those luxuries ourselves."

"We could save up. Let's just use less of what we buy and then bring whatever we accumulate to my relatives."

Pappa agreed, although he didn't enjoy going without his usual allocation of tobacco.

"Guusje, we may have another problem. We can't expect your relatives to provide for our big family. How can we take along enough money to cover our time there? We aren't allowed to take as much money as I'm sure will be necessary, and there's no doubt we'll be searched on the train."

Chills went up and down my spine as I listened to my parents from where I was seated in the tiny room. I didn't want to be anywhere near to German soldiers, and I certainly did not want them searching my parents. Perhaps going to Germany was a bad idea.

My parents continued discussing their predicament, and I eavesdropped with increasing dread. "Guusje, we have to take care. I've heard the border agents are very thorough and extremely hostile. What's more, if you're caught trying to bring in something illegal, the punishment is harsh." Pappa was pacing the floor with his hands behind his back.

Mamma frowned, then raised her finger in the air. "I know! I have an idea! We could use one of the children to smuggle money."

"No way!" Pappa barked. "Out of the question. I'm not going to expose my child to a *vuile rot Mof*." He crossed his arms over his chest.

"Wait, hear me out! They'd be okay, Cor. No one suspects children; they're so innocent."

Pappa held up his hand, but Mamma pressed on. "I'll sew each girl a headband matching their outfit. I'll put money in Meta's, because she's the youngest and so small for her age. Nobody will look inside a little girl's headband."

The blood drained from my face, and I felt a little dizzy, but I kept still, listening to what I was not meant to hear.

Pappa sighed. "I guess you're right, Guusje. If we have to, we have to. We'll do it, but I don't like it at all. Just in case the worst happens, I'll keep her by my side, so I can take the blame."

The very next day, Mamma sewed the headbands, putting money into the red one and then closing it up. Sieglinde immediately tried on her new headband but I was very reluctant and had to fake a smile. The problem was I knew what Mamma had done, and I was not okay with the plan.

I fully understood that I would be doing something illegal. Lying in my bed the night before we traveled, I tossed and turned, unable to sleep. I couldn't talk with my parents, because I was not supposed to have listened in; they didn't know I knew what was in my headband. I couldn't even discuss the problem with my sister.

All too soon, morning came. Suitcases and train tickets in hand, my family began the day-long journey to Germany. Our suitcases were heavy with coffee, tea and tobacco, and fear dragged at my every step.

As we marched, shoulders back and chins high, to the streetcar and disembarked near the train station, I felt what breakfast I'd been able to choke down swirling around in my stomach. After walking the rest of the way to the station, we climbed up the stairs into one of the passenger cars of the steam train, and I sank into a chair with my eyes closed.

"Meta, wake up!" Sieglinde shook my arm. "Look how fast everything outside is flying by!"

Pressing our noses to the window, we watched the bushes, trees, houses, and farms apparently moving towards the back of the train and chuckled at Ronald, who exclaimed over everything he saw. But the closer we got to Germany, the more ill I felt. My heart was racing, butterflies were fluttering around inside my stomach, and my hands were sweaty.

The train slowed down and stopped, and so did my heart. All the doors opened, and I knew that the border patrol soldiers, both Dutch and German, were climbing on board. Sweat broke out on my forehead as, through the window, I caught sight of der Stiefel. He was looking straight at me.

Panicking, I jumped out of my seat and ran to the tiny, smelly bathroom to hide. There I stood, trembling, feeling like I might throw up at any minute. I listened to the officious German voices just outside the door.

Finally, hearing nothing more, I decided it was safe to emerge from my rather unpleasant hiding place.

"Hey, I haven't seen you before. Did you just board the train?" a German soldier boomed.

I nearly jumped out of my skin. "No, I had to go to the bathroom," I squeaked in German. I hoped he thought the trembling voice was normal for me.

He sniffed and crossed his arms. "Don't you know you aren't allowed to use the toilet while the train is standing still?"

Looking at my feet and twisting my skirt between my fingers, as I'd seen Mamma do, I mumbled, "I had to go very badly." In this case, putting on a brave face would not have brought about the desired results.

Mamma came over and placed a protective arm around my shoulders. Just then, a shrill whistle sounded. The train was going to leave the station, and all soldiers had to disembark. Just in the nick of time!

My mother led me to my seat, where I sank down and closed my eyes, waiting for my heart to return to its normal rhythm.

"You know, don't you?" Mamma whispered.

I didn't bother to open my eyes, but nodded silently.

As soon as the train pulled into Oberhausen and stopped, my family and I tumbled off. I fearfully scanned the platform for soldiers while pretending to straighten my hair. There were none.

Dragging our suitcases with us, we mounted another train which took us to Bottrop, where most of our relatives lived.

When that train arrived at our destination, we saw my uncles waiting on the platform.

Mamma flew down the steps to greet them. "Wilhelm, Paul, how wonderful to see you!" She threw her arms first around Wilhelm's and then Paul's neck.

Pappa, who'd seen to the children and the suitcases, walked over and shook hands with them gravely. "It's been a long time, Wilhelm. Paul."

After greeting him, my uncles turned to the tired children. Wilhelm messed up my hair as if I were still four. "Here, Meta, give me your suitcase. You look so tired." I handed over the luggage and carefully straightened my headband.

With my mother chattering happily, we all walked to the new home Tante Ciska had been living in since her old house had been bombed flat. My mouth hung open as I gazed wide-eyed around me. There was war damage everywhere, even worse than what I'd seen back home. Until then, I'd not thought about what losing a war meant to the inhabitants of the country that lost.

Wearily, I dragged myself up the stairs to my aunt's new apartment. It was located in a narrow, tall building that, oddly, was set all by itself in the middle of a large meadow. The door was thrown open, and the rest of our German relatives greeted us. "Welcome! It's so good to see you, Gusti. And Cor. So, these are the children. How they've grown!"

"Here's the one you've never met." Mamma proudly pulled Ronald out from behind her skirt, so he also could have his cheeks pinched by the lady aunts.

"You all look so beautiful. Is that the famous new fashion?" Ciska solemnly touched Mamma's dress and then stroked the sleeve of my sweater.

"Thank you. Yes, it is. Of course, Meta and Sieglinde knitted their own sweaters. They're good knitters." My mother smiled proudly as Sieglinde and I each executed a twirl in response to the clamor of requests.

Pappa and the uncles, who'd lugged the suitcases up the stairs, now edged into the crowded room and dropped them to the floor, breathing a sigh of relief as they flexed their fingers. Gracefully kneeling down, Mamma opened one after the other of the cases. "Look, we brought you gifts!"

"Oh my! How did you get ahold of so much? And how did you get it all through the border?" Everyone crowded around to receive the coffee, tea, and tobacco that we'd dragged around for over a day.

With the relatives and Mamma distracted, I pulled off my headband and quietly passed it to Pappa. He raised his eyebrows, silently asking me what Mamma had already guessed. I nodded, and he slipped it into his pocket. I didn't care if I ever saw it again.

Soon, the conversation turned to the miserable, but looming, elephant in the room, and the adults began to discuss the war that had ravaged everyone's life.

"We don't have much to give you all, because we can't buy much since the war. But we're so happy you're here. It distracts us from our grief, as if that were possible." Ciska dashed a tear from her cheek.

Wilhelm hung his head and clasped his hands on his lap. "Since he was killed in action, I don't think anything has taken my mind off missing Emil." He reached into his pocket. "But here, Meta, I saved this ring that Emil made just for you. You still remind me so much of his sister, my little girl. If she had lived to be your age, I think she would have looked like you."

I solemnly received the ring and slipped it onto my finger. I knew that, now, my aunt and uncle only had their younger son, Bruno, left. "Thank you, Onkel Wilhelm," I murmured.

Cousin Bruno joined in. "The war was hell. I don't know how I survived it—probably only because I was in the hospital for so long."

I tried not to stare at the broken man, who was missing an eye, an arm and a leg.

Pappa agreed. "It's a wonder so many of us did survive. We in Den Haag starved, but I understand the German army also had no food."

"Oom [Uncle in Dutch] Cor, I have to admit that it's a very good thing we lost the war. If nothing else, I'm so glad about that. You understand we Germans had no choice but to fight. We wanted to win back respect, but it was such folly to make the war about Aryan people. There, we went totally wrong. And trying to exterminate all the Jews; that was totally reprehensible." Bruno spoke careful Dutch as his shoulders slumped. He covered his remaining eye with his remaining hand.

Onkel Paul added in a hushed voice, "I feel so ashamed of what happened. Some Germans have said '*Wir haben es nicht gewußt* [we didn't know],' but that's just not true. You know we did know. We discussed it with you even before the war. We just felt utterly helpless to do anything about it."

"We were scared stiff. If we'd protested the Holocaust, we would've been killed. Many, many people were. It didn't seem it would have done any good to let anyone know we didn't agree. So, we kept our heads down." Onkel Wilhelm didn't even try to hide the tears running down his cheeks. "I hate that we were cowards," he sighed.

After Mamma translated, Pappa shook his head and muttered, "Dirty politics!"

Bruno nodded. "The government and army did despicable things, no doubt about it. And we didn't protest. That makes me feel guilty to even be German."

Wilhelm put his arm around his son's shoulders. "We were focused on surviving, not on being heroes. And you've suffered enough."

My mother heaved a sigh. "Well, the war is over, and nobody can change the past. Tears don't change a thing. So, we move on." She winked at her younger brother. "Paul, how's married life?"

"Well, you've met my new wife, Renate. Obviously, it's great."

Mamma turned to her new sister-in-law with a twinkle in her eye. "I just hope you have enough jam in the house!"

Renate looked confused and glanced at Paul. "Whatever do you mean, Gusti?"

Mamma and her sisters burst out laughing while Paul blushed. The family never let him forget that, as a small boy, he really liked jam. One time, he stuck his hand in the jam barrel and put the jam in his pocket, just in case he wanted some later. Accompanied by much laughter, Mamma told his new wife the story of Paul's childhood escapade.

Finally, it was time for bed. I was falling over from tiredness. Sieglinde and I were shown to a pretty room with a white curtain-trimmed window that overlooked the meadow. I fell asleep gazing at the stars.

In the morning, I turned over and there, in the meadow, I saw a horse, grazing on the green grass. I kept my eye on him as I got dressed. Every time I looked out, he was eating. After breakfast I looked out again, and he was still grazing peacefully. It seemed the horse was totally unaware that he was standing in the shadow of an apartment building. I was very glad no one suggested I ride him!

After a week, my family and I went to stay with Tante Paula and Onkel Karl in their home in town. We approached the front door, and to my horror geese came swarming towards us honking loudly.

Being a city girl, I screamed and hid behind my father. "Pappa, those huge birds are going to bite me!" Mamma quickly picked Ronald up.

Onkel Karl, a darkly tanned man with a ready smile, had heard the honking and come out. He loped over to us, looking a little like a spider as he ran, and shooed the geese away. "They're our watchdogs, Meta. They protect us and our animals. They do a good job, don't they?"

I nodded silently, still clutching my father's hand.

As we walked up the path to the cozy home, I kept my eye on those fierce honking monsters, but they stayed back. Onkel opened the front door and called out, "They're here!" My plump Tante Paula came out of the kitchen, drying her hands on her apron. "Come in. Make yourselves at home. Would you like a cup of tea? We killed one of the fattest chickens for you, and I'm just preparing her, so perhaps you'd like to join me in the kitchen, Gusti."

I was mystified when I saw Tante wink at my father.

My mother turned green and backed away a few steps. "You didn't kill it yourself, did you? I don't eat chicken, Paula. You know that. I just... just... well, I don't." She passed her hand over her forehead. "I'll take a sandwich instead. And I'll sit with the family in the living room."

Paula burst out laughing. "I'm kidding, Gusti. You know I

wouldn't do that. I know how having to kill and pluck chickens as a child traumatized you. We slaughtered our pig last fall; we'll have wonderful sausages and sauerkraut tonight."

Mamma let out a long sigh. "That's so much better! Just the thought of eating chicken makes me gag. But I love your sausages. So, you still keep your own pigs?"

"Just one now. We keep it just out back." I began edging nearer in interest. "Do you want to come and see it, Meta?"

"Yes, please. I've never seen a pig up close. At least, not since before the war started."

"Well, come on then."

Sieglinde grabbed Ronald's hand and we went out to see the very dirty pig. My mind boggled to think that something that stank so much could taste so good.

The visit continued pleasantly—mostly. I just wished memories of the war would stop haunting me.

~

"Meta, did you see Eva? It's horrid! They shaved her head and covered it with red leaded paint! Her hair will never grow back. The poor girl is so embarrassed she wears a scarf, but she showed me..." Sieglinde's eyes filled with tears.

"What? Why would anyone do that?" I dropped the travel book I'd been reading.

"Someone said she had a German boyfriend during the war. I don't know if she did, but this was her punishment. Anyone who had anything to do with Germans is now suspect."

I shivered, remembering der Stiefel and the kinds of punishment I'd seen him mete out. But then, I gasped. "Uh, Siegie, we have a German mother..."

"Yeah, but she's Dutch now and married," she hesitated. "She helped the Dutch during the war, and she sure didn't date a German soldier!"

"Ugh. I just want to forget about the war. I hate passing the Oranje Hotel (nickname for the prison for war criminals) on my way anywhere! And I hate being hated. First, NSBers hated us if we resisted the Germans, and now the Dutch might hate us for having German relatives."

"Worse, we just visited them..."

I glanced around the room, just like Pappa used to when he grew nervous during the war. "You didn't tell anyone, did you?"

Sieglinde wrapped her arms around her legs. "I don't think so. I hope not. Oh Meta! It seems like the pain will never end."

"Let's think of something else. I wonder if Mamma will bring little cakes home from the shops today. Let's put the kettle on for tea." The problems of living in a formerly occupied and very broken country were forgotten—for a while.

A week later I came home with what I thought was great news. "Mamma, Pappa, my teacher says my schoolwork shows I'm capable of going to university. But since my school isn't set up for people who'll go to college, they want me to go to a special school. They say they want to meet with you both."

"Spilletje, that's wonderful! Imagine a daughter of mine going to university!" Pappa's face beamed. (Pappa had been forced to leave school when he was only II in order to support his family after his father died, so had never even finished school.)

"*Ja*, they say that, if I attend The Catholic Lyceum for Girls and then do further studies, I'll be able to become a doctor." I twirled from sheer joy. "My dream will come true."

Mamma looked doubtful. "Meta, women don't usually become doctors. Maybe you could be a nurse."

"Well, I want to try anyway. At least I'll be allowed to go to university."

Pappa's brow furrowed. "The Lyceum is a private school for wealthy children; it's very expensive."

I shrugged, determined not to let go of the euphoria. "The teachers know that, and they know us. Let's see what they suggest."

After some discussions between my parents, my teachers, and the church, it was decided that the church would pay my tuition; my parents would pay for the books. Since Pappa was both highly intelligent and very curious, I knew that I would not be the only person enjoying the books.

Preparations began in the summer. Because the Catholic Lyceum started with Latin and French, instead of English and German like my old school, I had to catch up. I studied Latin during my vacation, but there was no money to also learn French.

On the first day of school, I took the streetcar to the stop nearest to The Catholic Lyceum for Girls. As I walked towards the school, my steps slowed, and I became painfully aware of the gaping chasm between the run-of-the-mill student there and... me. First, I noticed the line of bikes parked close to the entrance of the school. I didn't own a bicycle. Some of the children milling around outside were wearing the latest fashions. My coat had been passed down from a neighbor to Corrie to Sieglinde to me. Everyone else seemed to know each other; nobody seemed to even see me.

A school official showed me to my classroom. As soon as I entered, the teacher called me to the front and introduced me to my classmates. I looked down at my feet, unable to meet the gaze of the roomful of beautifully dressed girls reeking of expensive perfumes. I was all too aware of my worn and faded dress—the best I had. I raised my chin. At least my clothes were clean, and my shoes had been polished.

"Meta, you'll sit over there." The teacher pointed to an empty desk in the second row on the left, right next to a tall, well-developed young lady, Sheila. She smiled at me, but I was too overwhelmed by the grandeur around me to grin back.

Once seated, I surreptitiously looked around and thought, I'm the youngest daughter of the little postman, living in the short street. The church paid my tuition, Pappa borrowed money to buy my books, and there's nothing left for the other things I need. What in the world am I doing here? Then I deliberately and nonchalantly arranged my school supplies on my desk.

That morning, my new classmates practiced *Le Bourgeois Gentilhomme* by Molière. I sat mesmerized, but I was inwardly stunned at the perfection of their pronunciation. I understood very little of what they were saying. My shoulders momentarily slumped, and I tucked my hands under my legs—until I remembered my brave face. Nonetheless, my forehead creased as I pondered this new dilemma: how on earth can I ever keep up here? I'm lost on the very first day!

Finally, the long day was over. I burst in through the front door of my home. "Mamma, I'm here!"

"How was it? How were the other girls in your class, and what did you think of the lessons? Sit down and tell me everything, Spil."

"It was great," I lied. "But so very different. We did a French play today that we would never have done at Cordi Sacratissimo. You should have heard them. They spoke with a perfect accent." I frowned. "Oh Mamma, I need French lessons so I can catch up!"

"I'll discuss it with your father."

That discussion did not take long. My parents were totally unable to raise the funds to pay for private French lessons.

"Class, I have exciting news. John Steinbeck is coming to speak."

I swallowed hard. Although this was amazing, it magnified my feeling of being a square peg in a round hole. I'd been thrust into the upper crust, and it was frankly overwhelming. I had nothing in common with these girls—they'd never starved, never worn recycled clothing, and their shoes had no holes in them. For them, private tutors and bicycles, let alone paying for food, were not an issue.

I decided to fake confidence and increase my participation in class discussions. During French, I raised my hand. "Juffrouw de Beer, *alstublieft*, could you say that phrase again, so I can hear how to pronounce it?"

There was no response. I thought that maybe the teacher considered me stupid because I couldn't produce the right accent, or she was ignoring me because I was so obviously poor. My shoulders rounded; I didn't have the courage to ask again.

But all was not lost. The next lesson was German, where I knew I would excel. After explaining the first lesson and having us listen to her pronunciation, the teacher asked me to read a sentence. Me! The one in the shabby dress! I stood and enunciated clearly. "*Guten Tag. Ich bin Frau Hohenzollern. Wie geht's Ihnen?*"

The blonde teacher crossed her arms over her flat chest, frowned, and questioned me, "Have you had German lessons before?" She pressed her lips together and her nostrils flared; she looked a lot like der Stiefel.

"Juffrouw, we had a year at my last school," I said, rather confused by her apparently negative response to my immaculate reading.

"That is not the accent one has after only having a year of lessons. You speak perfect German. Where did you learn that?" She spoke through stiffened lips while tapping her toe, making a clicking sound on the tiled floor that sounded like jackboots on the pavement.

Avoidance seemed a wise course of action. "I couldn't help but learn it during our five years of occupation, Ma'am."

"We all went through the war, but we don't all speak without an accent. Where did you learn to speak like that?" my teacher interrogated me, her icy-blue eyes narrowed.

I shrank back in my seat and confessed. "My mother is German. I've always spoken it." I held my breath.

You could have heard a pin drop. The teacher never engaged me again.

Most of the other students followed suit. Evidently, having German blood, I was beneath contempt. That week no one sat with me during lunch, and nobody talked to me. I was, quite simply, the enemy.

My anger about this unfair treatment gushed like blood over the street, but I tempered my reaction by remembering how cowardly and stupid the bullies I'd encountered had been. I shook my head slightly. Those who were mistreating me were so incredibly foolish. Especially the teacher. Didn't they realize their attitude was eerily similar to that of those they hated? The Nazis blamed all Jews for, among other things, the difficulties post-World War I Germany experienced. The teacher and some of my classmates were blaming all Germans for the horrors of the war. But not all Germans were Nazis. Including me, who was neither a German nor a Nazi. As I mused about this, I realized that the best course of action would be to evaluate people based on who, not what, they are.

Sheila, the beautiful daughter of the British ambassador, was a ray of light in that very dark school. I admired her greatly: she was both tall and wore a bra and make-up! She'd moved too often to really belong in any school, but seemed totally at ease with her situation. She didn't have to put on a brave face; she was brave.

We sometimes hung out after school, but I never invited her over. What if she were to witness the poverty of our home? My shame cut like a knife, even while I felt guilty for the feeling.

I was just starting out for home after another day of listening to a famous personality when I heard, "Hey Meta, you live my way, don't you? Let's go together."

I stopped walking and looked around, surprised that anyone was speaking to me. Evidently, Ellie, the lovely daughter of a local grocer, hadn't received the memo about my heritage. She pulled her brand-new bicycle out of the rack and joined me. "You ride it until the Scheveningseweg. Then I'll go to my house, and you catch the streetcar."

"Oh yeah, sure. I usually leave my bicycle at home," I lied nonchalantly.

～

After a year at the Catholic Lyceum, my parents decided that I should return to Cordi Sacratissimo, a prevocational school. I really wasn't enjoying the private school; the teachers didn't even try to assist me in my studies; the books were too expensive for my family to manage payment. As Mamma pointed out, there wasn't much point in continuing there anyway since girls weren't usually accepted into medical school.

Although relieved to no longer have to struggle at the private school, I was totally devastated. Lying on my bed, I mulled over what was left of my life. It had been my dream to go to university. But now, because that wasn't an option for children educated at Cordi Sacratissimo, it wouldn't happen.

Corrie was still very sick, and the doctors were scratching their heads. I'd so hoped to help people like her by becoming a doctor myself. But without university, well... And without going to any kind of further education, I doubted I'd ever rise above my working-class background. I'd never become wealthy enough to travel and see the world—another shattered dream.

Even more frustrating, none of this was my fault. None of it. I hadn't asked to have a mother whose parents had immigrated to Germany. I hadn't asked to be a girl. I hadn't asked to be unimpressive in stature. I hadn't asked to have working-class parents who were in debt because of my sister's ongoing illness. I hadn't asked to be the youngest daughter of the poor postman and his German wife living on the short street in the little town. I hadn't asked to be unimportant. Catching sight of Grietje, I grabbed her by the arm and threw her across the room.

Even though the war had been over for several years, the jackboots over my head threatened to crush me. In fact, I realized that der Stiefel had been keeping me down all my life. I could pretend it didn't matter, but it did. It really mattered. I buried my face in my pillow and screamed. Putting on a brave face would not change anything; the reality of my life remained. Should I give up? Maybe just go drown myself? I fell asleep with tear-streaked cheeks.

Hazy sunshine penetrated my curtains, and I awoke with a start. Der Stiefel with his icy eyes fastened on me and his arms folded was standing at the foot of my bed. I broke into a sweat and quickly ducked my head under the covers. What was he doing here? How did he get past Pappa? Was I dreaming?

Steeling myself, I slowly pulled the sheet from over my head. He was still there, just to the side of the crucifix hanging on my wall. I narrowed my eyes and stared at him. He didn't move; in fact, the image began to waver until he disappeared. Der Stiefel was only as real as I allowed him to be. The crucifix, however, remained.

"God, please help me," I whispered as I sat up to face the new day. Der Stiefel was gone; he would not win. I was all those things that kept me down—poor, a girl, short, and half-German—but I was more. Much more. I was me. I decided never to give up. If I couldn't fulfill one dream, I would go for another. There are always more dreams. I would do better than showing a brave face. I would both survive and thrive. I would be brave. After all, I thought, I am Meta.

I would go to school and immerse myself in my studies. If I then worked hard at a vocation, one day I would be able to work in an office. Maybe I could earn enough to travel. I distracted myself from despair by focusing on enjoying life here and now. After all, my neighborhood friends were at Cordi Sacratissimo, and I had nothing to hide from them. I didn't much like the rather clumsy and pimply boys, but the girls were still great. And I remembered that the teachers were helpful!

I threw back the covers, got out of bed, and stretched. Life was great. Then, I went downstairs and caught sight of Corrie.

~

Corrie, who had never fully regained her strength after her bout with TB, was growing progressively weaker while her neck swelled to a grotesque width. Eating had become almost impossible.

Dr. L. F. C. Mees, our physician and a professor at the Waldorf School, soberly examined my feeble, pale sister. As our family friend and a frequent visitor, he had loaned Corrie a violin and given her lessons, but now she was too unwell to do much of anything. I listened fearfully as he discussed options with my parents.

"I'm so sorry, but Corrie's only hope is surgery. If they don't do it, she'll die. If they do, she'll have a slim chance. Only slim." His brow furrowed, and he took a deep breath. "It's not a great choice, but it's all I can offer. Think about it and let me know what you decide."

Mamma sat with her arm around Corrie while Pappa walked Dr. Mees to the door. "*Dank u wel* for coming. We need to consider all you've said and talk with our daughter. She's old enough to decide for herself."

"Just don't take too long in coming to a decision. She's going downhill fast. Frankly, if she has surgery, she'll need to be strong to survive it." He sighed. "I'm not sure she is even now."

After a very intense day of discussions, Corrie and my parents agreed she would have the operation. Pappa once again borrowed money from his job to provide all she needed, both in the hospital and during recovery. The surgeon slit her neck from one side to the other, and after a week Corrie came home, even weaker than before.

Worse, she was totally unable to speak; the operation had damaged her voice box.

My mother nursed Corrie anxiously, giving her spoonsful of broth all day and through the night. Sieglinde and I spoke in whispers and tried to keep Ronald out of the way as much as possible. The house was gloomy and quiet. Even Pappa didn't smile. He just sat staring at nothing with suspiciously red eyes while he smoked one cigarette after another.

Dr. Mees came every day to check on Corrie, and every day he left shaking his head. Corrie ate only a little, mostly white bread soaked with warm milk. She grew increasingly gaunt as she lay on the little couch in the tiny room, finally becoming too weak to go to the bathroom. Much of the time she was only semi-conscious.

After pausing outside the tiny room to gather my courage, I entered to sit with Corrie. Would this be the day she died? My skeletal sister wordlessly offered me her bony hand. I cradled it carefully: her skin was almost translucent, and I could see every vein. Corrie's sunken eyes fastened on mine, and it seemed like she wanted to say something, but I didn't know what. I squeezed my eyes closed, hoping it wasn't, "Good-bye."

Even though it hardly seemed possible, every day was worse. Corrie's health declined until she was eating absolutely nothing and drinking only what Mamma spooned in. After examining her again, Dr. Mees gave us the bad news. "I'm so sorry, but it appears Corrie isn't going to recover. Death is approaching fast. She'll not see another week."

"Noooo!" The sound of Mamma's wail as she collapsed to the floor in anguish made the hair on the back of my neck stand up.

Pappa waved the doctor away and gently lifted her. "Guusje, don't give up. As long as she's alive, there's hope."

That night neither of my parents went to bed. I lay awake, desperately praying as I heard the dull buzz of their anxious murmurs.

In the morning, while I helped Mamma give Corrie a bed bath, Pappa sat by the smoking table reading the newspaper. Suddenly, he jumped to his feet. "Guusje," he called urgently. "Come and look at this!"

Mamma wrapped Corrie up in a warm blanket and hurried over. After touching Corrie's cheek, I went to peek over Pappa's shoulder at an article about Greetje Hofmans. I knew she was a lady who prayed for sick people—and sometimes they got better. *De Leugenaar* had been full of it when Juffrouw Hofmans hadn't been able to heal Princess Christina of her eye problem, but I knew people still flocked to her.

"Look, Guusje, she's in town. And as I see it, we have no other options left."

Mamma sighed. "Juffrouw Hofmans says she can't heal people, but God can, if it's His will... I sure don't know what His will is anymore, but we have to try."

Pappa nodded his head. "She says she will see those seeking prayer tomorrow morning from 7 am onwards. Let's go earlier—at 5 am. We'll take all our money and a photo of Corrie. Who knows? Maybe those will convince her."

Just before my parents left, they woke Sieglinde and me so we could sit with Corrie. They weren't sure if, when they got home, Corrie would still be alive. They did not want her to die alone.

Many hours later while Sieglinde was making coffee, Corrie opened her eyes, looked at me, and tried to get out of bed.

"Siegie, come here. Help me with Corrie!"

With both of us helping, our fragile sister maneuvered her legs out of bed and stood. Next, holding onto the wall for support as we hovered nearby, she slowly inched her way past the *kachel* and towards the WC.

Just then, the door opened. Pappa and Mamma were home.

"Mamma, Pappa, come fast. Look!"

My parents mounted the stairs in no time, screeching to a halt when they saw who was in the hallway. Pappa's mouth dropped open, and Mamma's eyes filled with tears.

Corrie gave us all a wan, but triumphant, grin.

Once Corrie was again safely tucked in and sleeping peacefully, we talked everything over.

"Mamma, Pappa, what happened with Juffrouw Hofmans?"

Pappa shook his head. "I don't know what to make of it. We had to wait for hours, but when we reached the front of the line, there she was. I could barely hear her; her voice was so soft. She just said, 'God loves you. Your daughter will be well.'"

"Did you give her the money?"

"No, it was the strangest thing. We offered her both the money and the photo, and she refused them."

Mamma wiped a tear from her cheek and explained further. "She said, 'I don't need to see her picture. I've seen her. Your daughter will be well. Put your money away. I don't do the work, and I don't need the reward.'"

"Oh, do you think it might be true? Will Corrie really finally get well?" I'd been praying, but without much faith.

Pappa walked over to the tiny room to gently stroke his sleeping daughter's cheek before he answered. "Maybe. It looks like maybe. Let's hope for the best. What else can we do?"

Later that very same day, Corrie drank some water and even ate a few bites of bread soaked in warm milk.

When Dr. Mees came to check up on his patient, his eyes popped in amazement. Pulling my parents outside the room, he whispered, "I was steeling myself to be told Corrie was gone. What happened?"

Pappa shook his head as he related the tale. "I don't know how, but after Juffrouw Hoffmans prayed, she turned the corner. Maybe it was a miracle..."

Dr. Mees cleared his throat. "I hope so. I'll be back next week to check."

He came back every week and so became another witness that gradually, gradually, without medicine, Corrie's health improved. Eventually, for the first time since the war, she was completely well. Although her singing voice was gone because of the surgery, she was even able to talk!

19

GROWING UP

"Come on, Meta. We're going to be late!"

"I don't care. I hate Wednesday afternoons."

"Well, if we want to be confirmed, we have to go to catechism." Sieglinde pulled on her threadbare coat and adjusted the scarf to cover her nose and mouth.

We raced to the Belgisch Park and arrived at Juffrouw Verwaand's home at the same time as some of the children from wealthy families.

"Hello, my dear Emily and Eva, come sit over here next to me on these red cozy chairs. Oh, and Marijke, you perch right here on the side of my easy chair, Schatje." Looking like she'd smelled something putrid, the gray-haired Juffrouw Verwaand peered over her glasses down her elongated nose. "Ah. There are Sieglinde and Meta. You two, sit on the floor over there by that door."

We sank onto the cold, tile floor, carefully tucked our dresses around our feet to hide the holes in the bottoms of our shoes, and prepared to listen to an hour-long lecture.

"Meta, stop fidgeting."

"My leg has gone to sleep! How long will that silly old crone keep droning on and on?" I whispered under my breath.

Finally, it was over.

"That's all we have for today, *Kinderen*, but just wait. I have a candy for all of you."

Juffrouw Verwaand reached behind her and drew out two bags. She handed chocolates out to all the warmly dressed children who were sitting on the easy chairs. Those who were sitting on the floor in tattered clothing were given something from the other bag: a *zuurtje*.

After kicking a stone down the street, I turned to Sieglinde. "I hate that ugly witch. It's just not fair! Why can't we have a chocolate?"

Sieglinde sighed. "Meta, don't upset yourself. A *zuurtje* is good, too. And maybe, when we get home, Mamma will give us a chocolate."

"Well, I'm sure God is angry about what Juffrouw Verwaand is doing. After all, He healed Corrie, even though we're poor. Obviously, we're not beneath His notice."

That evening I discussed the matter with Dickie. "I went to catechism today. Does your church do those lessons? Ugh! I detest them! The teacher treats us like dirt just because we're not moneyed snobs. Honestly, even our church does. We can't afford to pay for a seat in the front, so they act as if we're totally worthless."

Dickie looked confused. "Don't you guys go to Sunday school?"

"What's that? I've never heard of it. On Sundays, we go to Mass. It's in Latin, so I don't understand anything, but Mamma says we have to go. She says it's a good way for us to learn patience." I crossed my eyes. "So far, it hasn't worked!"

Dickie giggled. "I'll ask my mother if you can come with us on Sunday. I love Sunday school. Maybe you'd like it, too."

Mevrouw Heesterman agreed, and I went to ask my mother, who also gave permission.

So, it was that this Catholic girl went to the Prayer Chapel. Their Sunday worship started with everyone in the main sanctuary where everything was in Dutch, and I wasn't bored. We sat in the middle of the church instead of at the back, because no one had to buy a place. Even stranger, the congregation joined in with the singing. The atmosphere reminded me of our family doing the dishes together.

After the service, Dickie and I went to Sunday school. I was stunned when we were allowed to sit on chairs, and the teacher gave all of us milk and a cookie. She also answered our questions, even mine.

Arriving at home, I burst through our front door so full to the brim with stories that I could hardly catch my breath. "Mamma, Pappa, it was wonderful! They spoke Dutch instead of Latin, and I could understand it all. Everyone was so nice! I want to go to that church."

"Meta, we're Catholic." The subject was closed. But not forgotten.

∿

Catechism completed, Sieglinde and I were going to be confirmed. Even though we had no idea what it was actually all about, we were bursting with excitement about the upcoming celebration.

It was Wednesday afternoon, but we were free. "Girls, for your confirmation, you may choose a new dress. Let's go." Mamma's eyes were sparkling.

Mamma, Sieglinde and I took the streetcar into the city, went to shop and after shop, and tried on dress after dress. "How does this look, Siegie?" I asked, twirling to make the skirt float away from my legs.

"It's lovely, and the soft yellow really sets off your blue eyes. The white polka dots make the dress especially cute." Sieglinde held her arms away from her sides and looked down at herself. "What about me? Does this white dress suit me?"

"Of course. You're beautiful as always."

Sieglinde giggled. "We're a pair of extremely gorgeous ladies! I can hardly wait to show Pappa."

"Not so fast, Mademoiselles. You'll need new shoes, too."

Sieglinde and I looked at each other with wide eyes. Such extravagance!

We bought white shoes for the occasion. Since we would be kneeling in front of the bishop, it was very important that there were no holes in the soles. I hoped Juffrouw Verwaand would see our outfits from her front row seat—we wouldn't look poor now!

"Come on, my drei Grazien. Let's finish our very special day with ice creams at Florencia." Mamma's cheeks were flushed, and she was almost dancing as she led the way.

After buying our ice creams, we sat outside to eat, taking tiny bites to make the experience last. Sieglinde held her precious packages on her lap. "At our confirmation, what name will you choose, Meta?"

"Well, I think I'll take the name most girls pick: Maria, the mother of Jesus. Even though we're allowed to legally change our name, I'm not going to. I am Meta."

"Hmm, I prefer to be called Bernadette, but not for real."

Mamma smiled. "I'm glad. I like the names your father and I chose for you both."

The night before the confirmation, Mamma wet both of our hair and rolled it up in rags. That way, in the morning, when it was dry, it would hang in beautiful curls. Well, Sieglinde's would. The state of mine would depend on the weather.

In the morning, we slipped on our new dresses, the rest of the family donned their best clothes, and we all walked to church. I was pleased that it wasn't raining. Maybe my hair would remain curly for the entire service. I knew that I looked gorgeous and surreptitiously cast my eyes from side to side, hoping to spot an admirer.

On this special occasion the family was allowed to sit at the front of the church near the pulpit. Sieglinde and I, being confirmands, processed into the church preceded only by the bishop. At the confirmation, the bishop asked us for our new names, we knelt, he laid his hands on our heads, anointed our foreheads with oil, said a prayer and we got up. It was done. I turned and winked very deliberately at Juffrouw Verwaand.

Time to celebrate! Relatives came over and congratulated us, and we enjoyed little cakes with tea, lots of flowers and liqueur after dinner. Best of all, we were the center of attention. And I got a chocolate. Or two.

~

It was early evening when the doorbell rang. I pulled the rope and at the bottom of the stairs, saw a rather sheepish young man holding a bunch of flowers. "Is Celeste home?"

I frowned as I began to descend towards him. "Celeste? There's no Celeste here."

Corrie, who'd accompanied me into the hall, but could not be seen at the top of the stairs, whispered frantically, "Meta, Meta!"

"Just a minute. Let me check something." I smiled graciously at the now-perplexed youth, went back up the stairs, and raised my eyebrows in question.

"I'm Celeste!" Corrie hissed.

I nodded my head and went back down, smiling glowingly at the young man. "Oh, you mean Celeste! Of course. Celeste, it's for you." I trilled back into the living room.

A few minutes later Corrie came sailing down the stairs, a radiant smile lighting up her face.

A few weeks later the doorbell rang, and a different gentleman was standing there. This time Sieglinde opened the door. "I've come for Monique."

"Oh, you mean my sister, Corrie. Yeah, I'll get her." Sieglinde turned and rolled her eyes at the furious person breathing fire from the top of the stairs. Corrie simply didn't like her given name. It might have been good had she been confirmed!

"Corrie, isn't it time you start putting together a bottom drawer? You're into your twenties!" Sieglinde had her hands on her hips.

Corrie did a little twirl. "I'm finally well now, after having been sick for so, so long. Let me enjoy my life; I'm going to buy clothes, lots of them. And shoes. And maybe even a light blue coat. Hmm, and chocolates. Not sheets and towels—so boring!" She stopped and bored a hole in her sister with her eyes. "And *alsjeblieft*, Siegie, keep the secret about my names. I just want to have some fun."

"Well, you and I could begin collecting some things, Sieglinde. I'm going to start off by collecting towels—special ones." At 15 years old, I didn't have a job yet, but saved enough for a beautiful orange and green towel. I wrapped it carefully and put it under my bed. At least I'd begun.

Sieglinde bought a tablecloth to be embroidered and a set of sheets. They too were stuffed into the box she kept under her bed. Even though she had a job, it was difficult to acquire much more, because the money she earned helped pay household bills.

Pillowing my chin on my hands as we lingered after lunch, I asked Sieglinde what kind of boy she wanted to marry.

"I think someone who has a good personality—who is kind. And he has to have a steady job. What about you?"

"Mmm, I want a fine-looking man with a good figure, a well-formed face, and a generous mouth. And I want 12 beautiful children."

"What? That's crazy! I only want two. How are you going to pay for all those kids?" Sieglinde stood up and shook out her skirt as if shaking off my insane ideas. "Anyway, I'm off to see Lydia. Do you want to come?"

"Sure. I like hanging out with Jan."

"Meta, be careful. His parents are very determined that their children only marry Indonesians."

I giggled. "Don't be silly. We're friends, Siegie. I'm far too young to date!"

We walked over to the large Leidelmeijer home with its front and backyard and fascinating arrangement. All the bedrooms were on the second floor, but none of them had a closet. Instead, the entire family hung their clothes in a central common area with a huge circular railing.

Sieglinde, Lydia, Jan and I decided that, since it wasn't raining, we would walk to the Boulevard. My sister and her friend led the way chattering about their jobs while Jan and I became engrossed in our own conversation. "Meta, I got a new book out of the library. You'd love it. Come over. We can read some of it together."

"I'd like that, but will your parents allow me to visit just you?"

Jan frowned. "Probably not, but they won't know if you come on a Sunday afternoon when our whole family goes for a long walk. As long as you're out of the house before they return..." He winked slyly. "I'll buy chocolates for you."

I put my head to one side, thinking about his plan. "Okay, I'll come. But chocolate is too expensive. I like *drop* as well, you know."

"*Nee,* I'll get chocolates for you."

The very next Sunday afternoon, I went to Jan's house. We perched next to each other on Jan's bed and read while I let the chocolate melt in my mouth, and he enjoyed the licorice. It was heavenly. Until Jan looked outside. "My family's coming! It's too late for you to leave; my parents will be livid if you're here. Quick, hide! The wardrobe room will be best..."

We ran down the hall to the central room, and I slipped behind the girls' dresses. Jan pulled me away. "Not there. The girls may change before dinner."

So, I crouched down behind the boys' clothing to be as inconspicuous as possible. Before leaving me, Jan said, "Stay where you are. I'll come and get you when it's safe."

Jan went to innocently greet his family while I waited breathlessly. I heard the thunder of footsteps on the stairs as, yes, the girls came to change their clothes before dinner. Breathing as shallowly as possible, I listened to their chatter, wondering if I should just step out and confess. *Nee,* the consequences could be too harsh.

The delicious smell of Indonesian food wafted up the stairs, and I pressed my hand to my stomach which, despite being full of chocolate, was growling loudly enough be to deafening. Jan slipped into the room. "You can't come out yet. Maybe when we're all sitting down to eat..." He went back downstairs.

It seemed like hours before Jan finally came up and took my hand to pull me out from among the clothing. "The coast is clear. Quick, go out the back door so they don't see you. Stay as close to the hedge as possible, and leave out of the front gate. I left it open, so it won't creak."

With my heart in my mouth, I escaped. Jan and I remained friends for years, but I never tried that again.

❧

Armed with five balls, I sprinted down our stairs and across the street, determined to improve upon my previous record. I'd never managed to juggle more than four balls, even though I also practiced while helping to make dinner—with potatoes and apples—but maybe today would be the day.

To my astonishment, the garage door next to my practice wall was open, and the inside of the garage totally transformed into a workplace.

Peeking inside, I saw a diminutive man busily repairing carts and tunelessly whistling under his breath.

"Hello, Sir. I am Meta. Who are you?"

The dark-haired man looked up from his work. "I'm Meneer Poepa. It's ghood to meed you, Meda. I feenk I've *gesehen* you before. You leeve across ze zdreed, rright?"

It was difficult to understand Meneer Popa, because he spoke heavily accented Dutch mixed with German. However, I continued asking questions, speaking much more slowly and clearly: "What... are... you... doing?"

"I'm restoring dem. *Gesehen* dees one? Virst, I fixed and sanded, und now I'm staining, and tomorrow, I'll put on zee lacquer. I haf to leaf ze garage doors open, because of ze vumes." As Meneer Popa spoke, he gestured enthusiastically with his hands, which helped me to follow his words.

I cocked my head to one side. "Where are you from, Meneer Popa? I hear you using some German words, but my mother is German, and you don't sound anything like her."

"Ah yes, my accent is strong. I'm originally from Romania, and I left after the war. I've lived in many countries, but spent most of my time in Germany."

"How wonderful! I'd love to travel and really want to hear about the places you've lived, but not now. It's almost dinner time, and Mamma expects me home. Will you be here tomorrow?"

"Yes, I have to, if I want to finish the cart. There are several more to go, as well! I'll look forward to talking with you then, Meta."

In the morning, several friends accompanied me to meet this new person and watch him work his magic with the carts. Meneer Popa smiled and began explaining what he was doing to his audience.

"Uh, what language is that?" Mark scratched his head.

"Sshh, be nice," I whispered. "He just has an accent."

As Meneer Popa continued to try to communicate, some of the teens started to make fun of him, imitating his gestures and speaking gibberish.

Shocked, I stepped aside a little to indicate I wasn't part of the rude behavior. Because I had an immigrant mother, I knew from experience that having an accent did not mean a person was unintelligent. Far from it.

With a red face and even more passionate gestures, Meneer Popa let them have it—in Romanian.

The other young people first backed and then scampered away.

Once they'd gone, Meneer Popa continued to shellac the cart while I stood watching, now with tears in my eyes. Looking up, he winked and began to talk again. I listened closely, trying to hear the words he spoke, instead of how he pronounced them. It gave me a headache, but I could figure out most of what he said.

Meneer Popa's stories about life in other countries were absolutely fascinating, and I looked forward to our daily time. Hearing about Meneer Popa from me, my mother and some of the other grown-ups also began to spend time just standing in that garage and listening.

One day, I looked out of our front window and noticed the garage doors were closed. I figured everyone deserves a day off. But the days flew by, and now they'd been closed for weeks.

"Mamma, do you know where Meneer Popa is? Is he sick?" I bit my lip, remembering what had happened to Sjors.

"He's okay, but he's not coming back. His father-in-law told me he and his new family emigrated to Australia."

"Wow! Living on the other side of the world. Lucky..."

Later that day I pressed my nose to the window of the garage; the cart-fixing equipment was gone.

20

WALKING INTO MY FUTURE

Just before sunrise on Sunday morning, I heard a quiet knock on our bedroom door. "Girls, it's time to get up. Remember, we're going berry picking today."

We scrambled into our clothes, whispering so as not to wake up the rest of the family, and set out. The air was invigorating, the birds were chirping, the insects were humming, and the waves were pounding.

Pappa threw back his head and began to sing war songs. We joined in with *It's a Long Way to Tipperary* and *The Siegfried Line* while we marched along the Zwarte Pad.

Next Pappa started to sing opera, his bass voice filling the air.

"Oh, Pappa," I groaned. "Let's sing something else!"

"Okay, how about this one?" Pappa grinned mischievously as he began to sing from *La Traviata*.

We girls rolled our eyes; we didn't like opera. Worse, Pappa didn't know the Italian or French words to his favorite songs, so he just sang the sounds. And what he lacked in language, he made up for in enthusiasm and very robust volume.

Ah, relief—we were there. Pappa forgot to sing as he examined the bushes to find those with the best berries. Sieglinde and I quickly began filling our pails with the ripe, blue fruit. There were more than enough.

Mamma came into the kitchen just as we were dumping the berries into a bowl on the counter. "Oh Cor, I'm glad you're home. Joop said he'll be stopping by a little earlier than usual this week."

As Sieglinde and I set the table for breakfast, I thought about how life had changed. Now we could go to the sand dunes whenever we liked, we had no fear of bombs dropping, and we always had enough food. Peace was wonderful. If only the peace outside was always reflected on the inside.

I knew, even though der Stiefel was gone, the war had left scars on my heart. I was determined to be brave, but was only too aware I wasn't alone in my pain. Sieglinde cringed every time she heard a loud noise. Mamma never let us throw away even the tiniest morsel of food. Cousin Joop had it worse. Much worse. After World War II, he'd fought in the Korean war And when he came home after only two years, he was nothing like the happy cousin that had carried me around his living room. Pappa said he was a broken man.

The doorbell rang, and Pappa pulled the cord. "Come in, come in, Joop."

Joop bounded up the stairs. "Ome Cor, I managed to get another record of *The Pearl Fishers*. It's an oldie, but a goodie."

The two men made their way to the easy chairs on either side of the table. "Here, Joop, have *een Cubaantje* [a Cuban cigar], bought with money I won back in the lottery."

After they'd spent some time companionably puffing away, Joop pulled out the record. Pappa put it on the phonograph that stood in pride of place on the smoking table and wound it up. Then both silently sat back to enjoy the music. No one better knock the table or walk heavily; that would make the record skip.

"There will never be another Gigli. Even Caruso can't compete," exclaimed Pappa.

"Don't underestimate Caruso. Remember him singing, *O Sole Mio*? It was amazing!"

Pappa took a deep draw on his cigar while pouring gin into a special glass. "Give me that aria from *La Traviata* again, Joop."

Both men closed their eyes as they listened. We knew we'd better not talk. We sat quietly, either knitting by the *kachel* or reading a book. It was their time.

Cousin Joop and Pappa talked, laughed, listened, smoked and drank. But they never talked about Joop's wartime experiences in Korea.

Pappa told me that sometimes the most courageous thing a person can do is to go on living. Remembering doesn't help.

~

Mamma and I gazed into shop windows while strolling down the Haringkade. I pointed at a sailor's suit. "Mamma, Ronald is growing like a weed. What do you think about that outfit? I really like the color."

"He's shooting up; that's for sure. And he does need new clothes. Look at that ridiculous price—we really can't afford store-bought clothing. Trouble is, even fabric and wool are becoming unaffordable." Mamma sighed.

"You know, I'm off school for a month now. What if I got a summer job? That'd help, wouldn't it?"

"Oh Schatje, what a nice offer! And it would be amazing. But you can't."

"The school won't have to know," I murmured. As we continued on our way, we stopped to look in the window of Simon de Wit, a family-owned grocery store. "Look Mamma, they're hiring! I could apply here."

"Hmm, you know it's not allowed for school kids to have jobs. But it would be helpful..."

Seeing my mother wavering, I put on my puppy dog face. "Please! It'd be good experience, and I'd like to do it, and it will help the family."

Mamma held out for about three seconds. Then, she blew out her breath. "Okay, I'll go along with whatever you want to do—provided you do go back to school!"

This agreed, I pushed the door open, and we went in.

"May I help you, Madam?" The girl behind the counter addressed my mother.

"My daughter is looking for a job, and I see you're hiring."

"Oh yes, let me get the manager."

The balding man invited my mother and me into his office, frowning a little as he looked me over. "What are your qualifications? You look a little young. Do you have a high school degree?"

I shook my head. "No, Sir, I don't, but my parents need the money I'll earn. I'm capable, have good grades, and am a hard worker. Besides, I'm 16, old enough to have a job."

The manager turned to my mother. "Do you agree with all this?"

Mamma glanced at me affectionately. "*Ja*, she's a good girl, and I'm proud she wants to help us."

He scribbled something on the notepad on his desk and then looked up at me with narrowed eyes. "You know our policy states we do not employ students. Are you sure you want to drop out of school to work full time for us?

I nodded eagerly. "Oh, I love working with people. Being a shop assistant at Simon de Wit is my dream." I crossed my fingers behind my back, hoping I hadn't overdone my show of enthusiasm.

The manager crossed his arms and lowered his eyebrows. "Are you absolutely sure you won't quit on us?"

"Yes, Sir."

"Alright then. Since your mother agrees, you're hired. You'll start on Monday in our store in the Haagsestraat. That'll be much closer to your home, and we need someone working there."

My heart sank. That store was only two doors away from Meneer Langedoen, one of the teachers in my high school.

As we walked home, I shared my concern with my mother. "Mamma, if Meneer Langedoen were to find out I'm working, he would be most unhappy."

"Hmm, I see why you're worried, but usually women do the shopping. I doubt he'll even come in."

Mamma was wrong. Two days after I started work, Meneer Langedoen walked into Simon de Wit. Catching sight of me behind the counter, he did a double take. "What are you doing here, Meta? Don't you know school starts in three weeks?"

My boss was standing right there. "*Ja*, I know," I said, industriously scrubbing at the counter. "But I've decided to quit school."

"What? With only one year to go? You won't get a high school degree! And what in the world will you do without one of those?" Meneer Langedoen's eyes were huge.

I shrugged. "Well, I'll work here."

"Oh, Meta!" Meneer Langedoen's face crumpled. "Please think about it. You're so close. You're brilliant and a such good student. You just can't do this! This is no job for someone like you."

I stopped my cleaning to meet his eyes. He deserved the truth. "I understand, Sir, but my parents need the money. You know my sister was sick for a long time. That cost a lot."

"I think I need to talk with your parents. For now, give me a half kilogram of sugar, *alsjeblieft*."

I proudly measured out half a kilogram, filled a pointed bag and closed it such that nothing spilled when I turned it upside down on the counter.

Time passed, and now school was starting in just a week. I was supposed to give two weeks' notice of quitting, but had no idea how I could tell my manager. What could I possibly say?

Every time I tried to speak up, I lost my nerve. I'd cheated the school and lied to my work in taking that job and felt so ashamed.

"Meta," Mamma encouraged. "You have to tell them. Pappa and I want you to finish your education, so you can work in an office. And you gave me your word. The other kids have already been back for a month. Do you want me to do it for you?"

"*Nee*, Mamma. I'll do it tomorrow. I promise."

The next day, I gathered my courage in both hands and told my manager, claiming a conversation with my teacher had changed my mind. I was going back to school. He was disappointed, but said he understood. "I always thought it was a pity that a clever girl like you wouldn't finish high school."

I was six weeks late in starting my senior year.

~

"Pappa, people at church told Sieglinde and me that Anne and Wim Smidt will be starting a new beginners' dance class next week. May I go?" I waltzed around the living room, grabbing my father for my partner.

Pappa chuckled as he swept me into a dip. "What about school?"

"The lessons are on Sunday afternoons, so they won't be a problem." I executed a little twirl.

"And do you have money for them?" Pappa's eyes twinkled.

That stopped me. "Um, *nee*. Siegie probably does because of her job. But I don't." I took his hand in mine. "*Alsjeblieft*, may I go, too? Can you pay?"

Pappa winked. "Okay, I'll cover the lessons for my favorite Meta. Just be sure your schoolwork doesn't suffer."

That weekend, Sieglinde and I began what soon became our favorite pastime. We started with learning the Foxtrot, followed by the Viennese waltz and the English waltz. Floating around on the wings of the music together with our friends was a dream. All too soon, the beginners' classes were over.

"I'm going to sign up for the intermediate classes, Meta. What about you?"

"I'd love to, but I'll have to ask Mamma and Pappa. They may not like it, because I'm still in school."

"This class will be right after the beginners' class, still on Sundays."

"That's good, but I also don't have any money."

"Maybe Pappa will pay again," Sieglinde suggested hopefully. "It'd be nice if you could come with me."

Unfortunately, my parents just couldn't afford to pay for another set of lessons.

After church, I described the problem to Anne. I was no longer ashamed of being poor.

"I see your problem. Well, since you're such a good dancer, maybe you could help us with the beginners' class? As payment, you could take the intermediate class."

My parents gave their permission, and I became an assistant dance teacher.

On my first day teaching, Anne introduced me to Frits Evenblij. I tilted my head back to look into twinkling blue eyes set in one of the handsomest faces I'd ever seen. "Pleased to meet you, Frits. I'll be teaching you to dance."

As was recommended, we began without music, making a square on the floor with our feet. "Okay, you step forward while I step backwards."

Frits, eyes fixed on the floor, mechanically and carefully placed his feet onto the designated places of the square.

"Frits, your legs aren't made of wood. Try bending your knees a little bit." I smiled to diffuse the sting of my words.

He turned rather red, but attempted to do what I'd suggested, counting under his breath. "1, 2, 3, 4, 1, 2, 3, 4."

It didn't help. The music started, but Frits's dancing didn't improve. "Okay, don't count out loud. Just listen to the music and move with it. It doesn't matter if your feet don't make a perfect square. Follow me; I'll lead for a while."

That also didn't help. Frits had no sense of rhythm; he really wasn't a natural dancer. The lesson was over, and I'd been unable to teach him anything. I was totally exhausted, but now it was time for my class.

Sieglinde met me at the door. "How did your first day of teaching go, Meta?"

"Not so great. I was partnered with an older man."

"How old? Like ancient?"

"No, but he already has a job, so maybe even 24. He's absolutely dreamy looking with a great physique and the cutest dark, curly hair, but he sure couldn't dance. I think he smashed my toes to pieces."

"Ha! You must not be a good teacher then!" Sieglinde poked me in the ribs.

"Well, I tried, and I have the bruises to prove it."

"Maybe he just needs more practice. How about inviting him to the church dances?"

When I spoke with Frits about our idea, he was willing, but it soon became evident the Catholic church crowd wasn't about to accept this non-Catholic, partly Jewish young man. Hmm, another strike against the faith of my parents.

After discussing the problem with Sieglinde and our parents, Mamma suggested we hold our own dances—in our home—with our friends.

Frits became part of a group of young people that also included Sieglinde and me. We all hung out together on weekends, walking through the sand dunes and over the Boulevard. I eyed Frits, with his droll smile and twinkling eyes, as he kept everyone in stitches with his jokes.

I really liked him, but was well aware that I was only just 17. And he clearly preferred my sister. Most days, Frits met Sieglinde after work and bicycled home with her.

"So, tell me. What's going on between you two?" I asked, having spotted Sieglinde and Frits chatting through the front window just before she came up.

Sieglinde grinned at me as she put away her bicycle. "Nothing. The only reason Frits picks me up from work is that he hopes he might see you."

My mouth dropped open in shock. "What? That's crazy! He's too old for me." I paused for thought. Could it be true? "Anyway, if that's so, why doesn't he tell me himself?"

"He's not that old, Meta. The poor guy is only 18, he's shy, and he's crazy about you. Next time you have a chance, just spend some time with him."

I smiled to myself, hoping she was right.

Over the next few months, Frits and I got to know each other in the context of our group of friends. We all took walks, went to the library, danced, and went to parties, but I made sure I was always near Frits.

Gradually, we grew closer. I learned that while my mother was German, his was half-Jewish. While his father had died during the war, mine had kept us alive. While his family considered themselves upper class, mine was definitely working class. And while his family was undemonstrative, mine was, well, mine.

"So Meta," Sieglinde's eyes were twinkling. "You sure seem to be spending a lot of time with Frits."

"Siegie, he is everything I dreamed of. You know, I think we might belong together."

"You only just turned 17! Too young to have a boyfriend and way too young to be deciding that!"

I didn't answer. Why bother? I knew what I knew, and what my sister thought really didn't matter.

~

That school rule about sandals makes no sense, I thought as I snuck my new crisp white sandals into my school bag. As soon as I was out of sight of home, my shoes and socks came off. Hopping a bit, I slipped first one foot, and then the other, into the pretty, cool sandals. Despite my age and the heat, I then skipped the rest of the way to the school, feeling as weightless as a bird.

I flung open the front door of Cordi Sacratissimo and stopped in my tracks. I was late. I'd missed Mass and had completely forgotten about the assembly that was scheduled to occur right after it. Most of the students were gathered in the cavernous entrance hall right by the front door; the rest were standing on the sweeping staircase that led to the upstairs classrooms. The headmaster was at the top of the stairs.

All eyes turned in my direction as the huge oak entrance doors slammed behind me. Terror rendered me breathless.

"Bisschop! You're late again. You missed Mass. And what's that on your feet?" the headmaster thundered, his shaking finger drawing attention to my offensive footwear.

"Sandals!" I answered, my chin lifted, but my hands trembling.

"Bare feet? Where are your socks?" he snorted.

"Jesus wore sandals. And I'll bet He didn't wear socks. Everyone could see his bare feet!"

A shockwave passed through the entrance hall. After the collective gasp, you could've heard a micro-pin drop.

I felt a little dizzy, hardly believing I'd said such a thing, but it was out now.

The headmaster sucked in an enormous breath, looking like he might pop on the spot. "OUT!" he roared. "You are expelled—kicked out of school. You're never allowed back in!" He pointed furiously at the door.

I slowly gathered the things I'd dropped and walked towards the door, my head hanging. It was only a few weeks until my final oral exams. What would my parents say? I imagined Mamma's disappointment and Pappa's fury. How could I have messed things up so badly? I felt tears pricking behind my eyes, but determined not to let them fall. Whatever happened, I would be brave.

Just then, I heard someone calling my name. Meester [Master] Koster had followed me out the door of the school. I was friends with his daughter, Yvonne. I stopped to see what he wanted, and he put his hand on my shoulder.

"Meta, don't give up. Instead of going to school, come to my house every day. Yvonne will bring you the lessons of the day, and you study them there. Then, you'll be able to take the government exams with your class."

I inhaled shakily. "*Dank u wel*, Sir. I'll ask my parents if that would be allowed."

When I arrived home, Mamma was outside, cleaning the steps. "What are you doing home, Meta? Are you sick?" My mother put out her hand to feel my forehead.

"I'm fine. Kind of." I took a deep breath. "Mamma, I've been expelled."

My mother dropped her broom. "What happened? How could that be? You have to sit for your exam in a few weeks. What in the world did you do?"

"Mamma, this was the biggest mistake I've ever made in my entire life. But there is hope." After telling my mother exactly what had happened, I explained I could still take my government exams and graduate high school. I was registered, and had already completed the written part of the test.

"How will you prepare by yourself? Don't you have new things to learn?"

"That's the good news. Meester Koster said he'll help me—if it's okay with you. I sure hope I can do it." My mother wiped the sweat of her forehead and agreed that, every day, I should go to my teacher's home instead of to school.

"But don't tell your father. He'll not be able to handle this."

I was only too glad to comply.

So, every day, I went to my teacher's home instead of to school. I sat in Yvonne's bedroom and studied the lessons she brought home after school. There, I learned everything that was needed.

Because it was a governmental test, the oral exam was held in a large building at the zoo on the Malieveld, right where Pappa's cap had been shot while he stole potatoes. It was so hot I was sweating, but I wasn't wearing sandals.

After the exam, my friends and I gathered anxiously, awaiting our results. Finally, after what seemed like hours, they were posted. I looked under the "B's"; I passed with the highest marks in my class! Meester Koster congratulated me heartily as he shook my hand.

"Dank u wel for your help, Meneer Koster."

Just then, I spotted the headmaster making his way towards our group. He singled me out. "Congratulations, Meta. I'm so happy you passed."

I frowned and narrowed my eyes.

"Meta, I'm sorry, you have to understand I had no choice but to expel you. You were always skipping Mass, arriving at school late, and making your own rules. The sandals were the last straw. I had to punish your rebelliousness, because you were such a bad example for everyone. I hoped you'd pass anyway, and I'm glad you did."

I waited until he wasn't looking and then, grinning at my friends triumphantly, whispered, "Well, bla-di-bla bla bla."

At home, we celebrated my graduation with flowers and cake. My father never found out.

Now, I was a high-school graduate and nearly a grown-up. I'd already met the man who was to become my husband, and soon I would start my first office job. I was on my way to becoming the elegant, poised, lady I imagined Grietje had always been. But those stories are for another book.

21

EPILOGUE: MY BIG DECISION

I leaned out of the upstairs bedroom window of our house in Scheveningen. Tears welled up and left wet trails as they ran down my cheeks. The sea breeze ruffled my hair. I felt sad and a little bit anxious. I was so happy I wanted to dance. I desperately didn't want to leave, and yet I was breathlessly looking forward to going.

I'd lived in that town, even that house, for most of my young life. My family lived there. My beloved sea was only a few minutes' walk away; the music of the breaking waves had always been a constant and soothing background for all of my life. All of my friends lived nearby. But tomorrow, I was going to board a boat that would take me across the ocean, far away. I didn't know if I would ever see home again.

I wanted to go. Very much. I'd just married the love of my life: Frits. We were going to start our life together by emigrating to Canada. This was both exciting and frankly terrifying.

The people where we were going spoke a different language, ate different food, and probably had different customs. The city where we were headed was nowhere near the sea. My family and friends would not be coming.

I'd been through a lot in my life: cold, fear, hunger, poverty, loss, heroism, sacrifice, and the delightful warmth of family life. I'd not only survived; eventually, I thrived. But I wondered if I'd be up to this new challenge. I'd never before had to change absolutely everything or do without my close-knit family.

I worried about whether Frits and I would find a home in Canada. The job Frits was hoping for sounded neither promising nor secure. We had very little money.

Nevertheless, I knew that, from now on, I would have no choice but to manage. I patted Grietje where she sat on my dresser. I would leave her behind. She was no longer necessary. I raised my chin, and I was brave.

I never had my intended 12 children, but am totally satisfied with my five children, nine grandchildren, and countless great-grandchildren. I've lived in Canada, all over the United States and in England. I have traveled the world. I never became a doctor, but got a college degree as a 59-year-old and have lived a full and wonderful life. Der Stiefel did not keep me down, and I have no regrets.

PHOTOS

The coastal town of Scheveningen is just to the west of the Hague in the province of South-Holland (Netherlands-CIA_WFB_Map.png, Public domain).

Mamma at 18 years old.

Pappa at 24 years old.

*1935. This photo of me was sent to our German family. Mamma
wrote on the back that I was her little sparrow.*

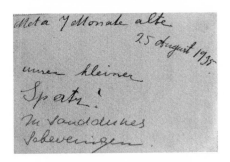

*1935. Corrie, seven years old, with two-year-old Sieglinde, and baby
me on the sand dunes.*

Leeuwardensestraat 1 in Scheveningen. We lived on the top two floors both before and after the war.

1908. Mamma on her mother's lap with Agnes on the left.

School photo of Corrie (left) and Sieglinde.

Vendors came through our street every day (Public domain photo from Pinterest).

A shop like the one Onkel Wilhelm owned in Bottrop, Germany (Public domain photo).

Sinterklaas arriving (Public domain photo found on Pinterest).

German paratroopers over Den Haag (Public domain photo).

German soldiers in Den Haag during the occupation (Public domain photo).

Dog fight over the sand dunes (Public domain photo).

The paper woven picture frame I made that Pappa kept until the day he died.

Hemalie, near Soesterberg (Public domain images from vakantiekolonie.nl).

Rolls of barbed wire blocking access to the beach (Public domain photo from Wikimedia).

Dutch WWII ration cards (Public domain photo from Wikiwand).

1943. Two of my future husband's cousins, Meriam and Edith, with their father. The girls, their brother Hansje, their mother, and her newborn baby died in Auschwitz (From: https://www.ramblingruminations.com/the-children-hidden-at-driebergen/)

An identity card.

The Kleykamp building before it was bombed

The destruction of the Bezuidenhout neighborhood (Public domain photo from Wikipedia).

1945. Ronald Alexander, who was born during the Hunger Winter.

1945. The liberation (Public domain photo by Menno Huizinga).

1946. My family and me on the beach in Scheveningen. From left to right (front), Corrie, Sieglinde (13), Meta (11), Ronald (2).

Me, at the age of 12, in an outfit Mamma made.

1946. My report card.

Weimerstraat 46

The dining hall at Hemalie (Public domain images from vakantiekolonie.nl).

The cots at Hemalie where we had to rest in the open air.

An envelope that contained a letter Sieglinde sent to me while I was at Hemalie.

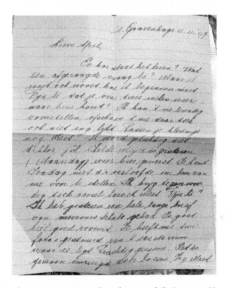

Corrie also sent many very long letters while I was at Hemalie.

The page from my diary where recorded Sjors's death (1947).

The Oranje Hotel, where war criminals were kept.

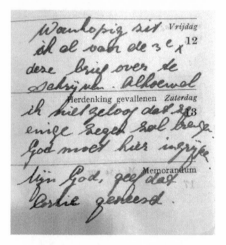

A prayer for Corrie recorded in my diary.

Greetje Hofmans, a famous faith healer.

The first addition to my bottom drawer: a beautiful green and orange towel, which I have to this day.

1951. Sieglinde (left) and me.

A Simon de Wit shop (public domain photo).

1952. Me, a week before I met Frits.

Me in my beautiful white sandals.

1952. Frits, 19 years old.

1952. School photo. Meester Langendoen is center back. I am to the left of him. Hannie is to the right. At the bottom left is Meneer Koster's daughter.

1957. The ship in which Frits and I sailed into our future.

ABOUT THE AUTHORS

Dr. I. Caroline Crocker

Caroline is both Meta's daughter and an immigrant to the US. Over the past 20 years, Caroline has worked as a biology professor, the chief executive officer (CEO) of a startup company, the president of a nonprofit, a private tutor, a technical writer, a research scientist, a consultant and a communications expert. Her last position involved teaching microbiology—very topical.

Caroline maintains a blog, RamblingRuminations, and is the author or coauthor of eight nonacademic books, including *Growing the Church 101* and *Free to Think*. More information on Caroline's writings can be found at https://ramblingruminations.com. Caroline is married to Richard and has four grown children, eight grandchildren, and a bulldog who snores very loudly.

Nonacademic Books by Dr. Crocker

Clemmy Gets a Family, Clemmy Learns to Talk, Clemmy Gets a Job, and *Clemmy Gets a Foster Sister*, 2018. This series of children's picture books featuring a brave and endearing bulldog is currently being rewritten [https://clemmy.org]. The first of the updated versions, published by Rambling Ruminations, will be available in 2023.

Ireentje Learns the Hard Way, 2017. A humorous children's chapter book about a Dutch immigrant child growing up in Canada [https://ireentje.com].

Growing the Church 101: Being Disciples Who Make Disciples, 2017. A Bible study co-written with the Rt. Rev. Keith Andrews.

Microbiology You Can Do at Home, 2020. A workbook for use by college and high school students who love bugs and germs.

Free to Think: No Intelligence Allowed, 2010. Leafcutter Press. A personal memoir written to expand on the movie, *Expelled: No Intelligence Allowed*, starring Ben Stein. The book contains some really cool, if provocative, science.

Meta A. Evenbly

Meta, who lived the story told in *Brave Face*, was born in 1935 to a Dutch father and a German mother and grew up in the Netherlands. When she had just turned 17 years old, she met the love of her life, Frits, who was born to Dutch parents in the Congo, but then grew up in the Netherlands. Meta raised her five children in three different countries, none of them her country of origin. She graduated cum laude with a degree in Liberal Arts from St. Thomas University in philosophy, psychology, and theology at the age of 59.

ACKNOWLEDGMENTS

Thanks to our wonderful families for their unending patience and love. Caroline's husband, children, in-law children, grandchildren, and Meta's four other children all gave us helpful advice, encouragement and support throughout this multi-year writing journey.

Special thanks go to William Crocker and Emma Brown for listening to/reading the story and giving their input; to Britten and William Crocker for their work in spotting typos; and to Megan and Emma Brown for helping us with editing the accompanying YouTube videos.

We are very grateful to Stan Crocker Petrov for his contributions regarding the use of imagery. The book is better because of him.

Thank you to our wonderful beta-readers, who gave valuable feedback during our journey, and to those who read the finished, but unpublished, manuscript and generously provided glowing recommendations. We are also very grateful to Chip Webb and James Crocker for their constructive comments regarding the foreword and preface.

Many members of Dutch Facebook groups gave us valuable advice in response to our numerous questions and made comments about the videos where Meta shares some of her experiences. We appreciate your help and encouragement during our journey to publication.

Last, but not least, thank you to Liesbeth Heenk, Helen Baggott, and the team at Amsterdam Publishers for patiently editing, giving advice, answering a multitude of questions, and spending the many hours it takes to bring a book to market. It was a pleasure to work with you.

GLOSSARY

alstublieft, alsjeblieft. please (polite and informal version)

banketletter. almond paste-filled flaky pastry; Dutch letters

Blitzkrieg. German bombing campaign designed to force countries to surrender quickly, literally quick war (German)

borstplaat. fudge-like candy

bosjes. little woods

boterhammen. open-faced sandwiches

dank je wel, dank u wel. thank you very much (familiar and formal)

Das Reich. The German Empire (German)

De Leugenaar. The Liar (what Pappa called the newspaper)

drop. licorice

eet smakelijk. enjoy your food

ersatz. substitute (German)

Frau. Mrs. (German)

Gelukkig Kerstfeest. Merry Christmas

gezellig(e). cozy, pleasant

Goedemorgen. Good Morning

Herr. Mr. (German)

hongerziekte. starvation sickness

Ich weiß es nicht. I don't know (German)

Ik weet het niet. I don't know (Dutch)

idioot/idioten. idiot(s)

ja. yes

Juffrouw. Miss

kachel. coal-burning stove

kapot. broken; in some contexts, it can mean "dead."

kindertjes, kinderen, kindje. children; small child

(echt) lekker. (very) yummy, not always referring to food

Gelukkig Nieuw Jaar. Happy New Year

Mamma. informal Dutch for Mom

meid/meisje. girl

Meneer. Mr.

Mevrouw. Mrs.

Motten. moths or have to (slang)

muisjes. chocolate, anise or fruit-flavored sugar topping for bread

nee. no

NSBer. Dutch Nazi, traitor/informer

Onkel. uncle (German)

Pappa. informal Dutch for Dad

Schatje. sweetheart

Schneckenkuchen. snail cake (made with jam; German)

Sinterklaas. holiday celebrating St Nicholas; also the name of the saint

spekulaasje. spice cookie

Spilletje, Spil. Meta's nickname, referring to her skinny legs

tante. aunt

ukkies. little ones

Van harte gefeliciteerd met je/uw verjaardag. Happy Birthday

vuile (rot) schoft(en). dirty (rotten) bastards

vuile rot Mof(fen). dirty rotten German(s)

zuurtjes. hard fruit-flavored, often sour, candies

Zwarte Pad. Black Path

APPENDIX

Abbas, Max. Jewish school friend whose family left during the occupation.

Bisschop, Augustine (Gusti, Guusje, Guusta). Mamma (The various versions of her name are as she was addressed by Germans, Pappa, and Dutch people).

Bisschop, Cornelius (Cor). Pappa

Bisschop, Corrie. Meta's eldest sister (7 yrs older)

Bisschop, Meta (Spilletje, Spil). Heroine of the book

Bisschop, Ronald. Meta's brother (10 yrs younger)

Bisschop, Sieglinde (Siegie). Meta's sister (2 yrs older)

Brandt, Agnes. Meta's aunt and Mamma's sister

Brandt, Albertine. Meta's cousin and Mamma's niece

De Haas, Jenny. Meta's friend whose Jewish father survived the camps.

Den Dulk, Sien (Sientje). Downstairs neighbor in Scheveningen

Evenblij, Frits. The man Meta eventually married

Graefner, Karl. Meta's uncle and Tante Paula's husband

Graefner, Paula. Meta's aunt and Mamma's sister

Heesterman, Dickie. Meta's friend at #3 Leeuwardensestraat

Heesterman, Mevrouw. Neighbor at #3 Leeuwardensestraat

Hijenga, Hendricka. Neighbor and Mamma's friend

Jansen, Ben. Hildegunde's husband

Jansen, Hildegunde (Hildie). Downstairs neighbor in Den Haag

Jansen, Maria. Hildegunde's daughter

Koster, Meneer. High school teacher

Koster, Yvonne. Teacher's daughter; Meta's friend

Kranenburg, Ciska. Meta's cousin and Mientje's daughter

Kranenburg, Joop. Meta's cousin and Mientje's son

Kranenburg, Mientje. Meta's aunt and Pappa's widowed sister

Kranenburg, Willie. Meta's cousin and Mientje's daughter

Langedoen, Meneer. High school teacher

Leidelmeijer, Lydia. Sieglinde's Indonesian friend

Leidelmeijer, Jan. Meta's Indonesian friend

Mees, Dr. L.F.C. Family physician

Popa, Meneer. Man working in the garage across the street

Streefland, Harry. Ronald's friend at #4 Leeuwardensestraat

Streefland, Rietje. Neighbor at #4 Leeuwardensestraat

Ten Bosch, Ciska. Pappa's half-niece

Ten Bosch, Helena. Pappa's mother and half-sister both had this name

Ten Bosch, Henkie. Pappa's half-nephew

Unknown, Bennie. Meta's friend at Montessori school

Unknown, Ciska. Meta's aunt and Mamma's eldest sister

Unknown, Dickie. Neighbor boy who lived on the Zutphensestraat

Unknown, Elise. Meta's friend at Hemalie

Unknown, Hannie. Meta's Jewish friend who was adopted after the war

Unknown, Lottie. Meta's friend at Hemalie

Unknown, Luuk. Pappa's colleague at the PTT

Unknown, Nellie. Meta's 6th grade friend

Unknown, Rainier. Pappa's colleague at the PTT

Van den Berg, Mevrouw. Lady living on Harstenhoekweg

Van Kruijsen, Alie. Sieglinde's friend at #17 Leeuwardensestraat

Van Kruijsen, Beppie. Meta's friend at #17 Leeuwardensestraat

Van Kruijsen, Cornelia. Eldest daughter of a neighbor at #17

Van Kruijsen, Meneer. Streetcar conductor living at #17

Van Kruijsen, Mevrouw. Neighbor at #17 Leeuwardensestraat

Visser, Jan. Vera's husband (fisherman)

Visser, Vera. Mamma's childhood friend from Bottrop, Germany

Weidemann, Bruno. Meta's cousin and Wilhelm's son

Weidemann, Emil. Meta's cousin and Wilhelm's son

Weidemann, Liesbeth. Meta's aunt and Wilhelm's wife

Weidemann, Paul. Meta's uncle and Mamma's brother

Weidemann, Renate. Meta's aunt and Paul's wife

Weidemann, Wilhelm. Meta's uncle and Mamma's eldest brother

Wieringa, Sjors. Meta's young friend who lived on the Harstenhoekweg

AMSTERDAM PUBLISHERS HOLOCAUST LIBRARY

The series **Holocaust Survivor Memoirs World War II** consists of the following autobiographies of survivors:

Outcry. Holocaust Memoirs, by Manny Steinberg

Hank Brodt Holocaust Memoirs. A Candle and a Promise, by Deborah Donnelly

The Dead Years. Holocaust Memoirs, by Joseph Schupack

Rescued from the Ashes. The Diary of Leokadia Schmidt, Survivor of the Warsaw Ghetto, by Leokadia Schmidt

My Lvov. Holocaust Memoir of a twelve-year-old Girl, by Janina Hescheles

Remembering Ravensbrück. From Holocaust to Healing, by Natalie Hess

Wolf. A Story of Hate, by Zeev Scheinwald with Ella Scheinwald

Save my Children. An Astonishing Tale of Survival and its Unlikely Hero, by Leon Kleiner with Edwin Stepp

Holocaust Memoirs of a Bergen-Belsen Survivor & Classmate of Anne Frank, by Nanette Blitz Konig

Defiant German - Defiant Jew. A Holocaust Memoir from inside the Third Reich, by Walter Leopold with Les Leopold

In a Land of Forest and Darkness. The Holocaust Story of two Jewish Partisans, by Sara Lustigman Omelinski

Holocaust Memories. Annihilation and Survival in Slovakia, by Paul Davidovits

From Auschwitz with Love. The Inspiring Memoir of Two Sisters' Survival, Devotion and Triumph Told by Manci Grunberger Beran & Ruth Grunberger Mermelstein, by Daniel Seymour

Remetz. Resistance Fighter and Survivor of the Warsaw Ghetto, by Jan Yohay Remetz

My March Through Hell. A Young Girl's Terrifying Journey to Survival, by Halina Kleiner with Edwin Stepp

The series **Holocaust Survivor True Stories WWII** consists of the following biographies:

Among the Reeds. The true story of how a family survived the Holocaust, by Tammy Bottner

A Holocaust Memoir of Love & Resilience. Mama's Survival from Lithuania to America, by Ettie Zilber

Living among the Dead. My Grandmother's Holocaust Survival Story of Love and Strength, by Adena Bernstein Astrowsky

Heart Songs. A Holocaust Memoir, by Barbara Gilford

Shoes of the Shoah. The Tomorrow of Yesterday, by Dorothy Pierce

Hidden in Berlin. A Holocaust Memoir, by Evelyn Joseph Grossman

Separated Together. The Incredible True WWII Story of Soulmates Stranded an Ocean Apart, by Kenneth P. Price, Ph.D.

The Man Across the River. The incredible story of one man's will to survive the Holocaust, by Zvi Wiesenfeld

If Anyone Calls, Tell Them I Died. A Memoir, by Emanuel (Manu) Rosen

The House on Thrömerstrasse. A Story of Rebirth and Renewal in the Wake of the Holocaust, by Ron Vincent

Dancing with my Father. His hidden past. Her quest for truth. How Nazi Vienna shaped a family's identity, by Jo Sorochinsky

The Story Keeper. Weaving the Threads of Time and Memory - A Memoir, by Fred Feldman

Krisia's Silence. The Girl who was not on Schindler's List, by Ronny Hein

Defying Death on the Danube. A Holocaust Survival Story, by Debbie J. Callahan with Henry Stern

A Doorway to Heroism. A decorated German-Jewish Soldier who became an American Hero, by Rabbi W. Jack Romberg

The Shoemaker's Son. The Life of a Holocaust Resister, by Laura Beth Bakst

The Redhead of Auschwitz. A True Story, by Nechama Birnbaum

Land of Many Bridges. My Father's Story, by Bela Ruth Samuel Tenenholtz

Creating Beauty from the Abyss. The Amazing Story of Sam Herciger, Auschwitz Survivor and Artist, by Lesley Ann Richardson

On Sunny Days We Sang. A Holocaust Story of Survival and Resilience, by Jeannette Grunhaus de Gelman

Painful Joy. A Holocaust Family Memoir, by Max J. Friedman

I Give You My Heart. A True Story of Courage and Survival, by Wendy Holden

In the Time of Madmen, by Mark A. Prelas

Monsters and Miracles. Horror, Heroes and the Holocaust, by Ira Wesley Kitmacher

Flower of Vlora. Growing up Jewish in Communist Albania, by Anna Kohen

Aftermath: Coming of Age on Three Continents. A Memoir, by Annette Libeskind Berkovits

Not a real Enemy. The True Story of a Hungarian Jewish Man's Fight for Freedom, by Robert Wolf with Janice Harper

Zaidy's War. Four Armies, Three Continents, Two Brothers. One Man's Impossible Story of Endurance, by Martin Bodek

The Glassmaker's Son. Looking for the World my Father left behind in Nazi Germany, by Peter Kupfer

The Apprentice of Buchenwald. The True Story of the Teenage Boy Who Sabotaged Hitler's War Machine, by Oren Schneider

The Cello Still Sings. A Generational Story of the Holocaust and of the Transformative Power of Music, by Janet Horvath

The series **Jewish Children in the Holocaust** consists of the following autobiographies of Jewish children hidden during WWII in the Netherlands:

Searching for Home. The Impact of WWII on a Hidden Child, by Joseph Gosler

See You Tonight and Promise to be a Good Boy! War memories, by Salo Muller

Sounds from Silence. Reflections of a Child Holocaust Survivor, Psychiatrist and Teacher, by Robert Krell

Sabine's Odyssey. A Hidden Child and her Dutch Rescuers, by Agnes Schipper

The Journey of a Hidden Child, by Harry Pila and Robin Black

~

The series **New Jewish Fiction** consists of the following novels, written by Jewish authors. All novels are set in the time during or after the Holocaust.

The Corset Maker. A Novel, by Annette Libeskind Berkovits

Escaping the Whale. The Holocaust is over. But is it ever over for the next generation? by Ruth Rotkowitz

When the Music Stopped. Willy Rosen's Holocaust, by Casey Hayes

Hands of Gold. One Man's Quest to Find the Silver Lining in Misfortune, by Roni Robbins

The Girl Who Counted Numbers. A Novel, by Roslyn Bernstein

There was a garden in Nuremberg. A Novel, by Navina Michal Clemerson

The Butterfly and the Axe, by Omer Bartov

Good for a Single Journey, by Helen Joyce

The series **Holocaust Books for Young Adults** consists of the following novels, based on true stories:

The Boy behind the Door. How Salomon Kool Escaped the Nazis. Inspired by a True Story, by David Tabatsky

Running for Shelter. A True Story, by Suzette Sheft

The Precious Few. An Inspirational Saga of Courage based on True Stories, by David Twain with Art Twain

Jacob's Courage: A Holocaust Love Story, by Charles S. Weinblatt

The series **WW2 Historical Fiction** consists of the following novels, some of which are based on true stories:

Mendelevski's Box. A Heartwarming and Heartbreaking Jewish Survivor's Story, by Roger Swindells

A Quiet Genocide. The Untold Holocaust of Disabled Children WW2 Germany, by Glenn Bryant

The Knife-Edge Path, by Patrick T. Leahy

Brave Face. The Inspiring WWII Memoir of a Dutch/German Child, by I. Caroline Crocker and Meta A. Evenly

When We Had Wings. The Gripping Story of an Orphan in Janusz Korczak's Orphanage. A Historical Novel, by Tami Shem-Tov

Want to be an AP book reviewer?

Reviews are very important in a world dominated by the social media and social proof. Please drop us a line if you want to join the *AP review team*. We will then add you to our list of advance reviewers. No strings attached, and we promise that we will not be spamming you.

info@amsterdampublishers.com

Made in the USA
Middletown, DE
13 December 2022

18386362R00170